Memories

Of My

Future

Anil Habib

Memories Of My Future

Ammar Habib

Anil Sinha

MEMORIES OF MY FUTURE

Published by Sinha Medical Device
Copyright © 2016 by Ammar Habib & Anil Sinha

FIRST EDITION

Printed in the United States of America
First Printing: July 2016

ISBN: 978-0-692-74528-1

For more information, to inquire about the rights to this or other works, or to purchase copies for special educational, business, or sales promotional uses please write to:

www.ammarahsenhabib.com

DEDICATION

Ammar would like to dedicate this book with love to:
His loving and supportive parents, Ahsen & Farah Habib,
His best friend and brother, Nabeel Habib,
His maternal grandparents, Muhammad Ashraf Khan & Khurshid
Musarrat Mirza aka "Achhi Baji",
His paternal grandparents, Waqar Habib & Khalida Waqar,
And to his adoptive grandmother, Ms. Grace "Nanni" Sooter, may her
beautiful soul rest in peace

Anil would like to dedicate this book to:
His loving wife, Laura,
And his wise grandfather, Ramashish, for teaching him morals and values
through stories

And special thanks to:
Dr. Vipin Tripathi for his assistance in creating the historical accuracy,
Jennifer Paris for her uncanny assistance in editing the story,
Jonathan Katzen for creating the title for this story,
Fiona Jayde for her incredible artwork,
And most especially to you, the reader, for your time and support

TABLE OF CONTENTS

A MESSAGE FOR THE READER

Dear Friend,

Today, there seems to be turmoil in every region of the world. Sadly, many of these problems seem to stem through the misuse of religion and politics.

The idea for this story began with a simple message of harmony, peace, and tolerance. From there, it grew into a complex story full of thrills as the main character goes on a journey where he slowly learns and accepts some universal truths about the world. And if you, as the reader are willing to travel down this journey with our hero, maybe you will understand these truths as well.

With Anil Sinha's upbringing as a Hindu and Ammar Habib's upbringing as a Muslim, we wished to tell a story that will exemplify the power different religions and different 'types of people' have when working together. Along with our differences in religion, there is a generational gap between us: Anil's background is as an accomplished surgeon who has run his own medical practice for nearly two decades while Ammar was still in college at the time this project began. To add to our own differences in beliefs, our friends and family who reviewed the novel stem from a wide variety of ethnicities, religions, and ages. We wanted this story to represent many major religions and cultures and believe that is reflected in the characters and settings of the story.

This is not a story that favors one religion or culture over the other. It is not one that preaches religion. Instead, it is one that shares a message of love and tolerance. A message advocating that it is not for us to decide which religion is right or wrong. Instead, it is for us to decide how we can work together while using our perspectives and strengths to think unorthodoxly to solve the problems that plague our world. And if we are willing to focus on our similarities while respecting our differences as we work harmoniously on the world's problems, we can truly make this planet a better place.

And maybe, we can create a bit of Heaven on Earth.

Sincerely,
Ammar & Anil

LIST OF CHARACTERS

Present Time (New York City)

Avinash Singh	*a cardiothoracic surgeon originally from India*
Martha	*a senior nurse and Avinash's confidant*

1250s (Bihar, India)

General Khau	*general in Bihar's army / Avinash's ancestor*
The Governor	*the political head of Bihar*
Bilal	*General Khau's most loyal officer*

1857 (Bihar, India)

Veeresh Singh	*respected farmer / Avinash's ancestor*
Pari Singh	*Veeresh's wife / Avinash's ancestor*
James Smith	*Colonel in the East India Company*

Present Time (Amaristan)

Jonathan Daniels	*a world famous philanthropist*
Lia	*a nurse originally from Spain*

CHAPTER 1
A STORM ARRIVES

The child was dead.

That was the only thought in Avinash's head as he had looked at the motionless corpse. It was now covered in a white sheet, concealing the child's lifeless eyes. But they had been burned into his memory. He would never forget them. He would never forget the dead eyes of the first child he had ever failed.

And then there were the eyes of the parents. Those blue eyes had been filled with a thousand emotions: sadness, loss, disbelief. They had lost their only daughter. And she was now nothing more than a beautiful memory for them. They could do nothing but weep over their eleven-year-old girl who they would never hold again. There would be no more birthdays, no more laughs, and no more warm smiles.

Now, there would only be a tombstone:

Estella Harp
May 31, 2004 – March 23, 2016
Beloved Daughter

As Avinash now sat in his office, he could still hear the weeping of Estella's parents. In his mind's eye, he could see the tears streaming down their faces. He could hear the monitor beeping go silent as the child's heart rate suddenly stopped during the surgery. Just when it looked like she would make it out of the surgery alive and better than ever before, her life ended. And Estella's dead eyes were no longer just burned in his mind; they were now engraved in the very depths of his heart. He could not get rid of them. They were with him now…and forever.

Sitting in his office behind his heavy russet desk and on his matching chair, his elbows rested heavily on the table. He was oblivious to everything as his head was in his hands, concealing his face. The only thing on his mind was the child and the parents he had failed.

The walls were decorated with framed degrees and achievements. Valedictorian of his high school. Top of his class in pre-medicine. Top of his class in medical school. Numerous honors related to surgery. He had accumulated more successes in his thirty-four years than most people could achieve in two full lifetimes.

But right now, he did not care about any of them.

They meant nothing. Neither did the name on his office door that read:

Dr. Avinash Singh MD, FACS
Cardiothoracic Surgeon

To Avinash, it was all useless: the title, the accolades, the degrees. Everything. What was the point of it all if he could not bring an eleven-year-old girl back into her parents' loving arms?

From the corridor, voices came in through the open doorway. The window opposite of the door had its blinds pulled down, blocking out almost all of the light. The only illumination in the room was the small, lit lamp on his desk. The rest of it was shrouded in darkness. Next to the lamp was a white, cordless phone. It had been taken off of its receiver, making it impossible for anybody to reach his office right now. Around it were neatly organized papers and forms that he needed to fill out before the day ended. But that was the last thing on Avinash's mind.

Several photos were tidily placed on his desk. One was of his parents who were now back in India's province of Bihar. Another was of him and his best friend in medical school. His friend, Mirza, was an average-sized man. However, standing next to the powerful figure of Avinash, Mirza looked like a midget.

Along the wall across from his desk were two bookshelves that matched the desk and chair. They almost extended to the 10-foot-tall ceiling and were completely full of novels arranged in alphabetical order. Since the first day he had been in this office, nearly two years ago, he had not touched any of those novels. He did not have the time for that. His work was more important than anything else. Avinash had sacrificed so much for it that he would not let anything get in the way of it now. He had given up his athletic career, his passion for writing, and any kind of personal life he could have had for medicine.

Since his first day in this office, he made a vow to be the best doctor that he could be. And he had made good on that promise. Just like he had done all his life, he had been the best. He had been as perfect as possible.

Of all his accomplishments, the one he held most dear was that every patient under his care was returned to the best health possible. Avinash had only lost a handful of patients on the table, but never a child. He was the one who other doctors aspired to emulate. He was the one who spoke at conferences about never giving up on a patient and always finding a way to win.

But that bubble had burst with the death of Estella.

Now, harsh reality had struck. Now, he had failed. For the first time in his life, he had not finished on top. He had not been good enough.

He had promised Estella's parents before going into the surgery that he would improve her heart condition. He had gone in thinking that it would be another predictable surgery. This was a new disease that had recently struck countless people here in the New

York City area. But Avinash believed that he had found the answer. It all looked perfect on paper. He thought he would be the one to solve the riddle of this new heart disease that nobody could understand.

And now his promise was broken.

He had not brought her back to good health. Instead, he had given her a one-way path to her grave. Now, rather than preparing Estella for her return home and showering her with toys, her parents would be preparing for her funeral and laying her body into the ground.

And many of the doctors who had held their breath waiting to see the results of Avinash's surgery would see that even he could not beat this disease. He was as helpless as they were.

As Avinash sat there, he did not notice the nurse standing in the doorway. Her curly grey hair showed her experience. On her nametag was the name "Martha" and in her hands was a document that needed the doctor's signature. But she did not dare step foot into his office right now. She had never seen him like this. He was always the most confident man in the room. He showed nothing but assurance and sometimes arrogance. But now as he sat in his office, he was a shadow of the man he had been just this morning.

Mustering some amount of courage, she took a step into the office. She knew that he felt her presence, but he still did not look up.

"…Dr. Singh?"

There was no answer or acknowledgement.

"…I…I have this for you to sign. It's a work release for Mr. Mathis."

Again no answer.

Moving forward, she took the few steps to his desk and put it right next to the lit lamp. She then softly placed the phone back onto its receiver. "Whenever you're ready."

Avinash took a deep breath, but did not look up at the nurse.

Knowing that there was nothing she could do, the nurse turned and left the room still not believing what she had seen.

***

Standing under the fluorescent lights, two young nurses were alone in the corridor. But unlike Martha's years of experience, one had only been here for six months after finishing up her schooling. The other had arrived only weeks ago.

All of the occupied rooms had their thick, brown doors shut while the unoccupied rooms' doors remained wide open. The polished floors rested between the recently cleaned and refurbished eggshell white walls.

"I can't believe what happened." The nurse with long auburn locks held her clipboard tight to her chest. On her nametag was the name: Julia. "I've never seen Dr. Singh like that."

"What happened?" The second nurse had black hair that had been tied into a long ponytail. "Nobody is saying a word."

"You should have seen his face, Erin. I've never seen him like that."

"Like what?" Erin's eyes were full of curiosity.

"He was...helpless. Completely helpless. Like a...I don't know how to explain it."

"Is this really the first patient he's ever lost on the table?"

"It's his first child," Julia replied. "Maybe that's why he's taking it so hard. We all thought that he'd cracked the case. But when the girl suddenly died...it was as if life left Dr. Singh's eyes as well."

Hearing footsteps echoing towards them, Erin and Julia turned to see Martha coming down the hallway towards them. The older lady had a distraught expression on her face and it was clear that her mind was elsewhere at the moment.

Erin took a step towards Martha. "Did you see Dr. Singh?"

Hearing Erin's voice, Martha was brought back to reality. She already knew why the inquisitive Erin was asking about the doctor. It seemed like everyone who was not in the operating room was caught up in this. And a part of Martha did not want to tell anybody a thing about it. But the other part of her knew that if she did not answer people's questions, rumors would turn this entire thing into a much bigger ordeal than it had already become.

Within a few moments, she was standing in front of her two younger co-workers. "Yes…only a few moments ago. Thank God his day is about to end. He needs all the rest he can get."

"How is he in there?"

Looking down, Martha slightly shook her head. "Worse than he was after the surgery. He's completely broken."

"Because it's the first child he's ever lost during an operation?"

Martha thought for a long moment. "…I've seen plenty of doctors lose a child on the table. It's always hard, but part of being a doctor is to keep fighting on and to not let fear deter you. I've never seen any take it as bad as he is."

"So what do you think it is?"

The older nurse did not reply, obviously lost in thought.

"…Martha?"

"His…his entire reputation has been built on being the best. But I think it may be more than that. And I think that his entire ego, his entire self-worth, may have been based on that whether he knew it or not. He went into the surgery thinking that he would be the one to find the solution for this heart problem. He thought that he would be the hero. But this…this failure…I think it has shattered his ego completely. The loss of the child only amplified it."

"You think it hit him that hard?"

Martha's wisdom showed in her words. "Maybe…but I think there's something else. And it has to do with the child's death. I don't know what. But what happened in there triggered something in him. Something he wished to forget long ago."

There was a short silence as Julia digested her older counterpart's words. "…But he'll get over it, won't he?"

Martha glanced down at the ground for another long moment. "I…I don't know. But we need him to. He has eight more patients with the same diagnosis. And there are many more children just in New York City who are afflicted with it as well. If their timetable is anything like we've seen with this disease, then they don't have long."

Erin and Julia silently watched Martha's frightened expression as she imagined losing the countless children who were slowly losing their fight against this heart disease.

"And they need him now more than ever."

***

The rain was falling hard when nightfall came. Its heavy drops loudly splattered and crashed against the high-rise apartment's windows. Out of nowhere, this thunderstorm had swept over the area. Nobody could have predicted it after how clear the early spring skies had been this morning. But nonetheless, it had come. And now the dark clouds showed that it would not be ending anytime soon. They sinisterly hovered over New York City and sent down their endless precipitation, flooding some of the streets.

In his light brown-walled living room, Avinash sat on his tan, leather couch. Tonight, just like most nights, he was alone here. A tall lamp in the corner of the room with a thick and stylish brown stem cast a warm glow. Next to that lamp was a window; its blinds had been pulled back and the endless storm could be witnessed through it.

To either side of the couch where Avinash was seated were two glass end tables. Their edges were black, and they were perfectly square. On one of them sat a cordless phone. It suddenly rang as somebody tried to get in touch with Avinash, but he did not bother to answer it.

Avinash heard his stomach grumble as the phone rang. But he did not have any intention of feeding himself. After all, how could he feed himself knowing that those parents would never be able to feed their child again? His head hung low and his eyes were shut.

The phone rang again. Avinash continued to ignore it as he listened to the endless splattering of the rain. There was a sudden flash of lightning followed by roaring thunder that woke up anybody in the city that might have been sleeping. The deafening clap of thunder shook the city. For a moment, it looked like the night had suddenly ended and day had come. The thunderous roar shook buildings in its wake and was louder than any that this storm had produced thus far.

But Avinash did not flinch.

The phone rang once more. Silence followed. But then there was a loud and long beep as the voicemail took the caller's message. As he expected, Avinash heard his friend's voice come out of the receiver.

"Hey Avi, its Gerald. I know your day finished up and you're probably asleep right now, but I wanted to see if we are still good for tomorrow. Hadn't seen you in a while since you're so busy with work and everything. Umm...there's a pretty great steak place I discovered. Me and Felicia went there a couple of weeks ago and I think that you'd like it. But anyways...give me a call back when you can. Felicia is out of town all weekend and I don't have anybody else to hang out with. If tomorrow isn't good, let me know what day is good...alright?...call me back when you wake up, bro."

There was another long beep as the message ended.

Avinash hardly heard a word of the message. His depression had turned into weariness and that weariness was now taking a toll on his body. He had not slept in over twenty-four hours. His brain wanted to shut down and rejuvenate itself, but he did not want to sleep right now. Even though it was killing him, he wanted to keep thinking about the surgery. He wanted to find out where he had gone wrong. It should have all worked out. It had been working. For several minutes, she had been on the path to recovery.

Estella should have been sleeping in a bed tonight. When the surgery ended, Avinash should have been looking into her blooming eyes. Instead, when it was all said and done, he had stared at Estella's lifeless eyes.

And as slumber slowly overtook him, those eyes haunted his dreams.

CHAPTER 2
WAKING UP

Not this again.

How many times would he have to live through this nightmare? How many times would his nightmares remind him that Akleshwar was dead? He had died once and yet Avinash had lived through it a million times.

Avinash's eleven-year-old eyes looked at the pyre. The wood was ready to be burnt. Tears were streaming down his cheeks as he sobbed uncontrollably. In his right hand was a lit torch. He held the burning end away from himself, but the flame's heat still crashed against his skin and made him sweat even more under the dark skies above. But most of the perspiration was not from the heat. It was coming from the feeling that he was stuck in the middle of a horrible nightmare. One that would never end.

On the other side of the pyre stood Avinash's father. He had a torch in his hand as he kept his eyes on the corpse between him and his living son. There were no tears rolling down his cheeks. He had already spent all his tears when his son had died.

On another side of the pyre was Avinash's grandfather. The man was nearly seventy-years-old, yet he was as strong as an ox. But even he was not immune to the death of a loved one. Even his heart was being crushed by the tears that he refused to let out.

How can he be dead?

Encircling the three of them, a crowd of men dressed in white watched on. Their prayers drifted through the air under the darkening clouds. Some were family. Others were neighbors. But none of their pain was anything close to the pain of the three men holding torches.

The three of them kept their eyes on the corpse of the young boy. The lifeless body was wrapped in white and surrounded by the wood. And at any moment now, it would burn like the sun, and its smoke would rise into the dark heavens.

Akleshwar can't be dead. This has to be a mistake. This has to be some horrible, twisted dream. I've prayed so hard...I've prayed so much. Why aren't they being answered!

A few pellets of rain came down on the procession, but it did nothing to hinder the ceremony. In the distance, a clasp of lightning lit up the heavens for a moment, and its thunderous roar could be heard for leagues all around.

Any minute now, I'll wake up—I will wake up and all of this will be a dream. Akleshwar's sickness. His year of suffering...his death. It will be nothing more than a dream.

The grandfather was the first to move. He stepped forward and brought his fire closer to the wood. Everything slowed down. Time stopped. Inch-by-inch, the flames came closer. Inch-by-inch, Avinash came closer to never seeing Akleshwar again.

No...no! Don't do this. Akleshwar can't be dead!

The fire touched the wood. And in the next instant, it spread like a virus. It ate up every inch it came across without any mercy. Just like the disease had destroyed Akleshwar without an ounce of pity, the fire consumed the pyre.

Stop it!

The father stepped up. He followed the grandfather's actions perfectly. Holding back his tears, his flames kissed the pyre. And the fire did what was in its and the virus's nature: it destroyed.

This can't be happening!

Now it was his turn. Now it was the turn of the brother.

Avinash stood still. He could not do it. He would not do it. This was not right. An unending flood of tears ran down his face. They completely dehydrated him, but he did not care. He shook uncontrollably, wanting nothing more than to hold Akleshwar close to his chest like he had done the night before he died. He wanted nothing more than to read him another bedtime story. He wanted nothing more than to see his brother's smile one more time.

But he could not. Not anymore.

***

A loud knock on the door suddenly woke the sleeping doctor. It echoed through the entire apartment with such power that it could have woken Rip Van Winkle himself.

Hearing the sound, Avinash bolted upright, unsure if it was happening in reality or not. His breaths were quick after the nightmare. Sweat covered his face as he tried to come to reality. He had no idea how long he had been sleeping. The doctor looked out the window. The storm was no longer in full rage, but the endless rain was still coming down and loudly broke its fall against his windows. The thick and dark clouds made it impossible for him to tell if it was night or day.

Hearing the knock again, he knew it was not his imagination. Rising to his feet, he walked over to his apartment's front door. He opened it without looking through the peephole.

On the other side was Martha.

The elderly nurse was soaking wet after having walked through the rain. Wearing an auburn raincoat, a brown vinyl rain hat, and matching boots, her partially open white umbrella was in her hands. But even all of her rain gear had failed to protect her from the ruthless storm. And her face showed how long she had been knocking.

15

The doctor's eyes showed his surprise. She was the last person he had expected to see here. If anyone, he had expected Gerald to be on the other side of the door since Avinash had not called him back yet. It certainly would not have been the first time.

Looking down, Avinash saw a full grown Siberian husky at her feet. The black fur on its top half and the off-white fur on its bottom half and legs had been recently trimmed only days ago. That was fortunate; otherwise, the dog would have been drenched by four times the amount of rainwater. Attached to the dog's collar was a black leash which Martha held in her hands. But it was apparent that even without the leash, the pet was not one to run off from its caretaker. The dog's tongue was hanging out of its mouth, and its tail wagged with excitement. Its loyal eyes were locked on him.

Avinash looked away from the dog and back at the nurse. Her frustrated expression was gone now. Her face now showed a little relief at seeing him answer the door.

The doctor was the one to break the silence. "…What time is it?"

"Time to wake up. Do you have any idea how long I've been knocking?"

"Sorry."

"You look like hell."

"Long night."

"It happens." She stepped through the doorway and the doctor moved aside, letting her and the dog in. He knew that there was no keeping her out. Inside of the hospital, she would respect each and every one of his wishes. But outside the hospital, nobody could tell her 'no,' not even the hospital's Director of Nursing.

Closing the door behind Martha, he watched as she slung off her raincoat and casually hung it on the nearly bare coat hanger. As she did, she kept the dog's leash in her hand and the pet kept its eyes on the doctor, trying to figure him out. Without a word or a glance,

16

Martha made her way through the foyer, and Avinash followed his guest.

"Quite a storm last night. I'm surprised you slept at all. I couldn't."

"Whose dog is that?"

"Yours. At least for the near future."

"I don't want a dog."

"It was actually my neighbors. Since she passed away, I've been taking care of the dog. She used to be a show dog, and now she's yours for the time being." Coming into the living room, Martha stopped and turned around to look back at him. "I need to make sure that you don't do anything stupid."

His eyebrows rose. "Stupid? You think I'm going to hurt myself?"

"I don't know what to think. That's why I'm here." Martha's gaze left him and travelled around the room. It went over the sleek television hanging on the wall, glass coffee tables, leather chairs, tall and decorative lamp, and the small plant. After a few moments, they stopped on the long couch he had been sleeping on only five minutes ago. Its roughed up and disheveled cushions screamed to her that it had been his bed the night before. "Did you forget that you had a bed?"

"Couldn't make it there."

She looked away from the couch and at the framed picture that hung a few feet above it. Within the golden edged frame were the bold, italicized words that read: *The 11ᵗʰ commandment: The day thou operates on a patient will not be their day of death.*

Avinash followed her gaze to the encased saying. It was the saying that he had lived his life by. The promise he had made decades ago when he had been at the first low point of his life—the day he laid his best friend to rest. But, like most people, he had not realized that the boy had been his best friend until he was dying. "I'm going to have to take that down."

"…I wouldn't." Martha's eyes came back to him.

"I failed that oath."

"So have a lot of good doctors. But I don't know any that have kept it for as long as you have." She looked over at the phone a few feet away and saw the blinking light, indicating that there was an unread voicemail. Without asking for permission, she went over and hit the button on the receiver. Avinash did not even raise a word of opposition, knowing that it would be useless.

In the next instant, Gerald's message from last night played throughout the entire room just as it had the night before. And the nurse listened to every word.

As the message ended, Martha looked back at him. "Have you called him back yet?"

"No."

"Planning to?"

"You know the answer to that, Martha."

"I thought so." She glanced down at her furry companion for a brief moment. "I don't suppose you've had breakfast?"

Avinash shook his head.

"Let me make you some."

"I'm not hungry."

"All the same…do you have any eggs in the fridge?"

***

Minutes later, the two of them were seated atop barstools next to one another at the black marble kitchen counter. The stove was directly across from them on the other side of the counter. Above it were russet cabinets. But the majority of the ingredients that would be needed to whip up even the simplest dishes were missing. To their left was the shining, steel oven that was hardly ever used. Above it was a similarly styled microwave. Next to it was a fridge and freezer that both matched the other appliances in the kitchen. They were stocked full of supplies. But the food inside had a better chance of rotting than being eaten.

To their right was a dishwasher stocked full of dirty dishes. The thought of having to empty it afterwards stopped him short of doing anything about it. The sink was next to the dishwasher, and above the sink was a window whose blinds had been closed. Had they been open, Martha and the doctor would have had a perfect view of New York City.

The dog was seated at the foot of the doctor's stool. Sitting down, her hopeful eyes were on the apartment's owner and the plate of food. Her tail was wagging and her tongue was out. And her mind was only on one thing.

In the background, the president's voice could be heard as he addressed the nation, promising to find a way to solve the new national health crisis.

But neither of them were really listening to the president's words. Avinash slowly nibbled at the plate of three eggs and two slices of toast that sat in front of him. Martha had scrambled the eggs just like she knew he liked them. The white and yellow had all been mixed together as its aroma filled the kitchen. The warm toast had been buttered, and the delicious substance now melted into the seams of the bread.

This was not the first time Martha had cooked him breakfast. Every time she came to his apartment, she made him something to eat, and he always appreciated her culinary skills. He did not know if it was customary for the senior nurse to behave like this. Maybe she felt like a mother to him. Or maybe she knew how lonely he really was.

Swallowing her bite, Martha looked down at the dog and then back at Avinash as he chewed on his delicious bite of eggs. "Her name is Taxi."

He looked over at her. "...What?"

"The dog. Her name is Taxi."

Avinash looked down at Taxi. "...She looks hungry."

"She hasn't eaten since lunchtime yesterday."

Without a second thought, Avinash scooped up some of his eggs and slung them at the ground next to the dog. Before it had even hit the ground, the hungry dog snatched it into her mouth and ate it without a second thought. Her eyes looked back at the doctor and showed her appreciation. Even if it had been a piece of leather, she would have been just as grateful.

Martha slightly smiled before a long and awkward silence fell over them. After letting nearly a minute pass without a word between them, she spoke again. "Avinash...I've always wanted to ask you something?"

"Shoot."

"The picture of the girl. Who is she?"

Avinash knew which picture she was asking about. It was a picture that was in his bedroom. Martha had seen it one day. While at the hospital, Avinash had asked her to run to his apartment and bring him his wallet which he had forgotten. Even though it was not protocol for a nurse to do such things, she had done so without a word of objection. And when she had gone into his bedroom to find the wallet, she had found it next to the picture of the girl.

The girl was in her early twenties. Her long, black locks hung freely. She was pretty. No, she was beautiful. Her black eyes were looking right into the camera and had so much joy and light in them. Her smile could steal away the heart of any man. Her fair skin was soft. Avinash remembered that when the picture had been taken, her

20

torso was covered with a sky blue top that seemed to be made just for her.

"…Avinash?"

Coming back to reality, Avinash refocused on the nurse. "…Isabel…her name is Isabel."

"Isabel." Martha softly repeated the name to herself.

He looked back down at his plate and shook his head. "I haven't seen her in years."

"Was she a girlfriend?"

The doctor again shook his head.

"A friend?"

"Not quite."

"Then what was she?"

"A false hope." Avinash's gaze fell back onto Taxi. Her tongue was out again as she looked at him pleadingly. Without a thought, Avinash picked up his half-full plate and got up off of his chair. Lowering himself, he put the food right at the feet of the dog. And in the next instant, Taxi was on it.

Feeling a little better about himself, he returned to his previous position. As he did, Martha broke the silence as she watched Taxi devour the food without any hesitation. "Do you want to talk about what's going on?"

Avinash took a deep breath. "Somehow, I don't think that is a request."

"It's not."

The two of them looked away from the grateful dog and back at one another.

"I won't have a doctor in the hospital whose head is not in the game. Whatever is going on, you need to talk to somebody about it, and it might as well be me. Something tells me you wouldn't trust anybody else at the hospital with it."

There was a long silence. Half of Martha thought that she might get thrown out for being too forward. But the other half of her knew better. Even though Avinash was too proud to ever mention it, he appreciated having a lady like her in his life. Since his parents had moved back to their ancestral land in India's province of Bihar, his closest relative was on the other side of the planet; Martha was the closest thing to a mother he had on this side of the globe.

The doctor finally nodded. "…Alright."

Martha leaned forward a little attentively.

"What happened yesterday—Estella's death—reminded me of something I thought I'd long forgotten." He paused for a long moment. "I…have I ever told you the reason I became a doctor?"

"Outside of moving to America when you were thirteen, I don't know a thing about your past other than all the awards hanging in your office."

After several moments, the doctor looked down at his lap. He slowly began to unlock the door that led to his past. "My birth was not normal. It was far from it. Probably further from any birth that you've ever seen. I was born prematurely, and I wasn't born alone. I had a twin brother. His name was Akleshwar. But there is a twist to the story." His gaze left his lap and came onto Martha. "We were both conjoined twins… craniopagus."

She softly whispered. "…Conjoined at the head."

The doctor nodded. "However, we were separated by a brilliant surgeon. It was a miracle what he did. An absolute miracle. Since that surgery, I have never had a health complication in my life." He took another deep breath. "But the same was not true for Akleshwar. I had gotten the best end of the stick. I was strong…while he was weak. He was always sick it seemed. He was small. He could not learn or think as fast as me. When I was in 4th grade, I skipped two grades while he was held back by two. He was scrawny and half deaf. And on top of that, he had a speech impediment. It's a miracle that he was not half blind as well. Whatever I was, he was the complete opposite...the antithesis."

The nurse could hardly believe what she was hearing.

"I was always the best. In school. In sports. In popularity. I was always number one. But Akleshwar...he was always the worst. The only reason he was never picked on and beat up by the other boys was because he was my brother. If anybody tried anything with him, I would always take care of it. I think I did it all out of pity. I never even thought of him as a human being. To me...he wasn't an equal. He was no more than a pet."

Martha listened on. She had never heard any of this before. Nobody at the hospital had known any of this. Dr. Singh had a brother? And a conjoined twin at that?

"But when we were ten-years-old, everything changed. He got sick...really sick." Avinash grew silent for a long time. He knew speaking about what happened next would reopen the Pandora's Box of emotions he had locked away a long time ago.

Not knowing if he had the heart to go on, Martha broke the stillness. "What was it?"

His gaze finally rose and locked with hers. "...His heart."

Those words drove a dagger straight through Martha's soul. He said those words in such a way that every syllable was filled with an overwhelming ocean of sadness. Every letter was filled with an unbearable amount of pain.

"There was nothing the doctors could do to fix it. I watched him go through torture for over a year. His heart was slowly dying, and the doctors could do nothing. His condition...it was so...so unique, so unheard of that the doctors could do absolutely nothing. They were dumbfounded. No procedure would have worked. Theoretically, he was as good as dead." As he said each word, the anger and resentment in his heart began to come out in his words. "And all I could do was helplessly watch as life slowly left his eyes.

The boy I had never given a second thought to—the boy that I thought of as a pet was now dying as each day passed. And the closer he came to dying, the more I realized what he had meant to me all along. Day by day he slowly died, and day by day I could do nothing but offer empty prayers. Prayers that went unanswered and prayers that did *nothing* but fill me with empty hope."

Avinash took a deep breath, calming himself. He looked away from the nurse. He could see Akleshwar's eyes as the boy sat in his hospital bed. His face was smiling at Avinash, but his eyes showed all the pain that he was going through. He did not even know if Akleshwar knew what was happening to him. He did not know if Akleshwar knew that he was dying. After all, how could he be smiling if he knew that death was nearly upon him? "Finally, the doctors had no choice. They had to try a heart transplant. Even though they knew he would die, they had to try. It was the only way they could at least give him a fighting chance."

There was another long silence. Martha did not dare utter a single word. Her heart was racing as Avinash told his tale. In all her years, she could never have imagined these words rolling off of his tongue.

"And he died." Avinash's eyes became angry as he relived the event. He could see it all happening again. The waiting room. The doctor coming out of the surgery with his face filled with sorrow. His parents' tears. His tears. The part of him that died with Akleshwar...his childhood and innocence. It was all coming back. "He died during the surgery. And all I could do was cry. All I could do was weep for the brother that died so that I could live."

"...I...I'm so sorry." What else could be said?

But Avinash acted like he did not even hear her words. "It was that day I made a vow. I was eleven years, six months, and nine days old. And I made a vow that I would never feel helpless again. I would do everything I could to never let a person—especially a child—die

24

like my brother. I would never let another parent bury their child. Never."

Martha could see the fire in his eyes. She knew that it was the same fire that had burned in his eyes the day that he had made this vow. It had never left him. That fire, that burning desire, was as real to him as Akleshwar had been in his last days.

"Estella—she was nearly the same age as my brother. And just like him, it was a heart disease that stripped her away from her family. When I saw her die…when I saw the life suddenly leave her eyes and found myself staring at her dead eyes…all I could see was Akleshwar's eyes." He took a deep breath, holding back any tears that swelled in his eyes. "And I was right back at the funeral."

She was speechless

"We moved to America shortly thereafter—The Bronx. I didn't speak English, and didn't know the culture. The experience was…challenging. I found myself surrounded by people who I could not understand for months until I taught myself English. As you can imagine, I was a target—an easy target—for my peers. Those were the toughest months and years of my life. Maybe it's because they didn't understand me or maybe it's because I was an outsider and an easy outlet for their anger. I felt what Akleshwar had felt his entire life. I felt the constant humility of being inferior to everyone else."

The nurse listened on.

"I had two bikes stolen, was chased almost every day, pelted with slingshots outside of my apartment complex, constantly blamed and relentlessly harassed for things I didn't do. The first time I stood up for myself, I was pushed into the deep end of the school's swimming pool when I didn't even know how to swim. My misery served as everyone else's entertainment. I never realized that people could be that cruel—I didn't think it was in our nature. But they proved me wrong. *Every single day.* It was a living hell I couldn't escape."

Avinash paused for a moment as the memories flooded his mind.

"But I learned that there is only one real way to rise above oppression: excellence. I taught myself English, taught myself how to fend for and defend myself; but above all, I taught myself how to win. I graduated from high school when I was 16-years-old. Top of my class. I got a scholarship to Texas A&M University. My parents had spent so much money on my brother that they couldn't afford to send me to college, especially one of that caliber. And so I figured out a way to get a scholarship. I was able to walk-on to the basketball team, and within a few weeks, I was the coach's favorite freshman. It was unheard of for a person as young as me to walk-onto the team, but I did it...I did it for Akleshwar.

"During the summers, I was working full-time to make up for whatever my scholarship did not cover. I was taking more than a full load every semester. Even with all this, I became the captain of the team. My coach begged for me not to graduate early. He said that if I stayed at the university for the entire four years or prolonged it to five years, I would be one of the most impactful players on the team. But I already had other plans for my life. I would not break my vow...*ever*. No matter the cost, I would become the surgeon who would never fail."

Any person would have been proud of these accomplishments, but Avinash spoke of them as if they were nothing. They had served their purpose in his life and that was it. As Martha listened to him, she could hear in his voice the love he had for his brother. And she slowly started to truly understand why he was in so much pain. She could see it in his eyes. She could hear it in his voice. And she could feel it in his aura.

"I graduated with my bachelors when I was 19 at the top of my class. After that, it was straight to Cornell Medical School. I graduated at the top. I had no problem finding a residency position at the Presbyterian University Hospital down on East 68th. During my residency there, I made a name for myself. I was soon doing my fellowship at the Cleveland Clinic. And before I knew it, I found myself here."

Avinash took a deep breath. His entire past since Akleshwar's death had flashed before his eyes, and it overwhelmed him. But now he was back here in the present. He was back again in this kitchen sitting across from Martha.

"I've always been the best. I excelled in surgery…especially when a child was involved. But now…out of all the things that could have happened, out of all the things that I could have failed at, I failed at keeping the *one promise* I made to myself. I failed at stopping another mother and father from burying their child. Once again, a heart disease has beaten me. It's…it's like the punch line to some *sick* joke. All my degrees, all my training, it means nothing." Without warning, his fist suddenly slammed onto the countertop, sounding off a thunderous roar through the kitchen that made Martha jump. "*Nothing!*"

Rage filled Avinash's eyes. He kept his fist on the table as he looked straight ahead. There was another long silence after the echo of his words died off.

He held back any tears from leaving his eyes. He had cried enough already and tears would not solve anything. He knew that from experience. "…even after all these years, I'm…I'm just as helpless as the eleven-year-old boy who watched his brother die."

Martha was silent. The man in front of her was in an ocean of pain, and she did not know how she could take even one drop of it away. Finally, she put her hand on his shoulder causing him to look at her. "I don't know about saving lives, Avinash. I've never been the one transplanting a heart or a performing a bypass surgery. But I do know one thing. You saved Taxi's life a few minutes ago. She was starving and you gave her food. And you did it without even thinking."

The doctor's eyes went down to the dog. Even through Avinash's flare up, the dog's thankful eyes were pinned on him as her tail still excitingly wagged.

"I suppose that counts for something."

CHAPTER 3
THE JOURNAL

Around midday, the storm had lessened. It was not raining quite as hard as it had through the entire night and morning, and the lightning and thunder had completely subsided. The meteorologist on the news channel was assuring his viewers that by nightfall the rains would end except for a few scattered showers. However, the heavy clouds would still hang over the city for at least the next day.

In Avinash's apartment, Martha and he sat on opposite ends of the long couch. Their dirty dishes were unwashed and lying in the sink. The television glowed as the meteorologist went on and on about the rain. It seemed as if nothing else was on except weather reports. A large part of the city had apparently lost power for the better part of the night, but most of the city's power was now restored.

Only an hour and a half ago, the doctor had spilled out the details of his past. He had thrown it up as if it was a poison that needed to get out of his system. Martha had clung to each and every word. He was not sure if telling his tale had done anything for him, but for the moment all his anger and rage had subsided. Since then, only a few sentences had passed between them. The nurse was still trying to digest everything that had been said and Avinash had no idea how to get her to leave his place. She had kept herself busy by looking through the dusty novels underneath the decorated coffee table, but her mind was not really registering anything.

After a long time, Martha looked over at him. "So…"

He did not take his eyes off of the television. "So what?"

"This girl...Isabel. How does she fit into your story?"

"You just couldn't help yourself, could you?"

Martha slyly grinned.

"I met her in my second year of medical school. I was almost twenty-one and she was eighteen. I used to work at a supply warehouse doing inventory. She was going to school for a degree in marketing. She was hired at the warehouse to help when we had an extra-large shipment coming in. She was the daughter of my boss' friend."

"Did you love her?"

"...What do you think?"

Martha got her answer. His eyes gave it away. Just the utterance of Isabel's name caused them to twinkle. But on the other side of that twinkle, she saw something else: sorrow. "Tell me."

Avinash shook his head.

"Unless you want me to stay here all day, tell me."

He did not say anything.

"Don't think I'm bluffing. I've been here all morning, and I have no problem staying here the rest of the day. I am already late for my granddaughter's birthday party."

After a few long moments, he let out a sigh. "Since when did you become my mother?"

"Since you started needing one on this side of the planet."

He slightly smiled. And as he did, his mind left this place. It left this time. It was back in medical school when he was a young man working at the warehouse alongside Isabel.

He could see her perfectly. It was as if she was only a few feet away from him. She was shaking his hand on her first day on the job. He could hear her introducing herself. Isabel Belo. He had never heard a sweeter voice or seen a warmer smile. Her hand was so soft in his as he shook it. And that scent of Jasmine. In it, he could smell a fragrance that he had never smelt before. Something about her made

30

him feel warm inside. He could not put his finger on it, but the moment he set his eyes on her, something about her captivated him.

"…Avinash?"

Coming back to reality, his eyes refocused on Martha. A smile slowly came to his lips. "The moment I met her, I think I knew what I felt. But I did not want to admit it for a long time. I was never one to be afraid to talk to a girl or ask one out on a date. But for some reason, I did not want to admit that there was something about her. Something no other girl I ever knew possessed. But nonetheless, I would catch myself staring at the back or side of her head for minutes on end without her noticing. And I would find myself lying in bed in the late hours of the night imagining myself with her."

"Did you ever tell her?"

"I tried…*God*, I tried. But something always came up. There was always somebody else. She was always in love with somebody else. She was always with somebody else and did not give me a second thought. She thought of me as a confidant, but nothing else. At this point in my life, I had been with three or four girlfriends. But nothing serious. I had imagined that she would be my first love. And about two years after we'd known each other, I told her that I loved her."

"What happened?"

"She didn't take me seriously. She was seeing someone at the time and thought that I was joking. Or maybe she knew that I was serious but did not want to face the reality. She laughed it off." He paused for a moment. "And one day, not long after that, she came into work the happiest person I'd ever seen. Her boyfriend…he had proposed…" Avinash's eyes became full of resentment as he relived that day again. "And she said 'yes.' She was showing the ring off to everybody. And the last person she showed was me."

Martha could feel his pain.

"I…I couldn't take it. I had taken her laughing off my true feelings even though it had taken me a mountain of courage to confess to her. I had endured her constantly talking about the man she was in love with even though I was madly in love with her. But now, for the first time in my life, I was almost at the point of hating her."

"…What happened?"

"As she was showing me her ring, I suddenly grabbed her wrist. I made her look me in the eyes. I mean, really look at me. And I told her…I told her that I loved her. I told her that there was nobody else that I loved more. And I told her that if she did not love me…if she did not say that she did, I would leave and never come back."

Martha was too afraid to ask what happened next, but deep down she already knew what had happened.

"I let go of her wrist. For a long time, she just looked at me. She did not say anything. Then…then she looked down at her feet not saying a word. I waited for what seemed like an eternity…but she did not say anything. She would not even look at me. For the first time since my brother's death, I wanted to cry. But I didn't. I would not in front of her. I turned around. I left. I walked away."

The nurse was silent.

His heartbreak, even after all these years, still showed in his words. "Ever since then, I became who I am. I became the untouchable doctor that you know. I became the man who always won. Who was the best at everything. I never got emotionally attached…everything was an equation. And I was a master at solving equations. I was the best…and I knew it. I believed it with every fiber in my being."

"…Until yesterday."

He slowly nodded.

"Yesterday, when the child died, it shattered your image. It shattered your entire psyche."

"The disease beat me. Just like Isabel…this disease got the better of me. And now…now I have eight other children who are afflicted with this disease under my care. And this disease is spreading through New York like wildfire. Hundreds of children are already afflicted by it. Thousands more have the dormant virus inside of them, waiting for it to strike. It will be the worst epidemic in the last hundred years." He looked up at the eleventh commandment that hung above their heads. "I'm failing. I'm failing the boy that made that oath. And I'm failing Akleshwar. I'm failing my baby brother."

Martha thought for a long time. She stared at the doctor as he looked down at the long coffee table in front of them. All his emotions showed in his eyes. And she could see that even through all this pain, he still loved the woman who had betrayed his heart. Furthermore, he still hated himself for never appreciating the brother he lost more than two decades ago.

After a long time, she broke the silence. "If you ever hope to beat the disease, there's something else you need to do."

"What?" He did not even glance at her when he replied.

"You need to remember who you are. Your entire self-esteem was based on your perfection. Now that it's shattered, you would be useless in surgery. You could not even do a beating heart bypass, let alone figure out this disease. And until you fix your mental issue, you're no good to any patients. Not until you fix this."

He finally let his eyes come back to her. "And how am I supposed to do that?"

"That's something you'll have to figure out for yourself. But right now, you need to get your mind off of this. It's the best thing you can do for yourself right now."

"…I can't."

"Here's what you're going to do. You're going to call back Gerald, and tell him you'll meet him for dinner tonight."

"Martha—"

"I'm not leaving until you pick up that phone and talk to him. Or…or you believe me, I'll stay right here until you do."

"You're being absurd."

Martha spit out her next words like rapid-fire. "Maybe I am. But one way or another, you're going to take him out to a nice steakhouse, or maybe he'll take you out. I could care less. He'll ask you about work, and you'll just give him the basic—everything is going great—answer. Then, you'll ask him about his work, and he'll say the same. He'll tell you all about his engagement and about how he's having second thoughts about his marriage the closer it gets, and you'll do what any good friend does and listen. Then, you'll come back here, and Taxi will greet you like any good dog should: she'll ask you for food. And you'll feed her. And as you do, you can let your mind ease back into your problems. Afterwards, you can figure out how you're going to rebuild your mind and put yourself back into the game. Sound good?"

Her words sounded just like his mothers. With a smirk, Avinash looked down at the long coffee table as he slightly shook his head in amusement. For a moment, he completely forgot about the predicament he was in.

"Avinash?"

He looked back up at her. With a sigh, he rose to his feet and took a step towards the telephone. "Whatever gets you out of my apartment."

She smiled.

***

The night went exactly how Martha said it would. Gerald and Avinash went to a Christos Steakhouse in Queens on 23rd Avenue. The steaks were some of the best in town, and the service was near perfect. The last time Avinash had gone to a place this nice was when Gerald and Felicia were celebrating their engagement. Gerald had an eye for these types of high-end restaurants.

When Avinash first moved to America, he had been a strict vegetarian. But by the time he was a senior in high-school, he had started eating everything but beef. And by the time he was in college playing basketball, he had thrown that rule out the window as well.

After asking Avinash how his work was going, Gerald immediately launched into talk about his upcoming marriage. Even though it was months away, he once again confirmed with Avinash that he would be a groomsman there. And not long after that, he began to list reasons why he was getting cold feet. What if he had rushed into this? What if she was not 'the one?'

Even though Martha had never met Gerald, she had predicted his every action to the 'T.'

And just like Martha foresaw, Avinash sat there and listened, offering a word of comfort here and there. After the first half hour, Avinash wanted his friend to shut up about the whole thing. But the doctor did not voice his thoughts.

Eating his medium-rare, twelve-ounce filet with a side of warm mashed potatoes topped with melting butter and another side of sautéed asparagus, Avinash tried to enjoy the evening. His food had been cooked to perfection. The steak was overflowing with its juices but was not drenched in them. Every bite was heavenly as the flavors danced in his mouth and its aroma waltzed in his nostrils.

Gerald had chosen the setting for its soothing nature. Soft music played through the restaurant. The place was designed and arranged in such a way that it never got loud even when there were a lot of people in it. The interior of the restaurant was decorated in whites, sky blue, and cobalt shades. The waiters were all calm in their demeanor. They had been trained to be like that. Wearing their black pants, white shirts, and black ties, they calmly carried out their duties without interrupting any of their customers' conversations.

But even in this environment, even with his friend sitting across the table from him, Avinash could not keep his mind on the present. It continued to try and drift into the past. Not the recent past of his failure yesterday. It went further back than that. It went back to the nightmare of Akleshwar's funeral. That dream had reminded him of another memory.

The memory of the journal.

***

It was two days after Akleshwar's funeral when his grandfather gave Avinash the journal. At the family's considerable farmstead in Bihar, Avinash was stopped by the old man in the home's corridor. The grandfather led him to his immense master bedroom. The room, like the house, was majestic in nature, and its enormous size was appropriate for the hundred acres of land that it sat atop.

Numerous servants were employed by his grandparents to work the land and tend to the animals. People in the village looked at Avinash's grandparents as if they were royalty. After all, they were by far the wealthiest and most influential people in the village. And in addition to all of that, they were Brahmins. They were the highest caste, and that gave them respect. However, the home's modest decorations showed that Avinash's grandparents were still the simple people they had always been.

Sitting Avinash down onto the bed, his grandfather went into the closet for what seemed like a long time. With his hands clasped together in his lap and his eyes looking downward, Avinash could hear the old man rummaging through a large chest that he always kept locked. Nobody, except for the grandmother, knew what was in that magnificent chest. Not even Avinash's own father, who was heir to all of this. The key to the lock was always with his grandfather. Like all Brahmin men, his grandfather wore a sacred thread at all times, the *Janeu*. The string went from his left shoulder to his right side. But unlike every other Brahmin Avinash had ever seen, his grandfather had a key hanging from his *Janeu*.

His grandfather emerged with something in his hands: a worn out journal. It's brown leather cover had been weathered with age. Its edges were now rough and uneven and its corners were bent out of shape. It was the smell of ancient times. Even its very pages had the same smell as his grandfather. A blind person could have sensed how old this journal was.

Coming to Avinash, the grandfather sat down next to the eleven-year-old boy. He took his strong arm, wrapped it around the boy's back, and laid his powerful hand on Avinash's shoulder. The boy looked down at the journal but then back up at his grandfather as the man spoke in the regional language, *Bhojpuri*. "...One summer when I was younger than you, there was a great drought here. Many died, including my closest friends. Dehydration is what sent them to the next life...and it nearly killed me too. But it *didn't*. Do you know why?"

Avinash had heard the story already but did not dare interrupt.

"Because we are *warriors*, Avinash. That is the blood that runs in my veins. And it is the blood that runs in *yours*. You will survive this. You will fight through this. *Bhagwan* let you be a Brahmin, and he let you be the descendent of your ancestors. It was not a decision made by accident."

Avinash had heard his grandfather say things like this many times, but he had never really listened to it until now.

"I know that you are hurting. But...but now as I look back, I know that no matter how much you are hurting, your parents are hurting more. You lost a brother...but they lost the one who they brought into this world." He looked down at the journal for a brief moment. "Right now, you have to be strong. Not for yourself...but for your parents. They need you to do that more than ever, even if they do not say it themselves. Do you understand?"

The boy nodded even though he did not understand completely.

"Good boy." The grandfather handed the journal to Avinash.

Avinash looked down at the journal and then back up at his grandfather.

"This...this has been of use to me many times. It has helped me find my way and find out who I really am. It's of no use to me anymore because I know it by heart. Your father has also read it many times, and it has been great use to him. You're too young for it right now. But I know that it will be of use to you one day."

"...What is it?"

The old man slightly smiled, which was something Avinash had thought the man incapable of doing. It almost scared him. "It's the story of where your blood comes from. It tells you why the name you carry is so special. It tells you what blood and passion runs through this family and where all this land under our family's name comes from. It tells you of warriors you descended from." He paused for a moment. "My child, this is the story of your ancestors."

***

It was late when Avinash came home from his steak dinner with Gerald. Since the rains had lessened, people had taken to the streets by the droves. The subway was congested as people tried to make up for the lost time the storm had caused. Unable to even get into the subway, he was forced to take an overpriced taxi and sit through one of New York City's infamous traffic delays. It seemed that the rates for taxis always spiked at times like this.

Arriving in the foyer, Avinash closed and locked the door behind him. The first thing he saw when he turned back around was that the coat rack had been knocked over and was lying at his feet.

Luckily, none of the wood had been chipped off, and nothing was broken. The salesman had not lied when he told him it was durable.

Taxi was several feet away. Her sheepish eyes were on him as she sat down.

The doctor sighed. "...Did you do that?"

Avinash did not need an answer. Without bothering to pick up the coat rack, he took off his raincoat and tossed it right on top of the fallen rack. He walked past the living room and into the kitchen as Taxi followed him. His eyes came upon the empty food bowl.

"Looks like you were throwing a tantrum."

Avinash refilled Taxi's bowl until it was nearly overflowing. No sooner had he finished than Taxi was eating as if there was no tomorrow.

"Don't eat it all at once."

Minutes later, Avinash was walking down the corridor and towards his home office. He passed by an open door that led into a nearly bare bedroom. The nice-sized room was empty of any furniture; at its center, a heavily-used black punching bag hung from a chain. It was in this room that Avinash practiced his Taekwondo forms. Although he had not taken a class in years, he kept up his techniques and practiced as a way to relieve stress. And on the far wall hung all of his belts from white to black.

Avinash soon came to his home office. It was the smallest room in the apartment, only half the size of his living room, but it was still a good sized room that could easily accommodate a queen-sized bed. The blinds were pulled back, providing a good-view of Central Park. The green and white lamp on the auburn desk illuminated the room. Its bright light bounced off of the sturdy bookcase that was almost completely filled with books, filing cabinets, framed photos hanging from the wall and on the desk, and a chest of drawers.

However, Avinash was not at his desk. Sitting on his knees, he quickly and impatiently rummaged through the bottom cabinet drawer. Digging through the numerous files, his mind was on one thing. He knew it had to be here somewhere. He had already looked through every other place it might be. If it was not here, he feared he would be out of options.

The fewer and fewer places he had left to look, the more this fear grew. His heart began to slowly beat faster and faster as he thought that he would be on the short side of fate. But these fears all dashed away when his hand touched something familiar. Feeling it, a small smile crept onto Avinash's face.

He pulled out the journal and for the first time in years, his gaze was on its brown leather cover. It looked exactly the same as it did when Avinash first saw it. Its pages had not been read since that day, but they still had the distinct smell that his grandfather had possessed. It was a smell that would allow Avinash to identify the journal even without seeing it.

Holding the journal in both hands, he rose to his feet. He could hardly believe that he had found it. Half of him feared that the journal had accidently been thrown away. But now it was here. And for the first time since he was a boy, it was in his hands once again.

Avinash went to his desk and sat down, but he did not take his eyes off of it. He ran his hands across the cover. It felt exactly the same as it had that day.

When he originally received the journal, he could not bring himself to read it. He was so destroyed by Akleshwar's death that he could not do anything but mourn. He had completely forgotten about the journal for a time. But ever since Martha had left and he had gone to dinner with Gerald, he could not take his mind off of it. The memory of his grandfather giving it to him had burned in the forefront of his mind.

He took a deep breath. He knew what he needed to do. If he had any hope of beating this disease, he needed to regain his confidence. Martha had told him that he needed to find something to build his self-image on. Maybe this was it. It had to be. His grandfather had told him that one day he would need it. And now, it was time.

Time to take a glimpse into the past.

CHAPTER 4
THE SUMMONING

The greatest gift God gave to Man is his mind. All we must do is unlock our mind, and we will find what we seek. And once the mind is unlocked, all the answers to Man's problems will be right before his eyes.

Those were the first words in the journal. Avinash did not know what they meant. How could all of man's answers to his problems already be in his mind? If that were true, would not the world be perfect already? It did not make sense. Maybe the writer had been hallucinating when he had written it. Or maybe he was mad. But Avinash read on anyways, knowing he had nowhere else left to turn.

***

According to the Christian calendar, it was the middle of the thirteenth century.

The exact year had never been recorded. But years are never important. What echoes throughout history is the courage and bravery of a people.

The sun was nearing its peak when General Khau was summoned to the governor's court. It was early October. The monsoon season had ended and the winter bitterness would not arrive for a few weeks. Today, the clouds were few and scattered. There was a mild breeze that blew between the trees, but it did not bother any of the people. In fact, it was welcomed after the humid summer that had captivated the people for the past few months.

The sun was warm, but not too hot. It looked down at the province of Bihar. Only a few decades ago, this same sun had watched the armies of the mighty Delhi Sultanate, led by the Turkish conqueror, Bakhtiyar Khilji, capture this land and integrate it into their vast empire. The invasion had been a dark time and with it had come much destruction.

But since then, there had been peace here in Bihar. Although the invaders had arrived less than half a century ago, they were now one people with the natives. Since the conquest, peace and prosperity had come to Bihar like the locals never could have dreamt.

The general proudly marched with his head held high and his gaze straight ahead. Born a Brahmin, he walked like a man of his status should. The noble blood that ran through his veins showed in every step he took. His lineage was blessed with strength. He was stronger and better built than any person he passed by, and his posture made him seem more magnificent than Goliath himself. He was not as dark as most people in these lands. With the build of an ox, he was covered in leather-like skin. Even with a white *dhoti* wrapped around his legs and a white *kurta* covering his torso and arms, his strength and powerful muscles showed through the loose clothing.

The white cloth around his lower body covered his legs and was knotted at his waist. The upper garment covered him from his neckline to his wrists and ran down to just above his knees, but a few decorative embroideries separated it from what the masses wore. Although the majority of the townsfolk walked around with their bare feet, he was wearing wooden sandals. On his face, the only facial hair was a well-trimmed mustache, signaling that his father was still alive.

Outside of the palace's gates, there was a nice-sized path that led from the palace to the capital city of the province. The straight path was only half a mile long and went through a sparse forest that separated the city of Patna from the palace's grounds.

As he made his way to the palace and walked through the small forest, Khau observed several *Marda* trees. Through the monsoon season, these trees absorbed plenty of water which they now stored inside. And now that the rains had ended, many people of Bihar would look to these trees to supply them with the water they needed. However, the people of Patna would not need to do so because their city bordered the west bank of the holy Ganges River.

Keeping his eyes on the path, Khau noticed a creature slithering from the grass and onto the walkway. With just a glance, Khau recognized the yellow and black striped snake as the *ahiraaj saamp*. But he did not even slow down or pause knowing full well that it was only dangerous to other snakes and would pay him no heed. When the general was a child, his older brother had been bitten by a snake. But unlike the one in front of him now, the cobra was no friend to man, and its venom killed Khau's brother after a long struggle. After the loss of his sibling, Khau made it his business to learn the lay of the animals.

Continuing down the path, General Khau saw a *Mahwa* tree. This was the most common tree in the forest, and this tree had plenty of evergreen foliage. However, only a few of its flowers could be seen this morning. Half a week prior, it had been full of flora. But numerous doctors had sent boys down to pluck it dry, intent on using its flowers for medicinal purposes. Many other villagers had come to collect the remaining edible flowers, nearly leaving the tree barren.

Close to the palace's gates, a few young boys could be seen plucking the leaves and stripping some heartwood off of a *Kino* Tree. No doubt, a village doctor from the town must have sent them to do so. Based on who the boys were, the general surmised that it must have been the healer, Ram. He needed the tree's

44

ingredients for his practice of *Ayurveda*. The Muslim rulers did not condemn Ram's method of herbal medicine even though it was slightly different from the alternative medicine they had brought with them. In fact, they had welcomed the opportunity to study it and had merged many of its aspects into their own medicine. After all, *Ayurveda* had been practiced for well over two millennium, and the people had never lost faith in it.

From the trees, a winged creature flew out and passed a few feet over the general's head. With a quick and unalarmed glance, Khau recognized the grey bird as the *Tee –Tar*. No matter where he went in Bihar and the empire, this bird always seemed to be there. Maybe it was just an animal that loved the land of Bihar just like Khau's people did.

He passed by an *Arjuna* tree and saw moths feeding on its leaves. In time, those moths would create the silks that the villagers used. And the general knew that before the month ended, the practitioners of traditional medicine would send their runners to retrieve even this tree's foliage to use in their medicine. Nearly half a millennia ago the wise man, Vagbhata, had realized that this tree could do more than feed the silk-making moths. It could be the treatment for heart disease. And a few months ago when the ingredients from the tree had saved the life of Lieutenant Bilal, the general had seen it firsthand.

But in Khau's mind, all healing came from God. These medicines were just His tools.

Although General Khau was never one to say it, it brought him joy to see his people going about their business unafraid of anything. Through the power and abilities God had given him, he and the governor had ensured that the borders of their land were always protected. No enemy that stepped foot into Bihar lasted very long.

Khau was almost upon the heavy gates to the palace's grounds. On either side of the entrance were thick red and off-white stone walls. Two soldiers were stationed outside of the open gate. Seeing their commander, the two men wordlessly came to attention with their eyes focused straight ahead. With five-feet-long spears in one hand and small circular shields in the other, the men were dressed in their iron armor from head to toe. The guards stood perfectly still as their commander came toward them.

"*Namaste,*" the two soldiers said in unison as their commander passed by them.

The proud general subtly nodded, but he did not glance in either soldiers' direction. Going through the entrance of the palace grounds, the path tripled in width and became perfectly leveled. There were soldiers spaced out and lined up on either side of the path all the way to the palace's entrance. Dressed in their military gear and with their eyes looking in Khau's direction, they all stood at attention like their brethren at the gate. Khau knew that the governor had ordered them to expect him.

Most were Hindus. Others were Muslims. And some were Christians. As he passed them, they all greeted him in their religion's traditional way slightly bowing as he walked by. But they all looked like brothers here and addressed Khau like any man salutes a respected older brother.

However, the general did not utter any response. His eyes stayed on the palace and its entrance, which was a little over two hundred yards down the path.

Guards were stationed throughout the grounds. And within the walls were numerous ancient trees that had stood tall for centuries. Not far from the palace, there was a beautiful and flourishing garden. It was full of greenery, vegetation, trees, and there were hedges that were full of flowers that matched every color of the rainbow. All these things were native to Bihar. But unlike the

46

forests and trees outside, these trees and hedges were trimmed and kept up on a regular basis. They could have put the Hanging Gardens of Babylon to the test.

From where he was, Khau could see several different types of birds resting on the branches and hedges. The dark and light brown *Buschat* birds were scanning the ground for insects. The *Shakkar khora* leisurely fed off the nectar of the flowers, knowing that there was more than plenty to go around here. But high above them all, Khau spotted a *Shikra* gliding through the air. Unlike the other birds, the *Shikra* did not feed on insects and nectar. And right now, it was deciding which unaware bird down below would be its prey this morning.

The general looked away. The walkways were meticulously paved and led the general all the way from the gate to the palace's entrance. Other paths broke away from the main one and led to all of the other areas of the palace's ground: the *masjid*, the gardens, the barracks, the stables, and the training grounds among other things.

Khau spotted several servants leading a large, male elephant towards the eastern gate. The grey and well-kept elephant was the leader of the horde and the flagship of Bihar's army. As it was slowly taken down to the waterhole outside of the gate for a bath, its loud calls were heard back in the streets of Patna.

Close to the barracks, on the other side of the palace, were the training grounds for the soldiers. Even from where he was now, Khau could hear his men battling one another on foot. Some fought hand-to-hand while others used wooden training weapons. All the men moved with skill and ferocity that was unmatched by any of Bihar's neighbors. They moved so precisely, and all the men seemed evenly matched in their near flawless skills. Khau's ancestors had perfected the art of hand-to-hand combat, and it showed in his men. And seeing them battle and train against one another brought pride to the general's heart.

47

Near the palace's gardens was a fully grown *Bodhi* tree. The first Muslim governor had planted it to show honor and respect to the Buddhists under his care. Over the past decades, it had grown into a healthy tree recognizable by its heart shaped leaves.

The governor had summoned him urgently under the pretense that the Sultan would soon be visiting, but Khau knew that it was a falsification. But if the governor had gone this route to send for him, Khau knew that he had his reasons.

Standing three stories tall, the large palace could be seen for miles and stood above the trees and the high stone walls that defended it. Flying on each corner of the palace was the banner of the Delhi Sultanate. At the edges of the palace were two-story covered walkways whose ceilings were supported by beautifully architectural pillars. Tall arched windows were spaced out throughout the palace's exterior. The building's walls were a decorative assortment of off-white and several different pigments of orange. Atop of the center of the palace rose a tall and impeccably built white dome. And flying above it was the largest banner of all. And on the banners were the proud words of *"La Ilaa Illallah"* which could be read for miles and miles around.

Arriving at the palace's open doors, a servant was waiting for him. Dressed in simple attire that mimicked the general's aside from the embroideries, he bowed respectfully.

"*Namaste*, General Khau. The governor is expecting you." Turning around, the young man led the general into the palace's foyer. Khau had been here hundreds of times before. A high ceiling supported by four thick columns looked down at Khau. On the top halves of these off-white structures, verses from the Qur'an had been colorfully inscribed.

Even though he knew the interior of the palace better than his own home, Khau let himself be led by the servant. Following him into one of the many corridors of the palace, he continued on his way without looking left or right to admire the adornments around him.

***

"The governor was in the *masjid* reciting the Qur'an, but he was notified of your arrival. He will join you shortly."

Khau soon found himself at the entrance of the governor's council chambers. He nodded without uttering a syllable or looking in the servant's direction. Seeing the gesture, the dark-skinned servant turned and left, leaving the general to his own devices. The general walked past the large open doorway and into the court.

On each side of the entrance were the heavy, iron doors that had been swung open. The blacksmiths had designed those doors so precisely that there was not a single flaw in them. Inscribed in gold on one door was the phrase "*La Ilaa Illallah*" and on the other was "*Muhammadur Rasullallah.*" Khau knew the meaning of both phrases. The words testified that there was no one worthy of worship except for God Almighty and that the Prophet Muhammad was his last messenger. Even though they were Arabic, every person in the empire—Hindu, Christian, or Muslim—knew what they meant. They were the core belief of the Muslims. They were the foundation of their faith.

It was a long room. Small, circular openings had been cut into the rafters measuring a few feet in diameter. Through them, beams of late morning sunlight came into the council chamber, illuminating much of it except for a few corners that were left in darkness.

Two rows of concrete pillars went from one end of the room to the other. Their thick stems were cylinders with square bases and tops. Sturdy enough to last for centuries, their surfaces were perfectly smooth. The banners that held the emblem of Sultan

Nasir-ud-din-Mahmud were hanging off each and every one of them and faced the chamber's main entrance.

But proud as the current sultan was, General Khau knew that had it not been for a marriage arranged decades ago, he would not be in power. Nasir was the grandson of Iltutmish, a man who had married the daughter of the empire's founder.

Walking atop of the pristine floors, the general knew that they had recently been washed. He could see the dampness that remained from the floor's regular up-keep. On the far end from the chamber's entrance was the governor's magnificent throne. It was the finest in all the province. Any grander and it would rival the sultan's own. The gold-plated seat was likely worth as much as the palace itself. It was slightly raised above the rest of the council. Embellishing it were countless rubies and sapphires the size of grapes. And a few feet from the throne was another open doorway. This one was considerably smaller than the chamber's main entrance and was only ever used by the governor or some of the higher-classed servants.

It took the general thirty steps to come from the entrance to the feet of the raised throne. The average man would have taken forty. Like many of his Brahmin brothers, he had been created to be a warrior. It was God's will and destiny for him.

Standing a few feet from the throne, General Khau studied it with his eyes. Although he lived a life of luxury and privilege, he was never one to think much of it. His father had taught him to love dirt, not gold. There was nothing more important than the earth. For without it, man truly had nothing. After all, riches and wealth would come and go as time and generations passed. But a family's legacy and honor would last an eternity.

Feeling a presence, his thoughts were scattered. He turned his head and saw the governor now standing in the open doorway.

"*Assalam-O-Alaikum.*"

General Khau slightly bowed in respect. "*Walaikum.*"

The governor returned the gesture. "Your haste in arriving brings this court honor, general."

"I wasted no time."

A plain white *thobe* covered the governor, running from his neck to his wrists and all the way down to the tops of his calves. Under that loose and comfortable garment was a matching *shalwar* that covered the governor from his waist to his ankles. There was not a single embellishment on the man's clothing. Whenever he went to the *masjid*, he would wear his simplest clothing to remind him that in the eyes of God, he was no better than the man begging on the street. His cheeks and chin were covered with short, well-trimmed facial hair. Were it not for the way he carried himself, his light-toned and smooth skin, and the awe that his presence gave off, a foreigner might have mistaken him for one of the palace's servants. But his voice still had a slight accent that showed his family's origins in the west.

Coming to his throne, the governor sat down while Khau remained standing before him. But before either of them could speak, a third figure entered the council chambers. He seemingly came out of the shadows that the beams of light had been unable to reach as if he had been there the entire time watching Khau like a snake. The man's arrogant footsteps echoed throughout the hall as he approached from behind the general.

He was dressed in a similar style to the governor, only his clothing was black. Golden-threaded designs had been sown onto his clothing, declaring the wealth and power that he came from. Just by his footsteps, General Khau knew who it was without bothering to turn around.

He stopped a few feet to the general's left. The whole way there, the governor had silently watched the man make his approach. The man's eyes were on the governor and neither he nor the general even gave each other the courtesy of a glance. As soon as the man came near the throne, the friendly atmosphere in the room suddenly dispersed as if it had never been there.

The governor's words broke the silence. "Abdul Latif, your presence was not at *Fajr* prayer this morning."

"You must have missed me, governor. I arrived late and was at the back of the congregation." Abdul Latif was a handful of years older than the governor and the general. On his cheeks and chin was a good sized beard, but it was trimmed and well taken care of. And on his head rested a white *Kufi* hat.

In Khau's opinion, it was all a vain attempt to show piety. The inside of that man's soul was anything but what he portrayed. He knew without any doubt that his words were a lie, but he did not challenge Abdul Latif's honor. A good warrior knew when it was time to fight and when to show restraint.

The governor did not respond to his advisor's lie and looked over the two men standing before his throne. "I called you here under false pretenses. Our sultan is not making a visit. I was forced to lie because what needs to be said must stay between us for the moment."

The two councilmen were silent.

"You know of the reports. Genghis Khan's family has conquered all of China. Our allies tell us that they are ravaging Rus', and a letter from the Persian Sultan tells me that they are pushing into the borders of his empire as we speak." There was a short pause. "However, three scouts came to me this morning with disturbing news."

The governor was silent again and slowly lowered his gaze. General Khau knew that apprehension regarding what needed to be said held the governor's tongue. A few long moments passed before Khau broke the silence. "Have they set their eyes on Bihar?"

With a slight nod, the governor looked back up at his counsel. "Our fears have been realized. We believed that they would not enter our lands if we showed no aggression, but that was a false hope. The Mongols wish to conquer all the lands and that includes our own. They have but one option if they wish to invade the empire...and that is through Bihar."

There was complete silence. It was a dead silence so quiet that a drop of water could have been heard crashing onto the ground. General Khau's expression did not change. He knew it would only be a matter of time. The Mongols were intent on destroying everything. They wanted to conquer the world. And to do that, they would have to raise their flag over his homeland.

But the same contemplative demeanor was not shared by the other councilman. As Abdul Latif digested the governor's words, his eyes were filled with panic. Terror consumed every inch of his body and every ounce of his very soul. The governor's words came straight out of a nightmare. His voice shook as he spoke. "N— negotiation...negotiation is o—our only option..."

"Genghis Khan's progeny are not ones to negotiate," Khau said. "They are conquerors, not diplomats. The only diplomacy they know is cleaving heads and burning cities. Asking to negotiate will only show them weakness. It will give them even more reason to invade."

The advisor looked over at his braver counterpart. Deep in his heart, he knew that the general spoke the truth. But he did not want to face the option of war. "What do you suggest? That we take them to battle?"

Khau kept his eyes focused on the governor. "No. I don't suggest we take them to battle. I suggest we *defeat* them in battle."

Abdul Latif took in what his foil said, unable to believe how much confidence the general had under such circumstances. The governor did not know if it was fear or haughtiness that drove his councilman to continue his argument. "Are you that arrogant, *Brahmin*?"

General Khau did not let his counterpart's demeaning voice get under his skin. "It is not arrogance that makes a man go to war. It is necessity, and the situation here dictates that war will be a necessity if our people are to survive."

"You fool!" Abdul Latif's words echoed through the council chamber and into the empty corridor. "The Mongols have not lost a battle in decades. And you wish to challenge them?"

The general's silent stare gave Abdul Latif his answer. He did not even give him the courtesy of a response. Slowly, Khau looked away from the advisor and back to his commander.

But Abdul Latif would not let the debate end that easily. "If that be the case, then your high caste has made you foolish."

The general's gaze left the governor. In an instant, he turned around to look straight into Abdul Latif's fear-stricken eyes. His voice held no anger, but the calmness was now gone. "Do not utter another word against my caste, or the next head I take will be yours."

Abdul Latif looked into the general's eyes knowing full well that the threat was not just mere words. He made a wise decision by not testing the general any further.

The governor rose to his feet causing the councilmen to end their power struggle. They looked back at the governor as he spoke. "This is a council of wisdom, not emotion. Logic and common sense dictate us in this court, not fear. And we all know that there is truly only one decision that can be made here."

Abdul Latif spoke. "My lord—"

Holding his hand up, the governor broke his advisor's sentence. "Your position has been noted. You may take your leave. I wish to speak to General Khau alone in the gardens."

54

CHAPTER 5
INTO THE FIRE

In the gardens, the governor and general walked under the shade of the tall trees and between the perfectly trimmed and flora-filled hedges. In the hedges and throughout the gardens, the two companions could see many Marigold flowers. The bright yellow flora ran rampant throughout all of Bihar. Almost every woman in Patna wore a necklace made from these flowers during regal and religious events.

As the governor and general made their way along the path, the governor was not one step ahead of the general as he had been in the palace. Here, where nobody could see them, they walked side-by-side. With both their eyes focused in front of them, the governor broke the peaceful silence. "As a governor, people look at you as a king. But I truly do not have absolute power. I have freedom as long as it does not impede on the sultan's wishes."

"Like the councilman who was given to you without your choosing?"

The governor slightly smiled. "Had Abdul Latif not been related to our sultan, I would have thrown him out of my court long ago. His council has been of no use except to create distrust within the palace walls. But our sultan's demands must be followed."

"But Abdul Latif's council need not be followed."

"He is not from here. Foreigners do not understand this place." The governor looked up at a butterfly that came out of the hedges and fluttered above their heads. Its soothing bluish-green colors and fluttering wings were so perfect. Only God could create something like that. "They do not understand the peace we have here in Bihar. They cannot see the mosaic that we make: Hindus, Muslims, Christians, and Buddhists. We live in harmony here. Just as no one could imagine this insect turning into something so beautiful, a hundred years ago the image of all these religions living peacefully in Bihar was a fool's tale. But we make this dream a reality every day."

Khau listened on to his friend's wisdom that echoed Khau's own thoughts.

"Here we are...a Muslim ruler and a Hindu general who commands an army full of Hindus, Muslims, and Christians. And yet we make it work day after day, season after season, year after year. On almost every corner of Bihar and throughout the empire, you will find a church, masjid, and temple side-by-side. As the people go in and out, they greet their neighbors with peace, regardless of what name they call their God." There was a short silence. "I have travelled to many parts of the world in my youth. I know that there are parts of the world where that is only seen in dreams...and I fear the day when that sight becomes extinct."

Continuing on the smooth path, the two of them could see the palace over the hedges and between the tree trunks. But out here, it felt as if they were walking through the forest. Had he not known he was in the palace's grounds, Khau would have half-expected to run into a leopard as had happened when he was younger. "When I was last in the sultan's court, he asked me why we are able to live in such peace and others in the world cannot."

The governor looked over at his friend. "What did you tell him?"

"That here, we know what tolerance means. It doesn't mean that I agree with everything you do. It means that I respect you as God's creation enough to let you worship and live however you please. It means that I understand what you call God by is a matter of discussion only between you and your Lord."

The governor put his hand onto Khau's powerful shoulder. "A wise response, my friend. Like your teachings, the Bible, and the Qu'ran say, we are truly all one people. And when we truly become one, we can best anything."

"Including the Mongols."

The governor slightly nodded as his smile faded away. "No enemy is unbeatable. Our beloved Prophet Muhammad—peace be upon him—taught us that when God is on your side, then no one can stand against you. At the Battle of Badr, the Muslims were outnumbered three to one, and in the Battle of Uhud, the odds were worse still. But both times, the Muslims did not fail. Bihar is a nation of pious people. Though we are divided as Muslims, Hindus, Christians, and Buddhists, every man, woman, and child follows His commandments in their own way. And whosoever is faithful to God, whosoever has dedicated his spirit to his Lord...well, then that spirit cannot truly ever be conquered by anything else."

"There is no doubt."

Khau's companion took a deep breath. "The Mongols are like a wolf—"

"A wolf in its prime."

The governor's eyes came back onto the general. "If legend holds true, you once killed a leopard when you were a boy. A full grown leopard according to the stories."

"The legend is true. I did kill the full grown beast. But the tale has been embellished. I did not kill it with my bare hands. I used the greatest gift mankind has been given: my mind. At the opportune moment, when the beast was most vulnerable, I struck the leopard with a makeshift spear."

"Our mind is what will defeat the Mongols. You are the Lion of Bihar. If any man can bring us victory, it is you. They are unmatched on horseback, and they have perfected the bow and arrow just as our ancestors perfected the methods of hand-to-hand fighting."

Khau nodded. "I was able to kill the leopard because it had a weakness. All creatures do. If I can find the weakness of the Mongol force, I will know how to defeat them as well."

"Our time is short. You must take a scouting party tomorrow at the crack of dawn. Every soldier is at your disposal. Observe them. Watch them. Study them. See their habits. And by God's mercy, may you find the weakness that you are looking for."

"I will take our bravest men, and I will find the weakness in our enemy."

The governor stopped moving and Khau followed suit. "And I pray that you do find it, general. You know that I think of you as a brother. I would sacrifice my own mother and father for you. But if you do not find a way to beat them in battle, I fear that Abdul Latif will use his relations with the sultan to get his way. And we both know that asking for negotiations will only make our enemy stronger."

General Khau glanced down for a long moment before looking back into the eyes of his friend. "It is a *Brahmin* tradition that when guests are at your table, you eat only when they have had their fill. And I swear not to return until I have every ounce of knowledge about our enemies to fill your belly. I will find it, or I will be martyred in the process. But I will not return in vain."

***

The night before leaving, Khau went to the Buddhist temple as was his tradition before leaving on any expedition. The monk here, Eshin, was the wisest man Khau knew along with the governor.

58

Khau found the monk in a state of meditation in an empty room at the monastery's center. The room was dark except for two candles on either side of him. Dressed in his yellow and red cloth, Eshin sat upright with his head bowed and his eyes shut. But sensing his friend, Eshin opened his eyes and looked up as the general took a seat in front of him.

Eshin smiled. "*Namaste*, general."

"*Namaste*."

"To what do we owe your respectable presence?"

"Advice, my friend...advice and good council."

"What is the matter?"

Khau looked down at his lap before looking back up at the monk. "I am facing an enemy. An enemy that may be unbeatable. They have yet to be bested, and I am now tasked with the duty of turning them back. Victory will mean peace. Failure will mean the end of our people."

Eshin was silent for a few moments. He shut his eyes and tilted his head downward as if he were looking within himself. Khau patiently waited knowing that his friend was trying to find the right words to say to him.

After a while, Eshin's eyes opened and he looked back at the general. He took a deep breath before speaking. "The greatest gift God gave to Man is his mind. All we must do is unlock our mind, and we will find what we seek. And once the mind is unlocked, all the answers to man's problems will be right before his eyes."

There was another silence.

"Do you understand, general?"

Slowly, General Khau nodded.

***

The next day came all too quickly. By the time Khau's expedition was prepared to embark on their perilous journey, the sun was still barely above the horizon, and its light had not yet filled the dawn sky.

But nevertheless, it was time for General Khau and his men to depart.

The fifteen-man party was all mounted on horseback. Their horses looked different from one another, but they were all the fastest in the army.

Last night, General Khau came to each and every man in this expedition and spoke to them about the situation. He told them of the risks they would be taking on this journey. But every man— Hindu, Muslim, or Christian—had taken an oath to protect their land, and now was the time to honor that oath. They had all left their homes under false pretenses, still not letting anyone but themselves know about the coming of the Mongols. Though they were walking into the den of hungry wolves, they could not even tell their wives about it.

The soldiers gathered at the top of a hill overlooking the city which was a mile away. Between the hill and the city of Patna was the mighty Ganges River. Only minutes ago, the scouting party had crossed it on a junk ship. The Hindus of Patna made their way to and from the waters as they conducted their daily rituals at the river. But no matter how many were in the river, its waters continued to flow in one direction, never returning from where it went. Many of the soldiers observing this prayed that their fate would not be the same.

Rather than being covered in heavy chain-mail armor, the men wore thick leather across their bodies. Five of the men were archers. They had wooden bows and quivers full of arrows strapped across their backs. However, during battle, the archers would wear their arrows on their belts for easier access. Also hanging from the

60

belts of the bowmen were long daggers that would be needed if the enemy came too close.

The rest of the men had circular shields thrown across their backs wide enough to protect their torsos and swords tied to their belts. Several of them also had four-foot-long spears hanging from their saddles.

The general looked over all of his men. Twelve of them were lined up in a straight line, and he faced them from a few feet away. They were all looking him in the eyes and awaiting his order to begin their journey. His two lieutenants, Ammar and Bilal, were on either side of him. The former was a swordsman and healer while the latter was the best archer in the province.

With his back straight and his hands confidently around the reins of his horse, Khau spoke to his men. "Hell is at our doorstep. At the border of our lands are the greatest savages the world has ever witnessed. And knowing who our enemy is, I chose each and every one of you. We may be facing Gog and Magog themselves if the scholars are to be believed. But if that be the case, I would want nothing more than to face our advesary in your company."

If there was any fear in any of the soldiers, they all masked it away as the words of their commander echoed through their souls.

General Khau looked over at Bilal and the lieutenant held up his fist. "*Allahu Akbar!*"

Four of the men, including Ammar, replied with the battle cry of the Muslim and Christian soldiers, "*Allahu Akbar!*"

General Khau raised his fist. "*Jai Bajrang Bali!*"

The rest of the men raised their fists and called with the battle cry of the Hindus, "*Jai Bajrang Bali!*"

The battle cries rang through the air. They were zealous enough that remnants of their voices were heard in the city itself as distant whispers. They showed that there was not a man in this company afraid of death. When the time came, they would embrace it with honor.

And with those words, they were off.

***

Three days of journeying passed.

From dawn to dusk each day, the company of warriors rode. With no map and no compass, they made their way to the border. Each man knew the land like the back of his hand. They were one with it. They gave it life, and it gave them life. Hardly any words were spoken during their rides. All that could be heard was the stomping of horse hooves. The men had brought no supplies except for water and medicine. When the time came for food, the Hindu men would pick from the land, while the Muslim and Christian men would hunt whatever lawful animal they could find. And when water ran low, they would cut into any *Marda* trees that they found if no streams or rivers were in sight.

The only time the men rested during the day was at the Muslims' prayer times. When those times came, the men relaxed for nearly half an hour before continuing on their path. At night, they built a fire and relayed stories and songs to one another as sleep overtook them.

But with each step, Khau knew that they were drawing closer to their enemy. The scouts had informed him that the Mongolian horde was right outside of Bihar's borders when they saw them nearly a week prior. The to-be-invaders were sending out scavenging parties to gather supplies as they waited for reinforcements. Then, they would set off on their path resulting in Bihar's destruction and desolation.

On each of the first two days, the expedition passed through small villages. Recognizing the men as soldiers in their army, the villagers were more than hospitable to the expedition, especially seeing the general in their midst. But when the evening of the second day came and the men left the small village where they rested and prayed, they knew the next people they would see would be the Mongols.

And no doubt, they would not be as welcoming as the villagers.

***

When nightfall of the third day came, they set up camp at the top of a steep hill. From this vantage point, the company would be able to see for miles and miles unhindered if it had been daylight. But even in the dark of night, they had a view sufficient to prevent any enemy from attacking their camp without warning.

The skies were clear and full of stars that brightly glimmered in the vast heavens. They broke the night's darkness and shed their light onto the earth below. With a single fire burning at the center of the small camp, the full moon's position and the number of stars visible told Khau that nearly half the night had passed.

The horses and most of the men were asleep, exhausted by the day's journey. But they kept their weapons close at hand, and none of them were truly able to rest knowing what tomorrow would bring.

Only two of the men were fully awake. Bilal was on watch at this hour. He had the eyes of a hawk, and he kept his sharp gaze on the surrounding lands. With his perfectly carved bow and deadly arrows in hand, he knew that if anything moved in the darkness, he would slay it before it took another step.

The lieutenant stood only a few feet from the fire with his back to it. He could feel its heat crashing against his back, but he did not let it bother him. After his last expedition in the northern mountain range had nearly ended in his death, he learned that it was better to be too warm than too cold.

Not far from Bilal's booted feet, Khau was seated. His sword was at his side as he stared intently into the burning flames. But it was clear that his mind was far from this camp and the peacefulness of this night.

Instead, they were looking into the nightmare that tomorrow might bring.

Most of Bilal's watch passed without a word. All that could be heard was the silence of the night, snores of some men, and crackling of the fire. However, when the time for his duty had almost ended, Bilal broke the peace but kept his eyes focused on his duty. "Sleep has escaped you, general."

The commander took a deep breath. "More than it ever has before. The last two nights, I have seen visions." As Khau spoke, he kept his eyes on the fire. "I saw my wife...my son...and my newborn baby. And I saw the Mongols doing what they do to every place they conquer." Khau could see the vision as clear as he could see the fire right now. "They were all dead. And...our entire land was ablaze...and I was nowhere to be seen."

Bilal was silent as he kept his eyes on the surrounding lands. The general was never one to share these types of things with his men. To them, he was infallible. But Bilal was different. Bilal was as close to Khau as his own son.

"Maybe it is a sign from my Lord. Maybe the Mongols are bringing the inevitable."

The archer slowly looked away from the plains and back at his commander. "Maybe it is, general. But if this is the end of everything, I want nothing more than for my death to be on my feet. I will be sent to God as a man who dies facing his death, not fleeing from it."

64

The general did not reply.

"You should retire for the night. Tomorrow will only be more treacherous than today."

After a long moment, General Khau answered. But he kept his eyes aimed straight ahead. "No doubt it will...and I fear that some of the men who sleep tonight may enter an eternal sleep tomorrow."

"We are soldiers. We have pledged our lives and will honor that pledge as men should. I swear to you that if one man survives tomorrow, it will be you. If *Allah* gives me the chance, I will surely lay down my life for yours."

His lieutenant's words brought Khau out of his nightmarish thoughts. The general slightly smiled as he looked up at his friend which was a rare sight for his men. "Had God given me a daughter, I would not have hesitated in marrying her to your son."

Bilal's eyes met his commander's as he smirked. The gleam in his eyes showed that he had taken the compliment to heart. "Would it not be sacrilegious for a Hindu girl to marry a Muslim man?"

"What is religion between blood?" Khau paused for a long moment as he looked back into the flames. "I believe the Lord of the worlds cares more about a man's character than what names the man calls his God by."

"Words of the wise. Tomorrow if a battle is to occur, the Mongols will not be able to tell us apart by our religion or family. When they face us, they will only see one people." Bilal said his next words with such confidence that it would have brought fear into the hearts of the Mongols themselves had they heard it. "An unbeatable people who have their Lord with them."

Hearing his lieutenant's words brought a sense of assurance to the general's own soul that had not been there before. For a moment, he felt certain that victory would be theirs and that the Mongols would surely be sent fleeing back to their lands.

There was a silence as, once again, all that could be heard was the crackling of the fire and the snores of some of the sleeping men. Khau kept his eyes on the flames, knowing full well that he might be leading his men into Hell itself. The Mongols were vicious. It was their legacy. For no other reason than to instill terror in the hearts of their enemies, they would slaughter cities of men and boys. And the things they did to the woman and girls put them on the level of Satan himself. It was why some people believed their conquest was a sign of Judgment Day.

But General Khau would not let them take the lives of any of his people.

"When your time as a warrior ends, what then general?"

Breaking away from his thoughts, Khau looked at Bilal. "...Lieutenant?"

"Surely you've thought of life after your duty as a soldier ends."

The general slowly nodded. A small smile crept back onto his face as he thought of the image that came to him in his happiest dreams. "I will do what any good man dreams of doing, what we were made by God to do."

"Farm."

Khau nodded. "I will get land near *Bhagwanpur*. It's known as the City of Gods. With my sons and serfs, I will become even more united with the land I have sworn to protect. Land is the thing that matters most. It's the thing that lasts. Combined with our most precious gift—our mind—we can turn a barren land into a fruitful garden. And that is what I will do. We were created out of dirt, and love for land runs through our blood no matter how noble we may be."

Bilal smiled. "As will I. Perhaps we can be neighbors."

66

The general let out a low laugh. "In this life and the next, my friend." Khau could see the image of his best soldier becoming his best neighbor. He took a deep breath before he rose to his feet. And as he did, the general picked up his enclosed sword off the ground and stared at its majestic sheath for a long moment. "Retire yourself, Bilal."

"My watch is not yet over, sir."

Looking at Bilal, he put his powerful hand onto the lieutenant's shoulder the way any older brother would. "Give me the honor of finishing it. You are all my sons, and it is my duty to watch over you."

***

The next morning came all too quickly.

An hour before the sun appeared, General Khau moved his force to the north still under the cover of darkness. And within the hour, they could see smoke rising from the enemy's camp. It was no more than a dozen miles away. After all the legends, after all the horrendous stories, after the long journey here, they would soon be face-to-face with their enemies. Had it not been for the enormous hills that rested all across the land, they would have been able to witness the distant Mongolian camp itself.

At the crack of dawn, Khau sent out his best scout, Rakesh, to reconnoiter around the enemy's camp. Rakesh had ridden off on his dark brown stallion without a word of protest or a hint of fear. He knew that a wrong step would end with his capture and tortured death. But if anybody would be able to successfully survey the land without being detected, it would be him.

Even after the sun emerged, the general could still see the smoke of countless camp fires in the distance as they drifted into the cloudless sky. He prayed that the number of fires burning was not a sign of the Mongol camp's numbers. But deep in his heart, he knew what the truth would be. However, he needed to know the specifics before moving in. Khau wanted to avoid a conflict today at all costs. Today was not the day for battle; rather, it was the day to find the weakness in the enemy.

But if it came to a fight, every man here would give their lives before surrendering.

From their vantage point, Khau and his party had a good view of the beautiful and aesthetic hill country. All around them were rolling green hills. Birds of many shapes and sizes could be seen fleeing from the smoke as they loudly cried out. No doubt, they had seen their brethren hunted for food by these outsiders.

And if the expedition looked even further past the smoke, they could see the magnificent mountains that touched the sky. None had ever ventured to the summits of those mountains and returned to tell the tale. But the mountains were so majestic and beautiful that they could only have been made by God's hands themselves. And it was those very same mountains that separated Bihar from its northern neighbor.

It was a breezeless day, and the air was completely still. At the top of a hill, the entire party was mounted on horseback as the warm sun beat down on them. Lined up in a straight line with the general a few paces in front of his men, they looked in the direction of the smoke and awaited Rakesh's arrival.

The sun had been up for two hours when the scout returned. Khau saw Rakesh and his horse appear at the top of a hill riding as fast as he could. Seeing him racing back to expedition so furiously made Khau instinctively touch the hilt of his sheathed sword, thinking that Rakesh was being chased.

But the fear quickly disappeared.

Rakesh made it to the foothills right under the company. He slowed his horse down a bit but still quickly made his way up to the rest of his comrades.

"What news did you find?" Khau asked Rakesh when the scout was near enough to hear.

Rakesh pulled back the reins of his horse, bringing it to a sudden halt when he was a few feet from his commander. The horse's weight went onto its back legs, and its front legs lifted off the ground a few inches before coming back onto the green grass. Rakesh was out of breath and panted as his eyes looked at the general. Beads of sweat ran down his face. "I...I have seen the Mongol's camp. They are inside o—our borders and only ten miles away."

Hearing those words, every man's grip tightened around the reins of their horse. Except for the general's. If he felt any fear, the valiant man did not show it, and his voice had the same reassuring quality that it always had. He had prepared his mind to hear this and would not show weakness in front of his men. "What were their numbers?"

Now at ease, Rakesh slowly gained control of his fast-beating heart. "I could not study their camp long. But in one glance, I saw a hundred at the least. But many were likely still in their tents, and I believe this to be only a forward camp."

Khau slightly nodded. "No doubt their main army will be no more than a day behind. Before long, thousands of these barbarians will flood across our borders."

The image of the invading army caused fear to crawl up every soldier's skin. Thousands of these barbarians? If the legends were true, then these invaders were truly unbeatable. And now the general was saying that *thousands* of them would be coming this way.

"What are the camps defenses?" the general calmly asked.

"They had patrols watching the area."

"How large?"

Rakesh took a deep breath. "I witnessed two patrols, and they each had either eight or nine men. I slipped by them, but a party of our size will not except by *Bhagwan's* miracle."

"For us to all move in would be folly." The general was silent for a short moment. "*Bhagwan's* greatest blessing is our mind, and we have to use it now." Khau looked over his right shoulder and scanned his men for a long moment. He took a deep breath as he looked into each and every soldier's eyes. "A few will accompany me to study our enemy, and the rest will remain."

Lieutenant Bilal nodded as his horse took a few steps forward breaking away from the rest of the pack. Just like his general, Bilal's voice held no fear or hesitation. "This is undoubtedly the wisest alternative. Allow me to be the one to go with you into the fire."

Seeing his soldier's bravery, General Khau smiled on the inside. "Bilal, you are undoubtedly the bravest man amongst the group, and if the time comes for battle, an archer of your caliber will be needed. The two of us will go forward. And Rakesh will accompany us since he knows the way."

"As you wish, general," Rakesh said.

Khau locked eyes with his remaining lieutenant. "Ammar, you will lead the men while I am gone."

"Yes, general."

"We are all here as one people, united in one cause. That makes us closer than any blood could make us. If the time comes, you are to fight for one another in such a manner."

Ammar put his closed right fist over his heart. "With my honor on the line, I swear to abide by those words, general."

"I have no doubt. And if we do not return by sundown..." Khau took a deep breath, "Then pray that our souls find forgiveness awaiting us on the other side of death."

CHAPTER 6
THE ENEMY

They were finally here.

The general and his scouting party could see the enemy's camp no more than half a mile away. Positioned right behind the top of the highest hill, they looked in the Mongol's direction. Lying on his stomach, the general was hidden and nobody from the encampment would see him with a casual glance. The scouting team's horses were behind them at the foot of the hill and well out of sight from the Mongolian camp.

The journey here was nerve-racking and tedious but uneventful. General Khau and his two men had slowly travelled through the hill country on horseback. Making sure not to move too quickly, they limited the chances of being detected. A few miles into their journey, the party had seen a pack of six Mongols riding on their horses as they patrolled the area. But being in hill country, General Khau and his men easily remained out-of-sight.

Now, Khau silently watched the camp. After all the legends, they now saw these unconquerable savages with their own naked eyes. Had it not been for the situation at hand, the feeling would have been surreal. A few feet below the general, Rakesh watched the party's right flank. And midway down the hill, Bilal scanned the land behind them as well as their left flank with his sharp eyes. Standing up straight, he kept his archer's gaze on the countless hills. With his bow in one hand and four arrows in the other, he would pick off any that came into view.

The sun was beginning to leave its peak now as it continued to send down waves of heat. General Khau had been silently studying the enemy camp for an hour. Rakesh had not exaggerated when he claimed that there were a hundred Mongols. In fact, in the time they had been watching the camp, Khau had counted nearly twice that number.

But the general did not let the strength of his enemies faze him.

There were countless huts in the enormous base. Some were bare while others were ceremoniously decorated. And between the huts, there were many smoldering fires that had been fully ablaze the night before. It was obvious that the larger the hut, the higher ranking the occupant. It seemed that even savages had a hierarchy of command. Some of the smaller huts had five or six men in them. And the larger ones likely held captive woman. Genghis Khan had taught his people by example how barbarians treated their captured woman and children.

Around the campsite, some of the Mongols were finishing up their meals. They ate like any savage would, without manners and etiquette. They had turned the once beautiful field into a filthy mess in the short time they had been here. They were like a pack of carnivorous animals that were always looking for their next prey. Even from where the two men hid, they could hear the loud and voracious voices of the invaders.

And across the plains, the Mongols trained. They had targets set up across several hundred meters. Countless archers rode on horseback, weapons in hand. But these were not the weapons of savages. Each bow was crafted by the hands of a master. They were made out of the best wood. Sturdy but flexible, they were the ideal weight for handling while riding a horse. Designs of the Mongolian tribes were intricately and flawlessly carved onto the weapons.

Their stallions were beasts of beauty. As much as the Mongols were savages, their horses were majestic. Strong and graceful, the horses glided above the grass. And they moved faster and with more control than any beast the general had ever seen. Even from where he hid, Khau could see the fine lines and powerful muscles of these magnificent horses. It showed that they had been bred for war. It was as if they had been made by God's own hands.

Expertly, the Mongolian bowmen rode past each target full speed ahead. But as they flew past each wooden board, they fired off a single arrow without slowing down a single breath.

Khau watched Mongol after Mongol run through the course only a few strides behind one another. It was as if each soldier was a clone of the next one. Their horses seemed to step in the same places as the one that went before them.

And no arrow missed its mark.

As arrow after arrow was fired, they were shot off with perfect precision. It was as if the invaders had been born and created to do this. This was their art and they were the masters. They were the rulers of horseback archery.

Khau looked away from the scene and towards Rakesh. He could see the awe in the scout's eyes as he watched their enemies train so perfectly.

"Do you see where their advantage lies?"

Slowly, Rakesh replied without taking his eyes off of their right flank. "...Advantage?"

"It's their ability on horseback. They have unlocked something anew." Khau's gaze went back onto the Mongols. "They can ride with just their legs. Genghis Khan learned to control a horse with just his legs freeing his hands from having to hold the horse's reins...I had heard the legend long ago, but I believed it to be a myth...until today."

Continuing to study his enemy, Khau saw the truth in his own words. Indeed, the Mongols did not use their hands to guide the horses as they came upon the targets. Using their legs and weight, they controlled and steered the stallions at their top speed. All the while, they kept perfect balance. And in their free hands, they held the bows and calmly pulled back their arrows. Somehow, they were able to keep their aim steady even while the horses raced at top speed. As they took aim, their eyes were focused on the target.

It all seemed like sorcery.

"It is what allows them to shoot *while* riding." Khau was silent for a long moment. "Do you realize what advantage this gives them?"

Rakesh was not sure if the general expected an answer or not.

"It has allowed them to beat every foe they have ever faced. This simple advantage has granted them a superiority no other army possesses. Genghis Khan and his followers have used their advantage to the fullest, making every foe play right into their hands." He looked at the scout. "It has made them invincible."

Rakesh was speechless for what seemed like a long time, never having heard the general utter the word 'invincible.' "...Do they have a weakness general?"

Khau's steady eyes stayed focused on the enemy camp. There was a brief silence. "From here, I see only a few: a lack of siege weapons, supply lines, and not knowing the lay of the land are the foremost. The latter two will make their army move slower than it otherwise would. But the Chinese knew of these weaknesses, and they still lost."

"...What do you command...sir?"

Khau took a deep breath. "There is nothing more we can do here but risk capture. All that there is to be seen here has been

75

witnessed. We must regroup with the others and ponder over what we have discovered. We must trust our Lord to show us to victory."

***

Not a word had been spoken when the group made it five miles out from the Mongolian camp. Moving slowly, it had taken them almost an hour to travel this far. They had yet to run into any of the Mongolian patrols but knew that they were undoubtedly at large. The trio of soldiers made their way down from the side of a steep hill. General Khau was in the middle while Bilal was two paces behind him on his right and Rakesh was to his left.

All was quiet except for the soft sounds of the horses' hooves as they lightly tread on the grass. The air remained still. Not a single draft had been felt all day as the afternoon sun continued to beat down on them. With both hands around his horse's reins, the images of all Khau had seen replayed in his mind over and over again. Where did the enemy's weakness lie? It had to be there. No army was invincible. The Mongolian army was just a group of men after all. They were no gods. He just had not unlocked the mystery yet.

Khau's eyes left the hills and slightly rose to the cloudless sky. He let out a whisper, but both his men faintly heard his words: "My Lord...my people need you now...I...need you now. There is nowhere else left to turn but you."

As the general's gaze left the heavens, his sixth sense was triggered. A moment after his prayer had ended, Khau felt something: an unwanted presence. Whipping his head around, he knew that it was already too late.

A pack of eight Mongols had discovered them.

Riding out from around the hill, they came into view. They were all armed with their majestic bows and deadly arrows. Around their belts were thin swords that did not weigh them down. They rode furiously at Khau and his party as four of them drew back their bows. Somehow, they had made no sound as they swung around the hill and tracked down Khau and his men. But now in plain view, the Mongols came at their foes full speed ahead as their loud hooves beat against the ground.

And mayhem was on their minds.

Four arrows flew through the air and at their targets. Instinctively, Bilal weaved his head to the side, and the arrow flew by him only inches away from his skull. The second arrow violently dug itself into Khau's horse, striking it in the head. The animal instinctively stood up on its hind legs and let out a final neigh—a neigh that was filled with the pain of death. And as its cry ended, the animal toppled over and died taking the general to the ground with it. But before being crushed by the carcass, the general kicked himself off of the falling horse, landing on the ground unhurt. As the horse crashed to the ground, the general's spear and supplies scattered and slid in every direction.

But Rakesh was not so lucky. The third and forth arrow struck him in the head and throat consecutively without giving him a chance to defend himself. And before he even fully knew what was happening, he fell off of his horse and collapsed onto the ground.

Dead.

And no sooner had Rakesh fallen that two arrows struck Bilal's own horse in quick succession, maiming the animal. As the horse staggered to its left atop its now wobbly legs and neighed in pain, Bilal leapt off the animal and landed crouched down a few feet away. A few arrows fell out of his quiver in the process. In the next instant, two more arrows intended for Bilal struck his horse and killed it. The dead animal's legs gave up, and it slumped onto the ground.

There was no fear on either Khau's or Bilal's face. If they had any terror in them, their enemies could not see it. All the Mongols could see were the eyes of provoked lions. General Khau stripped his shield off of his back and held it in his left hand. He swiftly turned around as he felt two of his foes behind him. With their bows drawn back, the two Mongols rode right by one another with their eyes on the general. Steadying their aim, they fired off their arrows, and the projectiles came at their target with enough ferocity to drive them through a rhinoceros's hide.

The general leapt to his right avoiding the first projectile by a few inches. Doing a quick roll, he came to his knee. He held his shield up before the second arrow viciously dug into it. A third arrow came at him from his rear, but the general sensed it right as it was fired off. Swiftly turning around, he blocked it with his shield as well. And when the fourth arrow came at him from his left, he easily broke it against his shield.

Bilal armed himself with his bow and arrow. Without wasting any time and still crouched down, he attempted to take aim and fire at the captain of the Mongols. But he was forced to shoot before he could properly take aim as he was nearly hit by two deadly arrows, causing Bilal's own shot to go wide left of the captain.

Bilal did a quick roll to his left to avoid another arrow meant to put him down. He took cover behind his fallen horse as he pulled three arrows out of his quiver. He felt more of his enemies' arrows bury themselves into the dead animal with loud thuds one after the other. Putting one arrow into his bow while holding the other two between his fingers, he rose up as he tried to take aim at another foe. But as he came up onto a knee, he saw another Mongol aiming at him. Ignoring that Mongol, he took aim at a fast-moving target and released his arrow.

But once again, the arrow missed its mark. Bilal was forced to fire before he could take proper aim and apply the right amount of pressure to his arrow. Ducking back behind his dead horse just in time, the Mongol's arrow flew right above his head. He quickly looked to his left and saw the general's spear lying at his feet.

A few meters behind him, General Khau's shield deflected and blocked several more arrows. Six had dug into the shield while countless others lay broken and scattered all around him. But these arrows were not just the ones aimed at the general. From his vantage, Khau was able to block any arrows fired at Bilal from the archer's unprotected rear. Khau was slowly backing up to join his lieutenant now only ten meters away. But as he did, he simultaneously watched the movement of all eight foes.

The Mongolian force was circling their two prey like a pack of wolves as they kept their distance between themselves and the soldiers of Bihar. Their ferocious voices filled the air, but Khau did not know the language of his enemies. And as the captain of the Mongols circled in front of the general, Khau saw the wicked smile on the man's face as Khau continued to block the fiends' arrows. The captain knew that these two men had no chance against his mighty warriors. He did not even bother blowing the alarm horn hanging from his neck.

"General!"

Hearing Bilal's words, Khau instinctively caught the spear tossed his way without looking back. Catching it firmly, he broke another arrow against his shield. A moment later, he launched his spear at a Mongolian archer.

The spear was aimed and thrown with absolute perfection. It soared straight at its target with blinding speed and powerful force. Before the Mongol had a chance to dodge it, it thrust itself into the side of his horse and came out the other side. With a cry of fear, the horseman fell from his steed and collapsed onto the ground hurt but alive.

But he did not last long.

Seeing what his commander had done, Bilal took aim. With the fallen horse protecting one side and the general protecting the other, he had the few seconds he needed. The archer drew back his bow and fired with all the focus required. Just as the fallen horseman rose back up, an arrow plunged right through his throat.

And just like that, the first Mongol fell.

Crouched down between the fallen horse and general, Bilal immediately put the small victory out of his mind. He looked away from the corpse and loaded his bow with another arrow. He could hear arrow after arrow being fired at them, but the general blocked each and every one from the archer's rear. The Mongols in front of him did not have him in their line-of-sight.

Only two feet away from his most loyal soldier, Khau was on his knee so that the shield would cover most of his body. Without looking back at his lieutenant, Khau spoke above the chaos as he deterred a few more projectiles meant for them. "I will mark the targets." He blocked another arrow. "You bring them down."

"By my life, I will." Bilal pulled back his string to ready another arrow. Eyes closed, he awaited his commander's order. "*Bismillah...*"

"Below the center of the sun!"

Rising up with his back against the general's, Bilal's bow was poised and aimed exactly where the general ordered and at the level where a horse rider would be found. Even with the sun's full glare in his eyes, he did not lose his concentration. With only a moment of hesitation required in order to change his aim from the chest to the neck, Bilal fired off the arrow. It cut through the still air as fast as a shooting star and struck its target in stride. The arrow sunk into the top of the man's neck. And in the next instant, the rider fell from his horse.

Bilal did not take a moment to reflect over his victory. He immediately sunk back down just in time to avoid two arrows meant for him.

"Why do they not move in?" Lying on his back, Bilal wasted no time drawing back his bow with another arrow. He could hear the Mongolians calling out to one another, and he could hear the captain barking out commands as the remaining five warriors fired at their two preys. But Bilal could not comprehend the language of his enemy just as the Mongols could not understand theirs.

"Perhaps they are playing to their strengths," Khau said as he knocked away another arrow, "As will we! Count to three, and then take aim directly to my left!"

With his eyes closed, Bilal counted the seconds. *One.* Another arrow dug into the horse's carcass. He focused his mind and held his bow and string steady. *Two.* A couple of arrows dug into the general's shield in quick succession. *Three.* The archer's eyes opened.

Rising up, he took aim perpendicular to the general and at the same level he had previously fired. With one eye shut, he saw his target approaching the arrow's line of sight. He had to release the arrow at just the right moment, otherwise it would miss. In the mind of the archer, nothing could be heard and nothing could be seen...except for the target. With a silent word of prayer, Bilal let go of the string.

He came back down before he could see if the arrow hit its mark. But the arrow flew towards its target even faster than the last one Bilal had fired. And before the Mongol had a chance to redirect himself, he rode straight into his death. The arrow plunged into his forehead right above his eyebrows with no mercy. His neck shot backwards before his lifeless body went limp and let go of his horse's reins.

"Your arrow met its mark!" Khau loudly spoke.

Again, Bilal reloaded his bow, silently awaiting his commander's next orders.

The Mongolian captain stopped twenty meters in front of General Khau. He realized what was happening and knew that he could not continue on this current course. Seeing his men shot down by a weakened foe made his wicked smile disappear. Khau did not know why the man did not blow his horn to alert the camp. Was it arrogance?

The captain shouted orders to his remaining three men, and as his words ended, the men ceased fire. Within a matter of seconds, they had joined him on either side. With only a few feet between each of them, they had effectively created a small semicircle around Khau and Bilal. And at his command, they all drew back their bows simultaneously aiming at the general.

Khau realized what was happening even before his enemies raised their bows. By firing at him from all different directions concurrently, he would only survive by God's miracle.

"To Rakesh's shield!" Khau roared.

Without any hesitation, the archer came to his feet, and the two of them raced to the fallen Rakesh only a few meters away. The Mongols fired away their arrows all at once. Coming to his fallen scout, Khau picked his second shield up off the ground just in time. Three of the arrows were fiercely buried into Rakesh's shield while the captain's and the remaining Mongol's arrows broke against Khau's own shield.

On their knees, Khau defended his archer from the onslaught. The Mongols fired another round of arrows in quick succession, but the shields covered the general and his archer.

"General! This defense will not hold. Even if I had a line-of-sight, I haven't the time to take aim!"

"Don't shoot at the archers, my brother. The horses are easier targets." Crouched down behind his shields, Khau looked back at Bilal. "The leader's horse is directly in front of me. Take aim. At the proper moment, I shall part my shield, and you will bring him to the ground."

"I shall not miss." Bilal took a deep breath knowing he had only a few arrows left. Each shot counted. There was no room for error. He drew back his bow and aimed straight ahead, still under the cover of the shields.

"Once the captain's horse is down, we shall use their confusion against them. Shoot down all their horses as quickly as you can. Then, I will send them to their death!"

"By *Allah*, I will."

Khau took a deep breath. He needed to wait for the perfect moment to make his move. His gaze fell down at his feet. Rakesh's fallen spear lay by his boots, and he knew what he would need to do once the captain's horse went down. The Lion of Bihar would be unleashed...

Khau's eyes came back into focus straight ahead. It was time to show these Mongols what bravery really was. "Now!"

Bilal released his messenger of death right as Khau parted the shields just a crack. The arrow flew out, and Khau closed the crevice immediately following its release. And no sooner did it happen that Khau and Bilal heard the sound of a horse dying and collapsing to the ground. Seeing their leader fall, the Mongols were all distracted for a moment as the captain tried to rise back to his feet.

And that was all that Khau and Bilal needed.

"To victory!" Khau roared.

The general dropped his arrow riddled shield and picked up the spear. Rising to his feet, he stepped forward and launched the deadly spear at the nearest Mongol. It plunged through the man's lightly armored chest and drove itself right through his heart. He fell from his horse like so many of his comrades had done today.

Bilal came to his feet. There was no fear in his eyes and there was none in his heart. Bilal wasted no time pulling out his remaining three arrows and loading the next one. He rapidly and expertly fired them all off consecutively within four seconds.

As the first Mongol's horse fell dead, the soldier leapt off of his stallion and did a quick roll before rising to his feet. He saw the ferocious general charging at him with the roar of a lion. In Khau's left hand was his shield, and in his other was his unsheathed sword.

The Mongol unsheathed his thin sword just in time to block Khau's first blow. But with two more quick strikes, the general masterfully disarmed his foe and gave him a long, deep gash across his right arm. The man let out a yelp of pain as his arm fell limp. He looked up at his attacker just as his sword fell to the grass. With no mercy, Khau cleaved off the Mongol's head.

There would be no clemency from the general.

By the time Khau had slain his foe, the last two mounted Mongols had been thrown off their horses after their steeds were shot down one after the other by Bilal. The arrows dug into each horse's exposed head, slaying them instantly. And as the soldiers rose to their feet, the angry lion charged towards them.

Knowing that their time was short, they quickly regained their composure. The two archers drew back their bows and launched as many arrows as they could at the charging lion. The arrows cut through the air faster than the untrained eye could see, but they were broken against Khau's shield.

And his roar was heard for a mile in every direction.

84

By the time each man had fired three arrows, the lion was on them. Both Mongols threw aside their bows and drew their swords. Khau took them both on at once.

They had the advantage in numbers, but their skill was nothing compared to the general's.

He expertly blocked both of their strikes with masterful ease, not missing a single step. The sound of their blades clanging against one another could be heard throughout the valley. Unbeknownst to the Mongol camp and Khau's remaining expedition, the lion in Khau had been unleashed.

With a quick move, he stepped up and forcefully cross-faced the first Mongol with his elbow. The man staggered back a few steps as he spit out blood. Turning to the second man, General Khau beat him back a few steps before knocking aside the man's sword. And he followed through by driving his sword through the man's stomach and out of the top of his back.

Khau put his right boot on the man's torso and wretched the blood-stained sword out. The first man came back at him, sword raised above his head. But it was in vain. In a handful of blindingly swift strikes, Khau ended the man's life with no remorse. The Mongolian fiend fell onto the bloodied grass with deep gashes across his torso and one across his face.

Khau turned around to see the Mongol captain attacking Bilal. The archer had no more arrows left in his quiver and no sword with which to defend himself. With a bow in one hand and a long knife in the other, he battled the captain. The Mongolian leader had a much better sword than the others. He beat the archer back, intending to slay the man who had killed so many of his own.

In one fluid movement, he knocked the dagger out of Bilal's hand and powerfully kicked him squarely in the chest. Bilal fell on his back as the captain stood over him, sword raised for the kill. He brought the sword down, but Bilal rolled out of the way and created space between himself and his foe before rising back to his feet.

Then he heard the roar of a lion.

The captain turned around and saw Khau only a few feet away. Khau's eyes were full of anger and his heart was full of hatred. And his blood boiled with a thirst for vengeance that could not be quenched.

"The arrow that killed Rakesh was yours!"

The captain could not understand the words of his foe, but he could understand the emotions perfectly.

"How many innocents have you killed? How many women have your people defiled? How many cities have you burned? I know why *Bhagwan* sent you here. It is so that I may send you back to him. Today will be your death! And soon, your army's death will follow!"

Khau threw his bloodied sword onto the grass a few feet away, leaving him completely unarmed. But his eyes stayed focused on the captain. The Mongol looked at the sword and then back at his unarmed opponent, knowing what Khau was doing. But he did not follow suit. A wicked smile crept back onto his face. As the grip around his sword tightened, the Mongol said something in his native tongue. Khau did not know what he spoke, but he knew the meaning of those words. He was saying that Khau would die today.

But he would be wrong.

In the next instant, they were upon each other. The captain brought down several quick and deadly strikes with his sword. But Khau easily ducked and weaved, dodging each blow. He moved with more speed and quickness than this Mongol had ever witnessed. Avoiding the swinging blade, Khau stepped forward and grabbed the captain's wrist. He followed through by smashing his elbow into the captain's face and then striking the man's neck with his open palm.

With his breath knocked out of him, the captain backed up as blood ran down his face. But he did not have a chance to recover. The lion was back on him. Grabbing the captain's arm, he twisted it forcing a cry of pain from the Mongol. But there was still no mercy in Khau's eyes. A moment later, he broke the captain's arm right above his elbow forcing the fiend to drop his weapon.

Khau powerfully smashed his boot into the captain's knee with all of his strength completely shattering it. With the captain now off balance, the general again skillfully and forcefully struck the captain's face. The Mongol released another cry of pain as his jaw was struck before falling onto a knee. Grabbing the captain by the side of his head, Khau brought the man's face down and slammed his knee into it, filling it with even more blood. With no mercy, Khau threw the helpless man to the ground. Crouching down, the general grabbed the powerless captain by his collar while his other fist prepared to come down once more.

"Get out of my land!"

Khau struck the invader again...and again...and again....

The battle ended. Crouched down over the captain, Khau's eyes were still filled with anger. He was shaking with it. His gaze was fixed on the body. His breathing was heavy, and his fists were dripping with the blood of his foe.

After a long moment, his gaze met with his archer's. Bilal had watched the entire fight from ten meters away. This was not the first time he had seen the lion unleashed. He knew the captain was as good as dead before the duel ever began.

The odor of death did not bother either seasoned warrior. Khau closed his eyes, regaining his senses and letting all of the adrenaline ooze out of his system. After a few deep breaths, his eyes reopened and looked at his most loyal soldier.

Bilal was at the corpse of his dead comrade. Crouched down at Rakesh's side, he pulled out the arrows and threw them to the side in disgust. He ran his hand over Rakesh's face and closed his eyes.

The general walked to Bilal. Looking down at Rakesh, he said a prayer over his fallen soldier. He took another deep breath as his gaze met Bilal's. "...I prayed to *Bhagwan* that if anyone was to meet their death today, it would be me. Of all the prayers that I ever make, this is the one that is never answered. It is always my brethren who are granted a martyr's death."

Bilal rose back to his feet but kept his eyes on Rakesh. "You were spared for a reason, general, as was I. *Allah* has greater plans for us than to be martyred on this field today."

Khau was silent for a long moment. After a while, his eyes met with his archers. "If that is true, then I know the reason. Our Lord has shown it to me. He has shown me where our victory lies."

CHAPTER 7
MIND UNLOCKED

Ammar and his men rested near their horses. Two men stood watch with spears and shields in hand while the rest were at ease but with their weapons close by. When Khau and his two loyal men had set out, the sun was still in its ascent. But now it was close to finishing its daily course. And with each passing moment, the fear that his general may have met his death grew in Ammar's heart.

But that fear instantly vanished when he heard one of the watchman's voices cut through the air. "The general is coming! Lieutenant Bilal is with him."

General Khau quickly galloped atop of Rakesh's surviving horse while Bilal, only two paces behind, was mounted on the horse of a deceased Mongolian fiend. And as they came from around the hill and into full view of the company, every man in the expedition realized that something tragic had occurred.

Rakesh, the great scout, was nowhere to be seen. Recognizing that the men were riding on horses that were not their own, every man knew the fate of their absent comrade.

The two riders were no longer slowly and quietly treading the land as they had when they began their mission. They were riding at a full gallop towards the company.

By the time the general and lieutenant reached the rest of the party, all the men had mounted their horses. Khau stopped his horse only a few feet away from his other lieutenant, and Bilal stopped right behind him.

The men could see the condition of their commanders. The two warriors were covered in their own sweat. Bilal's quiver was no longer full of his native arrows. Instead, it now held Mongolian arrows. Khau was covered in splotches of dried blood—the blood of his enemies. But the place with the most blood was his fists. Numerous arrow tips remained lodged in his shield, and countless other arrows had left their marks.

"General," Ammar began, "What has befallen Rakesh?"

"I was saved by *Bhagwan's* grace." The Lion of Bihar solemnly looked over his men. "But today was Rakesh's day to receive the death of a hero."

"We were ambushed by a pack of Mongolian fiends," Bilal said, drawing the gaze of the company. "They killed Rakesh with no honor, but we took many lives for his. And we now know that these invaders are not unbeatable warriors as the legends say."

Some of the Hindu men lowered their heads and muttered a quite prayer for their fallen brother. Their whispers could be heard by the general, but he kept his eyes on his lieutenant. "I have been shown the enemy's weakness. What we have learned will grant us our victory in battle. I must travel back to the governor with much haste."

Ammar's eyes showed his relief at hearing the news. "Praise *Allah*. Will you travel back alone?"

The general nodded.

"What is your command for your force?"

"Stay on our enemies. They will soon know of our presence. Keep your distance, and avoid confrontation unless it is unavoidable. Track them, and send messages every two days as to their movements. But if there is a sudden change, send a rider immediately."

Ammar nodded. "Yes, sir."

90

"I will leave Bilal with you. He will tell you of what we have learned." Khau tugged back on his horse's reins a bit. His eyes went back onto all his men, and they met his gaze. "Our Lord has shown us our path to victory. And He will keep his good favor on you as long as you have faith in Him." He raised his fist in the air. "To victory!"

The men raised their fists and simultaneously let out their cries. "To victory!"

With that, General Khau rode off into the distance.

***

Khau rode as quickly as possible without hurting the horse. He stopped for nothing except allowing the horse to rest when it neared exhaustion. Every second and every minute mattered. The longer he took to get back to the palace, the more time Abdul Latif had to use his leverage to follow his personal agenda.

And that would guarantee defeat.

So Khau rode his horse like a madman. Riding across the plains, through the small jungles, and across the hill country, he had his mind on one thing: returning to the palace as soon as possible. Dawn, day, dusk, and night. He rode through them all. During the journey, all he could hear was the beating of his horse's hooves as they crashed onto the ground. After a while, it became music to his ears.

Khau had his victory. In his mind's eye, he could see it as clear as day. But he needed to arrive back to Patna with ample time to prepare for the coming battle. For victory to be theirs, preparations were needed. He needed not only to defend the capital, but also the outlying villages that were not far from the Mongol's forward camp.

For that, time was of the essence.

***

It was the morning of the seventh day since General Khau's departure. In the ruler's court, the governor was seated on his throne, and Abdul Latif was not too far away. And around him were six other men. Four of them were ministers of Bihar while the other two were nobles. Of the six, two were Muslim, three were Hindus, and the last was a Christian. But they all supported Khau's directive of war with the Mongols.

But Abdul Latif was anything but supportive of General Khau. News had leaked of the Mongol's arrival to the people of Patna. Undoubtedly, the hand of Abdul Latif had been behind that. And like he had done every day since the general's departure, the advisor came to the governor's court to take advantage of Khau's absence. Since arriving into the council chambers at the crack of dawn, Abdul Latif's voice filled the halls as he argued his flawed logic. Not long after Abdul Latif's arrival, Khau's allies heard of what he was attempting to do, and they came to ensure the governor would not change his support of Khau's mission.

"Negotiation is the only way!"

"There is no negotiation with these conquerors!"

"Then you would have war brought on us?"

"If God is on our side and General Khau is leading the men, then yes. I will have war!"

"Your general will lead you and this nation to ruin with his warmongering!"

These words had filled the chamber for days now. And there was no end in sight. With all of the bickering between the noblemen and Abdul Latif, the governor was beginning to think that they would defeat themselves before the Mongols ever arrived.

The heavy iron doors to the chamber were closed shut. But the passionate voices of all the men could be faintly heard by the guards on the other side. The governor looked down and shut his eyes, trying desperately to regain his focus. His head was spinning from all of the arguing. Abdul Latif would not let his argument go. Every time his logic was proven false by another man, he threatened to use his position to get his way. The governor wondered if it was his arrogance and ego that blinded him from the clear logic of the situation.

But then it happened. The heavy iron doors suddenly swung open.

With one powerful shove, the warrior on the other side opened them wide and revealed himself to the court. Hanging on their hinges, the doors glided loudly a few inches above the ground until they almost ran into the walls. They creaked so loudly that it drowned out all the voices.

The discussions of the noblemen abruptly ended. Every gaze fell upon the open doorway. For a moment, they all thought that a apparition had arrived. Standing before them was the last person they expected to see.

The Lion of Bihar.

The general was wearing his light, leather armor. His shield was no longer with him, but his sheathed sword hung from his belt. Covered and drenched in his own sweat, he breathed heavily and quickly. He was completely fatigued, but still had the strength to complete this final task. And his eyes were that of a victorious warrior. His cheeks and chin had been cleanly shaven when he had last left them, but now a short, unkempt, and dirty beard covered the general's face.

"...General Khau," the governor said in disbelief as he slowly rose from his seat.

Seeing the look in the general's eyes, nobody uttered a word. His exhaustion was masked by his determination to come here. Even though he could barely muster the strength to stand, he still stood with every ounce of dignity that was in him. Without a word, Khau walked through the court. There was absolute silence except for the loud echo of his footsteps as his boots struck against the marble floor. All eyes were on him, and his ferocious gaze was on Abdul Latif.

"What has happened to you?" Abdul Latif finally asked.

Coming to them, Khau suddenly and piercingly unsheathed his sword. He threw the bloodied weapon onto the floor in the middle of the group. It loudly clanged against the ground and reverberated through the chamber and down the corridors of the palace. The governor and men silently looked at the sharp blade and the dried blood covering it.

"I have seen the enemy! I have looked them in their wicked eyes. And the blood of many of them stains my hands and sword!"

There was complete silence as the mighty general's words echoed.

"War is upon us. A brave brother of ours has already fallen. Another valiant soldier slew many Mongols with his noble bow. Without either of them, I would not be standing here today. And more may have joined the ranks of the dead since I journeyed back to you." Khau walked through the group as they parted for him. He stopped at the feet of the throne; his eyes locked with his commander's. "But I now know where our victory lies."

He said those last words with such conviction that every man in the room believed him, save for one. There was a short silence, but the advisor quickly broke it. "Victory against the Mongol's? That is a fool's dream."

Khau whipped around to face his foe.

"You will lead us all to ruin!"

Before the general could respond, the governor slammed his fist onto his throne's armrest, making every man look his way. But his own gaze was on his advisor, and there was no mercy or compassion in his tone. "Abdul Latif! Your presence is no longer welcome in this court."

The advisor blankly stared at the governor for a long moment, not knowing what to say. He was sure that his ears must have deceived him. How could the governor cast him out? "...My liege...do you wish to reconsider?"

"My mind does not waver."

"Do you forget, governor?" The arrogance in his voice showed. To be dismissed like this in front of all these noblemen was pure humiliation. "Do you forget who ordered me to serve on this court?"

"When the Mongols are turned around, the sultan will realize that your advice is folly. As is your presence here. And as I have cast you out of my circle, surely he will do the same." The governor took a deep breath. "Go now. Go with honor, or I will have you cast out like a leper."

Abdul Latif took the former. He knew better than to test the governor especially with the heated Khau only a few feet away. Without another word of protest, he turned around and left the court.

With his departure, all the noblemen looked back at the general as the governor spoke. His tone was back to normal. "General Khau, your arrival is a relief to us all. What did you find?"

"I know what we must do to achieve victory." Khau glanced at all the men and then back at his friend. "We must get the Mongols off of their horses."

Khau's words echoed through the court and were followed by an awkward silence before one of the noblemen spoke up. "...Please explain, general."

"The Mongols are strongest on horseback and with their bows. Riding their beasts, they are truly unbeatable. But...on the ground, on the ground and at close distances, they are no match for any of our trained infantryman. They continue to win their battles because they have mastered their strengths. And to beat them, we will have to master our own strengths." Khau took a deep breath. "We are the masters of hand-to-hand combat. We have perfected our strengths just as the Mongols have perfected theirs. And if we get them off of their horses, victory will be ours."

"And how do you plan to accomplish this feat?"

Khau looked at the man who had spoken. "Through fire."

"...Fire?"

"Horses are afraid of it. We will choose our battlefield wisely." Khau spoke slowly, seeing everything in his mind's eye before saying it. "We shall dig a ditch—a ditch that is a score foot wide—and it will be filled with bamboo poles, dry corn tufts...and kerosene." The more he spoke, the more Khau could visualize the scene in his mind. "We will draw them in close, so close that they will not be able to turn back. Then, we will light the ditch on fire causing the horses to go into disarray. Some will fall into the fire, others will knock their riders off in the chaos. And then, while the Mongols are in disarray, our army will charge across the hidden bridges and take down the invaders."

"You believe that strategy will send the Mongols back for good?"

"A sound defeat of their first wave will send the Mongols away. The Mongols have not tasted defeat in decades. They will not know how to react when they come across a true challenge...and they will retreat." Khau paused for a moment. "However, this plan alone may not be enough to fully defeat the Mongols. We may need to add to our plan."

96

"There is one more measure that can be taken," the governor quickly said. "It involves the *chakram*."

Khau knew which weapon the governor spoke of. It was the circular blade with a sharpened outer edge that his men used in warfare. They primarily used it as a throwing weapon. But many used it in hand-to-hand combat while wearing smaller versions of the blade on their sleeves.

"Since you have been gone," the governor continued, "I have had discussions with many of our brightest lieutenants. It seems that this weapon can be used to cut the Mongol's horses from under them, if the fire is not enough to stop them. Utilizing the basic functions of a slingshot, we can construct a mechanism that will fire the blades at the legs of the enemy's horses and take away their advantage before the Mongol's ever have a chance to fire an arrow. More than a hundred devices have already been built."

Khau slowly nodded. "How many more can be built in three days?"

"We can double that amount."

The general slightly smiled. "That should be enough. With the ones we have, we can begin training our archers to use them efficiently."

The last nobleman, who had not said a word since Khau's arrival, spoke. "Do we have the time to take these measures? Are the Mongols not already upon us?"

"We do. The Mongols will move slowly. They have no structured supply lines and will wait for reinforcements before moving deeper into Bihar. And that will give us the time we need."

The governor observed the faith in his general's eyes and heard it in his voice. Khau's hope was contagious. "If you truly believe we can win, general, then I am with you."

The Lion of Bihar looked at him. With a gleam in his eyes, he spoke with such a confidence that it bolstered the spirits of every man in the room. "Do I believe we *can* win, governor? No, I do not. That is because we have *already* won, governor."

The governor smiled.

***

The Mongolian commander could see the soldiers of Bihar in the distance. Half a mile separated Bihar's army from the deadly sea of invaders. The invader studied the opposing force. It would have been difficult for the naked eye to have seen the details of the enemy, but the Mongolian commander had the eyes of an archer. And he could make out the man who led Bihar's army.

A week prior, a scouting party had discovered eight Mongolian warriors. Seven were dead. But the last one, a revered captain of the Mongolian horde, had been beaten to his last breath. Before he died, the man told them what had occurred. These mighty men had been brought down by two soldiers.

In his last breath, the dying man described the Bihari commander who, along with his archer, had slain the men. And as the Mongolian commander looked at his foil across the battlefield, he had no doubt that this was the commander who had beaten the captain and slain the rest. This was the man who every Mongol in this army feared and saw in their worst nightmares. He was the one who had turned the Mongol's spirit of wolves into the spirit of hyenas.

He had showed the Mongols that they were not gods walking amongst the earth. They were just men. Because of him, the Mongols on this battlefield were not thinking about what spoils of war would be waiting for them when this battle ended. Instead, they were praying that they did not come face-to-face with any warriors like those who had slain their comrades.

But the Mongolian leader swore to slay this man today. Turning to his lieutenant, the general nodded. The lieutenant acknowledged the gesture. Looking straight ahead, he blew mightily into his horn.

And the Mongolian horde charged.

***

As Dr. Avinash Singh read the last lines of the journal's first account, the emotions it ignited intensified.

When the Mongols came into Bihar, they came like wolves.

They met the army of Bihar on the battlefield. But there was no fear in Khau's eyes. Nor did his men's hearts hold any terror. The Mongols charged viciously. The first wave of marauders came. But unbeknownst to them, they charged into the clutches of a trap.

As the Mongols came upon Khau's Army, the fire in the ditch was lit. Chaos consumed the invaders as their horses were thrown into disarray. No sooner was the fire lit that a slew of chakrams rained down on the oncoming Mongols. Countless were slain by the onslaught and many more were thrown off of their horses. And whilst the Mongols were in their state of panic, Khau and his men fell upon them. The invaders lost their advantage on horseback and were no match for their foes in hand-to-hand combat.

The Mongolian General realized what was happening as he saw his first wave of men beaten mightily. He recognized that the Lion of Bihar had discovered his army's weakness. If this was the trap he had for the first wave, what was in store for the rest of the Mongolian army? It was then he knew that there would be nothing but defeat for him this day.

So he did what any general facing certain defeat does. He fled. He turned back to his conquered lands, retreating back to the mountains and away from Bihar. For the rest of their lives, no soldier of Bihar ever saw another Mongol.

When the Mongols fled, they fled like hyenas.

The governor rewarded his friend by giving him the fertile land near Bhagwanpur. The general soon left the army and did what he had always dreamed of. Bilal was the best of neighbors. Khau and his children turned the land into a prosperous farm, and it has now been the home of his family for centuries. The love for Bihar is in the blood of Khau's lineage. For it was the bravery of Khau's men, a people of different creeds—a people who called their Lord by different names—but whose blood ran as one, that saved the land from destruction. And that is the true story of the land.

The greatest gift God gave to Man is his mind. All we must do is unlock our mind, and we will find what we seek. And once the mind is unlocked, all the answers to Man's problems will be right before his eyes.

CHAPTER 8
THE GENERAL'S DESCENDENT

By the time Avinash finished the first account in the journal, he was no longer in his apartment's office. Sitting atop his bed, he was under the blanket with his back supported by a wooden headboard. The bedside lamp was brightly illuminated. Its light bounced off the room's off-white walls, while the window curtains were pulled back. Taxi was on the bed next to him with her head in his lap and her eyes closed, but he did not mind. He had hardly noticed her come lay next to him while he read the journal. Avinash instinctively rubbed the top of her head.

The doctor found himself staring blankly at the last sentence of the first story. His mind was replaying everything he had just absorbed. There were several more accounts left in the journal, but he could not even think about reading on right now. His mind could only process so much.

It was well past midnight, but he did not care. Sleep was far from him this night. The story kept all weariness and slumber at bay. He almost could not believe what he had read and half of him thought that it was too amazing. As he read the words, he had been able to see it all play out in his mind's eye: the smells, the sights, the emotions. As the descendent of Khau had read the account, it was as if he had been in the middle of it all.

Avinash slowly placed the journal on the bedside table.

His eyes looked out the window and into "The City that Never Sleeps". Even from up here, even at this late hour of the night, he could hear the faint blaring of car horns and the sounds of streets that were still bustling with people and life. They all went along with the normal nightly routines, unaware of the paradigm shift that was occurring in the mind of Avinash.

He took a deep breath. Then another. The doctor looked away from the wall and down at the sleeping dog on his lap. He gently rubbed its head a few moments longer, admiring the former show-dog.

There was a string in his heart that the story struck, but he could not put his finger on it. But whatever it was, it had reinvigorated him. He knew what the journal was telling him. It was as if his grandfather had spoken to him from the grave.

It was as if Avinash was reborn.

General Khau had defeated the Mongols. He had defeated the enemy when no one else could. He had stood strong and fast when no one else had the courage to. He had figured out the weakness of his enemy when no one else was able to.

And just like his forefathers, Avinash was facing an enemy. This heart disease was popping up all over the map. Just like the Mongols had been hailed as the coming of Gog and Magog, this disease was being hailed as having the potential to be the worst epidemic in the last hundred years. But Avinash would beat it.

He knew it.

***

That night, Avinash dreamt of the first time he ever felt helpless.

A 13-year-old Avinash fell hard onto the floor as he collapsed at the foot of his locker. The top of his head banged against it and momentarily dazed him. When his vision returned, he looked up only to find the boy who had roughly shoved him towering above him. On the boy's face was a smug look as he looked down at the skinny, weak foreigner. There was a boy on either side of the bully, and they all had the same maleficent look.

Streams of people were going down the hallway behind the entire scene, but the most anybody did was give them a casual, passing glance. Nobody intervened. Nobody even gave Avinash a second look. This was a normal sight for them now. Nobody cared about this foreigner who could barely speak a lick of English and didn't understand America's customs. His torment was nothing but entertainment for them.

Why did nobody care? Was he not human? Was he so different from them because he could not speak their language and was not born in the same land? How could they be so cruel?

As he rose onto all fours, a swift kick sent powerful echoes of pain through Avinash's side, and he collapsed back onto the floor. One of the boys spoke, but Avinash could not understand what they were saying. But he saw what one of them was holding in his hands. It was a ball of brown sludge. It had the same stench as the mud outside the school. The bullies' eyes looked down at the face they would smear it on.

And there was nothing he could do.

***

Avinash jolted awake. The dream reminded him of what helplessness felt like. It was what he experienced when first coming to America, and what he again felt before reading General Khau's story. But no nightmare and no discouragement could take away what he felt right now. He was no longer that helpless child. He was born as the biological descendent of Khau but had now become his spiritual descendent.

A morning soon came at the hospital when Martha walked passed Dr. Avinash Singh's office and found it occupied. Even through the closed door, she heard the doctor's presence down the corridor. She recognized the familiar creaking of the floor when he would stand on it and shift his weight from side-to-side.

It had been nearly a week since she had seen him. The hospital's staff knew what was going on with him, and other doctors had taken over his duties. He had helped them all at one time or another, and this was the least that they could do to repay him. And since that rainy day at his apartment, Martha had not even received a call from Avi. She had heard that he was alive and well from a few nurses who had spotted him making quick visits to his office. Martha knew that it would only be a matter of time before she caught him here as well.

The door was unlocked. As her hand gripped the doorknob, Martha looked down the corridor both ways and saw that it was empty. Hugging a chart close to her chest, she slowly turned the knob and gently pushed the door open without making it creak. The nurse hesitantly walked in.

Behind Avinash's desk was a white board propped up on a stand. His back was turned to the nurse. Without even glancing her way, he continued to scribble illegible words across the board's surface with his black marker. And on the desk were scattered stacks of paper that seemed to be in no particular order. Some appeared to be notes while others were research articles and files.

Martha quietly and slowly closed the door behind her, but kept her eyes on the doctor. "Dr. Singh…I did not expect to see you here today."

Avinash did not answer as he continued to write on the whiteboard. He was faintly muttering something to himself under his breath. Martha's ears barely picked it up, not comprehending what he was saying.

"…*Dr. Singh?*"

Again no answer. He kept his back to her. It was as if the doctor could not even hear the nurse's words or feel her presence. He continued to softly talk to himself as he worked on.

Martha took a few hesitant steps, not sure what mental state her friend was in. He was not in the best condition when she had last seen him. Had she left him alone too long? She set her charts atop the paper stacks on his desk as she slowly passed them. Stopping a few feet from him, her gaze went from the back of the doctor's head and onto the whiteboard. Avinash's handwriting had never been the best. But like any nurse, she could always decipher what he inscribed. But right now, the board was covered in unrecognizable hand drawn diagrams and unreadable scribbles. The one thing she could read on the board was a name that looked like "Khan", although she could not make out the last letter completely.

She hesitantly and lightly placed her hand on Avinash's shoulder causing him to suddenly realize her presence. In a swift move, he whipped his head around, and his eyes came onto the older lady. His cheeks and chin had not been properly shaven for several days. His eyes were red and the edges of his dry lips were curved into a slight smile. His body was slightly trembling, but it was all from excitement—the same excitement an artist has when creating.

The doctor's smile slowly grew when he saw Martha. And every ounce of his voice carried enthusiasm. "Martha!"

"…Avi, are—are you okay?"

"*Okay?* I've never been better!"

Martha breathed a sigh of relief inside as her hand left his shoulder and fell back to her side. Her eyes went back onto Avinash's artwork. "What's all this?"

Avinash looked back at the board as if it was his Mona Lisa. "This?" He took a deep breath before his gaze left the scribbles and came back onto his nurse. "What do you know about Genghis Khan?"

105

Martha's eyebrows furrowed closer together. "I barely passed world history, Avi."

"Do you know what he and his people did?"

"No, but what's your point?"

"Just—just listen, Martha. *Genghis Khan*…he—he and his army were hell-bent on one thing: conquering the world. And they made good on their mission. They conquered all of China, much of Russia and Persia, and were virtually unstoppable—"

"When exactly was all this?"

"The 1200s—but that's not the point." Avinash held up his hand. "Just listen. I want you to pay close attention to this."

"I'm all ears."

"The Mongols were unstoppable. Nobody could stop them. Everybody who tried failed, and they took countless lives." Avinash was talking so fast that he had to take a deep breath to calm himself down. As he spoke, he waved his hands through the air as excitedly as when he had been writing on the board moments ago. "Do you know who outsmarted them, Martha?"

"Should I?"

Avinash said his next words with a heart full of pride. "My ancestor."

Her eyebrows rose. "…*Your* ancestor?"

The doctor nodded. Without looking, he pointed back at the name that Martha had mistaken for 'Khan.' "General Khau was the man who figured out their weakness. He was the first person to turn them away."

Martha did not say anything.

"Combined with the efforts of his Hindus, Muslim, Buddhist, and Christian comrades, General Khau defended his homeland from destruction. He beat the unbeatable virus of the invaders by thinking outside-of-the-box."

"…How exactly did you learn all this?"

106

"My grandfather. He told me."

"I thought that he passed away?"

"He left me a gift. A journal that has stories of my forefathers. This was the first one. It was…" The doctor moved by the nurse and came upon his desk. At the top of a stack of folders was a worn out and ancient journal. Avinash took it in his hands and showed it to the nurse. The book's brown leather covers were worn out, and its edges were now rough and uneven while its corners were bent and torn. "It was as if he was speaking to me. And…it—it's made me realize something, Martha."

"…Tell me."

"That this virus—I've been looking at it all wrong. I've been thinking too traditionally, and that's why I can't beat it. That's why the Chinese and others could not defeat the Mongols for so long. They weren't thinking right. They couldn't…couldn't unlock their minds to see their enemy's weakness." He paused for a moment, trying to form his thoughts into words. "When I was a boy in Bihar, my grandfather taught me how to fish. But we didn't use any fishing rods or bait. We used our minds. And just with that, we could catch half the fish in a pond if we wanted to."

"How'd you manage to do that?"

Avinash put the journal back onto his desk, but his eyes stayed on it as the memories replayed in his mind. "What we would do was build a dam in the middle of the pond. Then we'd drain the water out of one half and dump it into the other. And what would be left were a bunch of fish flopping on the ground. We'd take what we needed and then break the damn down, refilling the pond."

Martha silently listened on.

"That's the kind of thinking I need here—nontraditional thinking. That's how General Khau beat the Mongols." Avinash took a deep breath as he looked back at his nurse.

"But how will you change up your approach here?"

"That's exactly what I'm figuring out. General Khau—my ancestor fought with a sword. He fought with a sword in his hand and courage in his heart. And he won. And this...this knowledge is *my* sword. And with it, we are going to win *this* war."

CHAPTER 9
AVINASH'S ARMY

Sleep became a luxury for Dr. Avinash Singh over the course of the next three weeks. Just like Khau had faced sleepless nights before battling the Mongols, so it was for his descendent. For every moment he wasted on rest, the children under his care drew closer to death.

He scheduled a minimal number of surgeries, and they were all simple procedures. Heart bypasses, valve replacements—these were things that were routine to him before. But now they were easier than ever. He did not know if it was his reinvigorated soul or newfound passion that made it so.

As always while performing surgeries, there was jovial music playing throughout the operating room. But instead of his favorite Jamaican music playing—Shaggy and the likes—he was now playing traditional *Qawwali* music. Even the nurses had started to enjoy it without understanding the lyrics of the songs and poems. Avinash knew that if he wanted to think like the victorious General Khau, he needed to embrace the man's character from head-to-toe.

Something had happened to Avinash's soul. The way he talked, the way he walked, the way he thought, the way he felt—it was all different now. It was all better. He did not know what had happened inside of him.

But whatever it was, he did not want to lose it.

The descendent of Khau had become something more than a doctor. He had become what every man dreamed of being, what every man had deep inside of them.

He was almost living in his hospital office now. In the little free time he allowed himself, Avinash practiced his Taekwondo forms. It seemed to do more than relieve his stress now. Doing it now made him feel closer to his ancestors.

The hospital's director, Dr. Cheng, knew of Avinash's work. It had taken him less than half a second to give his full support. He had been more than willing to give many of Avinash's duties to other doctors freeing up more time for Dr. Singh's quest. After all, the hospitals were under increasing pressure to figure out this disease. The media was blowing it up ten times bigger than they had hyped Ebola. And when the dust settled, the people would want someone to blame. Everyone knew that people like Dr. Cheng would be the easiest targets to hang if this became an epidemic as so many feared.

So Dr. Cheng did what he could. He checked in daily with Avinash and continued to maintain full faith that the hospital's most courageous doctor would find the answer if there was one to be found.

But more importantly, Avinash believed in himself.

***

Hours ago, Avinash walked into the office of the famed Dr. Ashraf Waqar. Not only was he the best infectious disease specialist in this hospital, but he was arguably the best in New York City.

The door to the room was shut, keeping their conversation private. The window blinds had been closed, cutting the two off from the rest of the world. On the desk between them were a few folders Avinash had brought with him. Many of his documents and drawing were now scattered across the table.

Ashraf was a well-liked man. He was born in Pakistan in the city of Sialkot. He was never one to speak of his background. But the rumors were that his father died when Ashraf was only ten. After

110

finishing his primary education, he went to medical school while still working to support his family. After graduation, he came to America and began work as an infectious disease specialist. But to this day, twenty years after coming to America, he still sent over half of his salary back to his family.

He was a strong man, and it showed in his build. But stronger than his physical body was his mind. It was that mind that earned him such an esteemed reputation in the medical community.

Ashraf thought for a moment before slowly nodding. Although he had lived in the states for decades now, a bit of his accent still remained. "I'm liking everything you've told me, Avinash. This approach you're suggesting, it's…it's very unusual to say the least."

"Do you think it's feasible?"

"I do. However, the two of us will need to work out the details of it all."

Hearing those words was a sigh of relief to Avinash's heart.

"Everything you're suggesting is based off the theories and research that Duke University has been looking into for some time now. Only, they're thinking of using this approach to treat brain tumors."

Avinash silently nodded, already knowing all this.

"I've followed their studies closely since they first started. And—as I'm sure you've found out—just about everything they have produced has been more than promising."

"Yes, it has."

"And in theory, what you have put together should be able to kill the virus. But what works in theory does not always work in reality."

"That's why I want to work out exactly how the treatment and procedure will occur step-by-step with you. We can't predict what will happen, but we can have everything prepared to the best of our abilities."

"Of course. But there is also one more thing. According to the autopsy, your last patient died when a colony of the virus and debris was swept into her bloodstream and went into her brainstem. Even if this treatment works to kill the virus, you'll still need to go in and repair all the damage the virus has done to the heart valves. And during that time, virus and debris could embolize into the bloodstream like before."

Avinash nodded. "I know. And I have thought of something that could contain any potential threat of embolization. But I wanted to run it by you and see how we can make the idea work."

"Please do."

There was a brief silence between them as Avinash dug into the file folder closest to him to pull out his diagram. But he stopped and looked back at Ashraf as the man spoke again.

"We're pushing the boundaries here, Avinash. There is no denying that." Ashraf grinned mischievously. "But that's why we became doctors, isn't it?"

Avinash smiled without replying.

***

A little more than a week later, Martha was called back into Dr. Singh's office. She found him standing at his desk, his foot tapping on the floor and his fingers drumming on the polished wood. A ten-page document was on his desk, and his eyes were glued to it. But hearing Martha enter, he immediately looked up at her. She could see the weariness that consumed his face. Over the past three days, he had merely slept six or seven hours collectively, and he had not bothered to shave during that same time.

He wasted no time with a greeting. But today, there was no smile or hint of happiness on his face. "Fiza was just here. She brought me Alice's test results."

Martha knew who he was speaking of. The eight-year-old girl was one of Dr. Singh's patients afflicted with the heart disease. Her heart had been deteriorating like clockwork. Last night, Avinash ordered Nurse Fiza to run some more tests on Alice to reevaluate the patient's timetable. "What did they say?"

"She's deteriorating quickly. She won't make it another three months at this rate."

The nurse's heart froze as she heard those words. She could not move.

"I've asked Julia to convey this message to Alice's parents."

"...My God." As she uttered those words, a heavy weight settled onto her heart and crushed her soul. She was silent for a long moment. They had all known that Alice's body could not beat the disease, but Martha never would have suspected that the young girl's life would be ending in a matter of months. "Alice...that poor girl. She's..."

"No." Avinash slightly shook his head. "No. She won't."

"How—"

"I won't let her die. She won't join the list of the dead like Estella did." Every ounce of Avinash's voice was filled with unbreakable determination.

"Have you figured the disease out?"

In his heart, Avinash knew that he did not truly have the answer to that question until this procedure was actually performed. But he spoke with enough confidence that the nurse did not doubt his decision. "I know what has to be done—I know what we can do to give her the fighting chance that Estella never had. I'm going to speak to Dr. Cheng now."

"What did you find?"

"I had some theories and took them to Ashraf. He and I turned my ideas into a practical treatment. We've found a way we can change our approach. "

"A new procedure?"

Dr. Singh adamantly nodded. "I've been reviewing the autopsy report."

"A lot of people have."

"They haven't been looking at it in the same way I have. This…this virus it—it's…" He lightly shook his head trying to form his thoughts into words. "We all know that this virus is attacking the heart's valves. The autopsy report shows us how the death occurred." Avinash took a deep breath. "Estella Harp lost her life because a small colony of the virus and debris embolized to the brain stem causing instant death during surgery. There was nothing I could have done differently to stop it."

Martha solemnly nodded.

"And knowing all this, I now know where this virus can be beaten. I know the angle we need to attack it from. All we have to do is stop thinking so traditionally—stop thinking so by-the-book and start thinking nontraditionally."

"…What is it?"

"We inject our patients with the polio virus."

Martha was silent as she tried to register what Avinash said. What was he thinking?

"When the polio virus is injected, the inflammatory response to the polio will attack and kill the heart virus." His voice was overflowing with excitement. The more he spoke, the faster his words came out. "Our immune system is unable to fight the heart virus. It cannot create the antibodies necessary which is why we are left helpless. However, everyone in this country has been vaccinated for polio and is immune to it. Our bodies'— including every patient of ours— immune system *can* create the antibodies needed to kill the

114

polio virus, and it will do so quickly. But by the time it does, the polio antibodies will have killed off the heart virus, and then all we have to do is replace or repair the damage already done by the virus." He took a deep breath. In his mind, he could see the procedure as clear as day, and it showed in his eyes. "All we need to do is get approval from Cheng to deliberately inject our patients with the polio virus, and we can carry out the procedure."

Martha's mind was moving quickly to stay up with Avinash's words. It all seemed so simple. Too simple. After hearing his solution, she could not believe that no one else had thought of this. "…that— that's amazing, Avi. But…do you think he'll give you the green light to do the procedure?"

Avinash picked up the stapled document. He left his desk and slowly made his way past Martha and towards the open doorway. "He doesn't have a choice. With every day that passes, he's under more pressure as are all the hospital administrators. He will have to give the parents the final say about this."

The nurse shook her head as she thought of Cheng. Without any approval, especially from the Institutional Review Board, she knew proposing this idea to Cheng would be useless. No matter how good it sounded, Cheng was never one to take any risks. "He won't approve it, Avi. Whatever you're planning on doing hasn't been fully tested or even submitted for approval by the IRB. He'll shoot the idea down."

"Don't worry about Cheng. I want you to go to Alice's parents. Make sure that Julia conveyed the test results properly…and tell them that I'll be seeing them within the hour." With those words, Avinash left.

***

"Dr. Singh, you do realize the implications that will occur if I sign off on this, don't you?"

Sitting across the desk from Dr. Cheng, Avinash looked him confidently in the eyes. It was only minutes since he had spoken to Martha. Behind the director was a large window, its blinds pulled back. A flood of sunlight spilled through and almost directly into Avinash's eyes, but he ignored it. That was the least of his concerns.

Before coming here, Avinash freshened up. Cleanly shaven with all the weariness in his eyes gone, he sat up straight with hands clasped on the desk. On the desk were a few pages that Avinash brought for the hospital's director to initial and sign.

Avinash spoke with a calm demeanor. "I do realize what may happen. But we both know what *will* happen if you don't sign these. We both understand the situation, Dr. Cheng. When the dust clears and this…epidemic is over, the people will blame somebody for the deaths of all these children. The easiest target will be people like you that are in leadership positions. Neither of us went to medical school to get involved in a media circus, and that's exactly what will happen if you don't sign off."

"You're asking me to sign off on an entirely new and untested procedure."

"It's not completely untested, and it's not something entirely new. As we speak, researchers at Duke University are researching ways to use this approach in combating brain tumors. And the results we're seeing from their research is very promising."

"Brain tumors are far different than what we're dealing with here."

"I'm using their concepts, not techniques. I've modified everything to fit our situation. I've kept you in the loop, and you know that my theory is sound. We're taking research—*sound research* that has been going on for over ten years and has the support of many medical communities—and we're adapting it to our situation."

"And that's what makes it new." Dr. Cheng glanced down for a moment and took a deep breath before looking back up. "You've had my full support this whole time. I wholly expected you to find the treatment to this disease if anyone would. However, we both know that I never expected you to carry it out so soon. What we need to do is take your findings and present them to a higher authority and receive their support. That's the next step here, Dr. Singh…not injecting our patients with *the polio virus*."

"You think I made a mistake?" If Avinash felt any annoyance, he hid it well. "And you're willing to let a girl die because of your apprehensions?"

"It's not that I don't have faith in you, Dr. Singh. You are by far one of the best doctors in this building. But since…" Dr. Cheng took a deep breath. "When the young girl died during your operation, I know it hit you hard. And that makes me believe that you may be too emotionally involved in this to make a sound decision about your findings."

"But you've seen our work. And you know that it will succeed."

"There is still a hole in your theory. You have not solved the problem of what will happen if a colony of the virus and debris embolizes again. If the virus and debris get into the bloodstream, your patient could die just as your last one did."

"I have. I've spoken to Dr. Ashraf about this and—"

"You've brought him into this?" Cheng's eyes widened in surprise.

Avinash ignored the comment. "And he's helped me design a version of a Greenfield filter that can be placed in the pulmonary artery and the aorta that will catch any debris that embolizes from the valve. Once it catches the debris, the filter can be removed by a catheter after the valves are replaced. Implementing this filter will prevent any future complications from occurring from this procedure.

117

Ashraf believes wholeheartedly that this will take care of any possible embolization as do I. He and I have worked out the details of how this would be done." He paused for a moment. "What happened last time won't happen this time. I'll do everything in my power to make it so."

Cheng was silent for a long moment. He stared at Avinash's face, but his expression made it impossible for Avinash to know what he was thinking. Finally, Cheng spoke. "Maybe you do have the answer—a part of me believes that. But we can't execute it on such short notice. Other surgeons and medical boards have to look at it. You *need* their endorsements." He leaned in a little closer. "We don't operate on theory. You know that. A successful treatment on paper and a successful treatment in a living patient are two different things."

"That may be. But if we don't act, the girl—Alice Richards— an eight-year-old girl who should be surrounded by dolls and not medicine—is going to *die*." Avinash's open palm slammed onto the table's surface. "And her parents will bury her just like Estella Harp's parents buried her and just like my parents lost my brother." Avinash was silent for a long moment. "I won't let that happen. We don't have a choice here."

If Avinash's words had any effect on Dr. Cheng, the director was not showing it. "I do have a choice. This...this procedure you are recommending...how can I possibly sign off on it? There are too many variables involved. Too many things that can go wrong. It would be morally irresponsible for me to sign off on it without letting a medical board look at it. And I could very well lose my job along with anyone who is associated with this. For God's sake, think about this. You're injecting somebody with *polio*! Think about how that sounds."

Avinash took a deep breath to calm himself down. "You're not looking at the situation clearly. If you do sign this, then every outcome is a good one for you regardless of how the surgery turns out."

118

Dr. Cheng stared at Avinash for a few long moments. "...Explain."

"I'll start with the obvious. You sign off on this treatment, and the treatment is a success—and I can assure you that it will be a success. And when it is, you'll be hailed as a hero. The fact that you approved the surgery without letting it be evaluated won't matter. You won't lose your job. In fact, you'll probably get a better one. People will see you as the man who made the gutsy call—the maverick—the gun slinging cowboy. Nobody with any real power will come after you with repercussions. They won't dare touch a man people are hailing as a hero."

"And what if it's not successful?"

"Then the blame won't fall on you."

The hospital's director leaned forward a bit.

"Even if you sign off on this, Alice's parents have the final say. And if the treatment doesn't go well, the media will look at this as a poor decision made by parents who had no other choice but to give their consent. Nobody with any real influence in the papers will bat an eye at you. It'll just be another failed attempt and a last ditch effort made by a helpless mother and father whose backs were against the wall."

Dr. Cheng did not reply as he stared at Avinash, digesting the man's words.

"But say that you don't sign off on this." Now Avinash leaned in a little closer as he confidently stared the director in the eyes. "Then when the dust settles, the media will look for somebody to blame. They always do. And say if I was able to later prove that this would have been the cure...all the children that die from now until this is over—well, you can just imagine how the media will hang you. They won't care about what excuse you have. You'll be the scapegoat for everybody." Avinash glanced down at his lap for a quick moment. "So...*Dr. Cheng*, we both know what you have to do here."

Again, there was no response.

"…So what will it be?"

***

"What is it, doctor?" the mother asked. She was a sweet lady in her early thirties. Her long brown locks were tied back into a lengthy ponytail. Dried streams of tears were still visible on her face.

In the nearly empty corridor, Alice's father sat next to his wife on a bench. He had not shaven in at least two days and had not slept during that time either. He looked as if he had not eaten all day.

"Mr. and Mrs. Richards," Avinash took a silent, deep breath as he stood in front of the couple. In the hallway, only a few nurses could be seen making their rounds and attending to their duties. The fluorescent light brightly lit the hallway, but it did nothing to brighten the dark tunnel that the mother and father were trapped in. "I'm sorry to have to pull you away from your daughter."

"Julia explained the test results. Is—is there… anything you can do?"

"Not conventionally, ma'am. But…" The doctor briefly glanced at the nurse at his side. Hugged to her chest was a folder full of paperwork, and in her coat pocket was a pen. "But there may be a way."

Mr. Richards thought that his ears were deceiving him. "…A…a way to save Alice."

Avinash solemnly nodded.

There was a quick flash of hope in the mother's eyes. "Tell us."

"To put it simply: on paper, a treatment for Alice's condition has been discovered. I must tell you that it is an untested procedure, and it is an unorthodox method. No medical board or medical

120

authority has thoroughly examined it other than myself, Dr. Ashraf Waqar, and Dr. Cheng."

Mrs. Richards' clenched fist came over her heart as she let out a gasp of disbelief. She would have broken down into tears had she not been in complete shock. Her husband's hand grabbed hers as they both stared at the doctor in disbelief and awe. It was as if his words had suddenly brought a light into the darkness. His words were their north star. "...But will...will it work?"

"The director has signed off on it."

"But do you believe it will work?"

Avinash nodded with every ounce of confidence he had. "Life and death are not in my hands. I cannot promise you that your daughter won't die. But what I can promise you is that if you give me the chance to help Alice, I *will* do my best. I can promise you that. Enough children have been claimed by this condition. She won't be."

"Then you have our vote of confidence." Looking into the doctor's eyes, Mr. Richards did not have any wavering in his voice. He could see the gleam in Dr. Singh's eyes and that was enough for him. The father recognized it from his time as a lieutenant in the Marines. This was the gleam only a soldier's eyes could have. "When will the procedure take place?"

"Alice has to be injected with the polio virus first. Then Dr. Ashraf will check her antibody levels. When they are high enough, he will give us the go. I'd estimate that we have a few weeks. I will spend the rest of the time going over everything with the nursing staff. Martha will fill you in on the details of what we are going to be doing. And God-willing, Alice will be back home soon."

Mrs. Richards spoke. "...Thank you, Dr. Singh."

"I haven't done anything yet, ma'am."

"But you will...I know it. If anybody can save our daughter, it will be you."

Avinash nodded in thanks. "Is Alice awake?"

121

"She was when we left."

"I'd like to see her."

"Of course."

***

Alice's eyes looked up at the doctor as he walked into the room. With a friendly and fatherly smile plastered on his face, he looked down at the child. Her long, light brown locks were a mess as she lay down on the propped up bed. Wearing a blue patient's gown and half covered with a blanket, her gaze was set on a *Sesame Street* episode when Avinash entered the room.

Rays of the early afternoon sunlight came in through the window. Even up here, the distant and bustling street could be heard. Under the young girl's gaze, the doctor made his way around her bed and took a seat on the chair next to her bed. Still smiling, he reached out and took her small hand in his. He could not believe it, but on the face of the girl was a smile.

The same smile Akleshwar wore when his death had approached.

"How are you, Alice?"

"I'm good." Her light blue eyes stayed locked with his. Like any child's voice, hers was pure and sweet. But it was more true with this girl.

"Have the nurses told you the good news?"

She shook her head.

Avinash acted like he was completely surprised that Alice was in the dark. "You're going home soon!"

Her eyes lit up almost immediately. She could not say a word as the doctor's words rang though every corner of her heart. She had been here so long that she never could have imagined leaving this place. But now it would all be over. This nightmare that she had never fully understood would come to close.

Avinash reached into his coat's large pocket and brought something out. It was a stuffed brown bear that he bought from the gift shop downstairs. "I even brought a very early going away present for you, Alice."

The little girl could not believe it as she took the bear into her arms. She instinctively hugged it close to her chest and squeezed it tightly; her smile tripling in size as everything sunk in. "Thank you—thank you!"

Avinash affectionately rubbed her head as he nodded in gratitude. "All that's left is one last treatment. Can you be a brave girl one more time for me?"

"Yes!"

"Thank you. And…once that's over, you'll be able to go home before you know it."

***

The weeks leading up to the surgery went by quickly. Time seemed to have sped up, and the day of the operation was upon them before they knew it. Dr. Cheng explained everything to the parents. According to Martha, who had been in the room, he had subtly tried to discourage the parents from signing off on the procedure. But they had been adamant. During the meeting, Mr. Richards said several times that he knew that it would work. His instincts as a father and as a soldier told him that Dr. Singh would win this battle.

Avinash explained the treatment to each and every member of his nursing staff. They ran through it countless times. But Avinash wanted them all to know their roles perfectly. They all knew the risks of what could happen to them if the treatment went awry. But each and every member of his staff was loyal to their commander. They would follow him with all their passion.

It was time. Alice's antibodies that would fight off the polio virus were finally at the therapeutic level. The deadly virus was no longer multiplying. Now was the time to repair all the damage that the virus had done. Doing so successfully would mean that the treatment was a success. But if any of the virus and debris embolized and traveled up the bloodstream once again as it had with Estella, then all this would have been for nothing. Another child would join the list of the dead.

It was a few hours before Avinash and his staff would conduct the procedure to repair the damage. Everything was in place. The stage was set. The players were ready. Half an hour ago, he called his nursing staff to his office, and now he looked at them all from behind his desk. Each and every one of their eyes was full of determination and faith. It matched his own resolve.

And as he looked at them, he realized something for the first time.

The older nurse, Martha, was closest to the door. Only a few feet away was the accomplished Dr. Ashraf Waqar. Next to him was a nurse wearing a *hijab*, Fiza. She had joined the hospital's staff only days after Avinash had come. Across the desk was an African-American, Adam Wise. He had played college football at Ohio State, and it showed in his physique. Dr. Wise would be the assisting surgeon and had been with Avinash for many months now. If there was any doctor that Avinash trusted with his life, it was Dr. Wise.

The brunette Julia and the blonde Erin were to Avinash's right. The former was the type of person who visited the Synagogue religiously, and the latter was a strong Catholic. To Avinash's left was Quinn. Unlike the rest of the staff, she was the perfusionist in the crew. In terms of age, she was right in the middle of all the other nurses, and her features showed her family's origin from western China. She was a practicing Buddhist.

For the first time, Avinash let the reality of it all sink in. He did not know how this had ended up happening. Maybe it was in his nature to make it so. Or maybe it was God's will. But just like General Khau led an army made up of different kinds of warriors with varied backgrounds, so did Avinash. And just like the army of Bihar, Avinash's army was united in one cause: *to save the life of a little girl.*

***

Dr. Singh began with the words of his forefathers, "The greatest gift God gave to Man is his mind. All we must do is unlock our minds, and we will find what we seek. And once the mind is unlocked, all the answers to Man's problems will be right before his eyes." He paused for a moment. "I believe that our minds have been unlocked. We can see this opponent clearer than anybody else, and that is why we have the upper-hand."

There was complete silence in the room as they waited for the doctor to go on.

"I know it's unorthodox for me to call you here a few hours before a procedure. But the fact is, we all know what we're going to do today is all a little unorthodox. We know what we are trying to accomplish. But what we *need* to do is remember *why* we are doing this. The implications of a success are that we will put an end to this disease. But that's not what is driving me today...it's the fear of failure and all that failure will bring about. Failure means a girl—a daughter— a sister—a human being is going to die. I won't let that happen...and I know that it won't. We all know what the procedure entails, and we all have our duties. This surgery will go like any other that we have done in the past."

Avinash took a deep breath.

"Last time, I went into a surgery expecting to save a life. This time, that's not what I'm expecting. Because I know that it's not me who will be saving the life. I don't give or take life. But what I can do is my best—I can do that and leave the rest up to God. And if we do that…then we've done enough."

***

When the time for the procedure came, there was no tension in the room. Moments before entering the operation room, a peace fell over Avinash Singh. And with every fiber of his being, Avinash believed that it was the same peace that had come over General Khau moments before he entered his battle against the invaders.

Coming onto the stage, everything was as it should be. The off-white walled room had its florescent lights nicely illuminated. The floor was made up of white tiles throughout the perimeter of the room while around the table were sea-green tiles. More lights hung from the ceiling aiming at the table. The table itself was padded by a black cushion.

And next to the table was the intricate cardiopulmonary bypass machine. It was what made open heart surgeries a possibility. Once the surgery began, it would take over for the heart by replacing the heart's pumping action while adding oxygen and removing toxins from the blood. Quinn would be the one in charge of operating this machine. Two large screens were on the longer walls on either side of the room. All the equipment was where it should be. On a stand next to the table was a tray full of every handy tool the doctor would need: lancets of all sizes, hemostatic forceps, and retractors among many more.

There was music gently playing on the speakers. The smell of the sterile equipment was similar to that of the clean and germ-free room that had been scrubbed down several times earlier today. The

126

first thing Dr. Singh did was tell one of his nurses to put on a disc by Shaggy and turn up the volume a bit.

The sedated patient was gently placed on the table under the bright lights and soon put to sleep. As the entire nursing staff took their positions, Dr. Singh made a light comment. "Once we succeed here, everyone can write a best-selling memoir about all this and retire to a tropical island. Then you won't ever have to put up with me again."

There were light chuckles from the surgical crew.

Avinash took a deep breath. Looking away from the girl, Avinash looked at the nursing staff around him, smiling under his mask as the music continued to play.

"I bet you are all glad that music from Bihar is gone and that Shaggy is back to drown out our sorrows. Don't think I don't know about how much you all hated my country's music."

"What makes you say we hated it?" Julia sarcastically asked.

Avinash looked over at her. "I'm a doctor; I know everything."

There was some more brief laughter.

The doctor looked over at Adam. "Hey Adam, what does a graduate from Ohio State call a graduate from Texas A&M?"

"What?"

"*Boss!*"

Adam smiled as he shook his head.

And then it began.

As the surgery got underway, there was no heavy burden on Avinash's soul. There was no boulder of immense pressure crushing down on him. Instead, it was the complete opposite. He felt free. He was an artist, and this was his canvas. Time seemed to stop. The entire thing felt surreal, almost like a dream.

He performed this surgery so many times in his mind over the past weeks and in rehearsal over the past days that he had every movement and every word down to perfection. He even knew which

127

light-hearted comments to make at which points during the surgery to keep the spirits of the team uplifted and make sure that it did not get too serious in here. That would be the worst thing. Without a second thought, he knew what strokes to make where and what instruments to use when. He could have done the surgery perfectly even if he was not at his best.

But compared to the last time he tried to save a child's life, this time felt different. As he performed the surgery, he did not have his mind on the outcome. Just like Khau, he understood that the outcome was out of his hands. All he could do was what was in his power. As the Lion of Bihar knew that all he could do was find the weakness of his enemy and plan a strategy accordingly, Dr. Avinash Singh knew that all he could do was what he had trained and practiced to do. All he could do was carry out *his* own strategy.

The rest would be left to a higher power.

CHAPTER 10
SPOILS OF WAR

Two months later:

It was an hour before his workday began. In a coffee shop only two blocks away from the hospital, Avinash sat at the auburn circular table for two. The chair opposite him was unoccupied. The small café was full, and nearly every seat was taken. People sat and worked on their open laptops while others wrote down notes or spoke to people from across their tables. The aroma of hot coffee filled the room. The sky was clear, and the city was alive. Rays of morning sunlight flooded in through the glass windows, making the yellow lights that dangled from the ceiling almost useless.

Men in fancy suits and women in business attire filled the place as many of them stopped by on their way to work. A line of them had formed from the ordering counter to the glass doors that led onto the busy sidewalk. Behind the polished brown counter were several employees dressed in their white uniforms. The illuminated and bold words "Ray's Coffee" hung from the wall, and under it was a menu of drinks and breakfast options. However, most patrons did not have the time to enjoy their morning coffee here and ran out the door as soon as their orders were in hand. The loud sounds of orders being filled, baristas calling out, and people chatting amongst themselves consumed the small shop.

But Avinash was in no hurry today.

His coffee cup was on the table, and one of his hands was clasped around it. Dressed in his green scrubs, he held his smartphone in his free hand. He leisurely scrolled through his emails looking at their subjects and senders but not intending to reply to any of them at the moment. None of the emails received over the past few hours were pressing.

A sleek, flat-screened television hung from the wall only a few feet behind him. Its volume had been turned low and a morning news report was being broadcasted, but Avinash gave it no attention. Instead, he enjoyed this start to a beautiful day where he was not rushing to the hospital through heavy traffic or a crowded subway.

He took a sip of his coffee and set it back down on the table. Coming to the end of his email list, he saw the last one was from Dr. Cheng. It was labeled as "Urgent." Avinash was halfway certain that the message was anything but urgent. Cheng had a knack for exaggerating this sort of thing, but he opened it anyway.

Dr. Singh,

I have received another request for an interview with you. This request is from the well-known reporter, Dena Allen. I am sure that you recognize her name from the New York Times. *I informed her that you will seriously consider the request. I would advise you to go ahead and take it because it would give the hospital, along with yourself, some good publicity. I have included her telephone number and email below. Let me know once you have contacted her.*

Below was the reporter's contact information and Cheng's signature. Avinash slightly shook his head. He had lost count of how many interview requests he had received over the past few days. He had only taken one up on the offer and disregarded the rest much to Cheng's displeasure. The hospital's director, however, had done all the interviews that came up. Dr. Cheng's job was to help foster the public image of the hospital, and he was doing it perfectly.

One of the patrons turned up the television's volume. Hearing a voice come from behind, Avinash turned around and looked at the news anchor on the television screen. The well-dressed, middle-aged lady spoke as she looked into the camera. On the top right corner of the screen was a screenshot of the hospital's logo.

"Today, thirteen more children who were afflicted with the heart condition were released from hospitals after undergoing the new treatment that was developed by Dr. Avinash Singh and Dr. Ashraf Waqar. The procedure, which was first performed without any approval from any higher medical authority, has now been approved by the FDA along with governing surgical bodies and is currently the method being practiced all across the country. This morning, Governor Paris declared the medical state-of-emergency to be over. Tonight, we will be featuring an interview with one of the men who was the backbone of this miracle: Dr. Huang Cheng. We have also requested an interview with Dr. Singh, the man who developed the treatment. However, we have yet to receive any word back from him. Dr. Singh has done his sole interview with CNN's Jennifer Martin. We will be re-airing that interview at the top of the hour."

Avinash got out of his chair and looked away from the television. If they were going to be showing his one and only interview, he would rather not be in the room to be recognized. He slipped his phone back into his pocket. Coming to the trash bin a few feet away, he tossed his quarter-full cup of coffee into it. He put a couple of bills into the 'tip' jar as he passed the ordering counter and left the coffee shop.

He walked out to the bustling street. Dressed up men and women quickly made their way to their offices, briefcases and purses in hand. Many of them were using their phones in one way or another and not paying attention to where they stepped. They passed by the street vendors who tried to attract as many customers as possible to their stands. The aroma of freshly cooked bagels, pretzels, donuts, and coffee filled every inch of the sidewalk. Traffic slowly moved down the one-way-street as people blared their horns out of frustration.

The chaos of the street, the voices of the pedestrians, and the sounds of the vendors all mixed to make the city what it was. And mixed with the aromas and smells from the street, this place had the ambience that New York City was known for. It was this feeling that Avinash had grown to love since moving here.

He took a deep breath before joining the river of pedestrians. Looking down the road, he could see the hospital only a few blocks away. It stood the same as it always had. But today, it seemed different. Today, it seemed to be standing taller than ever.

Avinash did not care that Dr. Cheng was unhappy at him for turning down so many interviews. If he had performed the operation for himself, he would have failed. That was why he failed the first time. Booking the interviews and going on a tour for fame would dishonor the memory of Avinash's forefathers. It would dishonor General Khau and all that he stood for. Avinash had developed the treatment and conducted the surgery—he had dedicated himself to it—because he had the ability. That alone made it his duty to use his abilities for the betterment of mankind.

And that was how he would honor Khau.

***

The famous interview between Dr. Avinash Singh and Jennifer Martin was re-aired. In the break room at the hospital, all the nurses and doctors stopped what they were doing to watch it unfold. Had the news station known that this would be Dr. Singh's only interview and that it would be their highest rated interview in the past ten years, they would have polished up the setting.

But that was not the case.

The interview was a simple one. Avinash sat on a white, leather armchair across from the reporter. The room's walls were a shade of light brown and went perfectly with the carpets. Cameras were set up so that the viewers at home could see the upper halves of the interviewer and interviewee. Avinash was dressed in black, tailored suit that accentuated his powerful frame.

The questioning began with the usual pleasantries. The reporter introduced his guest, stating his prior accomplishments and background. She then asked the doctor to describe what he had accomplished at a level that a common person could understand. The first few minutes were nothing to remember and nothing out-of-the-ordinary for an on-set interview.

But the final minutes were what would be remembered.

"Dr. Singh," Jennifer said, "People are calling you a hero. What do you think of that?"

"I'm not a hero. The real heroes are the ones who were afflicted with this condition and faced it with unwavering courage, patience, and faith. I'm a man who used my abilities the way that any person should use their abilities."

"And what is that?"

"For the betterment of mankind. That's our duty."

Jennifer appeared taken aback upon hearing those words. "…That's a powerful thing to say, Dr. Singh."

"It's the truth. I don't think we're given abilities without a purpose."

"People are wondering what gave you the inspiration to come up with this—this cure. What do you say to them?"

Avinash glanced down at the ground for a quick moment. "The greatest gift God gave to Man is his mind. All we must do is unlock our mind, and we will find what we seek. And once the mind is unlocked, all the answers to Man's problems will be right before his eyes."

Jennifer was silent.

"Unorthodox and critical thinking is what people—your ancestors and mine—used to solve problems…it's what we've lost.

It's what makes man the dominant species on this planet. And it's what I used to figure out this problem. The important thing is to know where we come from. Every man and woman should know what blood flows through their veins. It is the blood of one people. When we set aside our differences, when we unite and use our energies for the betterment of mankind, then the power that we possess is an unstoppable force that can achieve anything."

***

Avinash walked down the halls of the hospital. His confident footsteps echoed down the nearly empty corridor. Having just finished a successful stent procedure an hour and a half ago, he was still dressed in his scrubs. The operation had gone like clockwork aside from a few minor adjustments he called for mid-operation. But nonetheless, it had been nothing out of the ordinary, and the patient would be out of the hospital on schedule.

His heart was full of happiness knowing that the patient would be better coming out of surgery than he had been going in. There was always an indescribable joy that filled Avinash's heart when he used his abilities to make a person's life better. But now the doctor's stomach was empty. He could hear and feel it begging for food having digested his small breakfast hours ago. After stopping at his office, Avinash would head down to grab a late lunch in the cafeteria.

With his back straight and his head held high, he passed by Julia as she made her way back to her station. It took a moment for the nurse to register the fact that Dr. Singh was wearing green scrubs instead of his normal blue ones today.

The doctor politely nodded in her direction. "Hi, Julia."

"You're looking good in green, Dr. Singh."

"Julia." Avinash looked at her with all the playful seriousness in the world. "I look good in everything."

The nurse let out a light laugh as the two of them passed each other and went their separate ways. A couple of turns later, Avinash came upon his office. However, it was not as he had left it. He distinctly remembered closing and locking the door before leaving. But it was now open, and the lights were switched on.

Avinash's first thought was that it must have been the cleaning crew, but in the back of his mind, he knew that they only cleaned his office during afterhours. He was not expecting any visitors, but maybe a nurse had left something in his office and was looking for it. He stepped into the doorway and looked into his office. Everything was in place.

Except for one thing.

A man sat at Avinash's desk opposite the doctor's chair. Dressed in a dark suit, he sat with his back to the doctor. His hands were in his lap as he looked over all of the medical accolades hanging from the walls. His trimmed blonde hair was perfectly combed over.

Avinash knocked on the door, announcing his presence. His guest turned around, and Avinash's brown eyes locked with this man's blue ones. The man had a strong jaw, and his fair-skinned face was cleanly shaven. Dr. Singh did not recognize this man, but it was obvious that he knew who Avinash was when the stranger shrewdly smiled at him.

"…Can I help you?" Avinash left the doorway and walked into his office.

"Dr. Singh." The man got out of his seat and met Avinash halfway. They both firmly shook hands. "My name is Nate Hopkins. It's a pleasure to finally meet you in person."

"Do we know each other, Mr. Hopkins?"

"Not formally, no. I've seen you on the television and done my research on you, but this the first time we've met in person. And please—just call me Nate."

Avinash kept his eyes on the man as he took his seat.

Nate came back to the chair he had been sitting in. "Your nurse—I think her name is Faiza or Fiza—"

"Fiza."

Nate nodded. "Right. She let me in when I told her who I was."

"And who exactly are you?"

"I'm representing the New York City Medical Center. No doubt you've heard of us."

Avinash was silent for a few long moments. The New York City Medical Center? They were the most prestigious hospital in the entire state and one of the top hospitals in the nation. Nate uttered the name so casually as if it was just another hospital. At first Avinash did not believe it. But he could not say anything and found himself in total shock as he watched Nate flash his badge to prove his credentials. As Nate put his badge away, Avinash blankly stared at the man's face not knowing what to say.

"You have impressed a lot of people, Dr. Singh. Not only by your skills, efforts, and guts, but also because of your character. A lot of people would have taken what you did and made it their claim to fame...but you haven't. You've only done one interview and denied the rest. Why?"

Avinash took a deep breath, still digesting all of this. The words 'New York City Medical Center' still rang in every corner of his head as he quickly registered what was happening. His hunger was suddenly gone. Half of his mind thought that this was all a dream and that he would wake up at any moment. But he kept his voice calm. "...Why? It's simple really."

Nate leaned in a bit.

"I did the operation to save a girl's life, not for fame. I don't deserve the spotlight any more than a teacher or police officer. I did the one interview to give my message to everyone that would listen, not for glory. I don't want to become a part of this media circus and

136

lose myself in it. We all have a duty…a *duty* to use our abilities to make the world a better place. And that is all I did. Nothing more, nothing less."

Nate slightly nodded. A small smirk came to his face as he heard the doctor's words. "That's exactly the type of response I was hoping to hear."

Avinash nodded in appreciation. He was silent for a couple of moments before asking what was on his mind. "…If I may ask, Nate, what exactly is your business in seeing me?"

The guest leaned back in his chair. "My boss—the CEO of the hospital—has sent me to deliver you an offer. We want you to work with us. We want you to continue your research with us, and we have the best resources and substantial funds to offer you for your research."

Dr. Singh was speechless.

"And we are prepared to pay you much more than you are making right now."

Those words were spoken so calmly that Avinash thought he misheard them. Was this really happening? He was at a loss for words, expecting to wake up at any moment from this dream. He could only think of one thing to say. "…I…I have a contract here."

"And we will buy it out. I'm sure it can easily be arranged. We like you, Dr. Singh. Not just because of the doctor you are, but because of the *man* that you are. You think uniquely—which is a hard thing to come by in our field—you're a maverick and you have empathy for your patients. You see things that others don't, and you fight until the end. But most importantly, you're modest."

Avinash could not believe what he was hearing. He looked down at his lap and lightly shook his head. He knew that Nate could see the complete shock and disbelief in his eyes. His eyes slowly came back to his guest. "…I…I don't know what to say. This feels so—so unreal."

"And you don't have to say anything. I'm not a salesman, and I'm not here to get you to sign a dotted line. I'm just bringing you our offer." Nate reached into his inside coat pocket and brought out a business card. He put it on the desk and slid it towards Dr. Singh. "Here's my number. Think it over, and give me a call in a few days."

Without waiting for a response, Nate got up, turned around, shook Avinash's hand, and left without another word. Before Avinash knew it, he was alone in his office. But now nothing was in its place. Everything had changed.

***

The rest of the day went by quickly. As the afternoon passed, Avinash found himself walking through the motions, unable to keep his mind on the tasks at hands. He saw countless patients throughout the rest of the day. Some were post-surgery evaluations while others were pre-surgery appointments, but there were no more operations scheduled for the rest of the day. Avinash skipped lunch and did not bother eating another morsel of food until his day ended.

The nurses knew that something was off but none of them mentioned it. At one point, he thought Martha would bring it up, but she did not. She did not ask him who his guest was, and he did not bring up their conversation or the offer. Before he knew it, his day's work had ended. He took a cab but did not go home directly. Instead, the doctor stopped at a café for a light meal. The café was crowded by sharply dressed men and women. They all looked like they had just gotten off work. Many of them had their laptops out as they went over information and projects with one another. Their voices filled the overcrowded restaurant as each tried to speak over their neighbors.

As he sat there with a warm and mouth-watering four-cheese-flatbread in front of him, he paid no attention to the aroma of the

138

food or hear the voices all around him. All he could think of was his conversation with Nate Hopkins.

When Avinash had seen the man sitting in his office, his first thought had been one of hesitancy. But by the time Nate left, all the doctor felt was disbelief.

Was this really happening?

It seemed too good to be true. That morning, he walked into work with his mind clear. He went in expecting nothing more than to use his abilities to keep making the world a better place. But when he left, his mind was anything but clear. Nothing was the same.

***

It was late night when Avinash found himself unable to sleep. He was up in the living room sitting atop the long sofa. The clock had nearly struck midnight, and he was on the phone with his parents. It was time for his semiweekly catch-up with his folks; if he did not call on the dot, they would worry themselves to deaths. Because of the time zone difference between New York and Bihar, he always called late at night or early in the morning.

He had been speaking to them for the past twenty minutes. Sometimes this conversation lasted an hour; other times it did not make it to ten minutes. It depended on how much his folks had to say. It seemed that almost every minute, the phone would switch hands from his father to mother or vice versa as they remembered what they wanted to ask him. Outside of asking how all the relatives were doing, Avinash did little more than answer questions. How was work? Have you been eating enough food? Have you seen any friends lately? When are you coming back to visit us?

The soothing voice of his mother poured out of the phone. *"How was work today?"*

"Good." He did not bring up the offer from Nate Hopkins. Something stopped him. "It was as normal as any day should be at a hospital. I had one surgery and a lot of appointments."

"Avinash Beita...I was listening to your interview again." His mother's voice was as caring and loving as any mother's voice could be. *"You looked so handsome and spoke so eloquently—I couldn't believe that it was my son who was up there..."* She sounded as if she was about to burst into tears of joy. *"It was* my son *who was being given so much respect."*

Every time his mother saw the interview, she called and told him this word-for-word. But he did not mind. He smiled warmly as he heard her words and knew that she could feel it.

"I'm so proud of you, Avinash."

"Thank you, *ma ji*. It's only from your blessings."

"No. It's from Bhagwan *answering my prayers."*

"Of course."

Before his mother had the chance to say another word, Avinash's father came onto the line. Unlike his mother's sweet and caring voice, his father's voice was that of a stereotypical martinet. *"I must speak to you about something important, Avinash."*

He knew what was coming.

"Have you taken up any more interviews?"

"No, *pita ji*. One was more than enough."

"You still *haven't? What are you thinking?"*

"The one I did was covered nationally and even broadcasted in some other countries. There's no need for me to do other interviews—"

"Why is there no need, Avinash? This is the time to let your words be heard throughout the nation. It is the time to shine a light of honor onto you and your family."

"What I wanted to tell the world I have, and people have heard it. The interview is still being broadcasted and watched so why do I need to waste my time giving more? All I would be doing is repeating myself and letting myself become a part of this circus we call 'the media'…and how does that bring honor to the family?"

The rest of the conversation went as good as could be expected after Avinash talked back to his father.

Placing his cell phone on the table once the call ended, Avinash leaned back on the sofa and let out a long yawn. He had sent countless clippings of what he had done back home so his parents could read about it. They had taken the liberty of showing them to the entire village, and now, the people there wanted him to return so they could give him a hero's welcome. Avinash decided it was best not to tell them of the job offer for the time being.

The apartment was quiet except for the soft and continuous ticking of a clock. To the right of the table, Taxi was curled up and had fallen fast asleep. The doctor's eyes slowly came to her. The beautiful animal was as graceful as ever. He knew that once he stood up, she would somehow feel it and wake up to follow him into the bedroom.

It was about time to call it a night. He had not mentioned a word of Nate Hopkins' offer to anyone. He did not know why. He should have been ecstatic about the offer. Anyone else would be. To be offered a position at such a prestigious place was the opportunity every doctor dreamt of. What more could he want?

But there was something, something deep in his soul that stopped him from jumping at the offer. Something that told him he needed to think about it before making a decision.

His phone vibrated once more. It was a soft vibration, but Taxi's eyes suddenly shot open as she felt it. Avinash looked at the screen and saw that it was an unrecognized number calling him, but the '832' area code told him that it was a Houston number.

At first, he had half a mind not to answer it. Maybe telemarketers had resorted to calling at this late hour of night. It would not surprise him. But he answered it anyway. Putting the phone to his ear, he spoke. "Dr. Singh here."

"I hope you're not expecting me to start calling you Dr. Singh."

As the first syllable had been uttered, Avinash recognized the voice on the other end. It was the last person he expected to hear from tonight, his best friend and roommate from medical school: Mirza.

Avinash's eyes lit up. "Mirza! My *God*, I can't believe it's you."

"Glad to hear you're excited. I've been following the news. I believe congratulations are in order."

"I would not expect you to be starting a new habit of congratulating people, Mirza."

He heard Mirza's smile in his friend's voice. *"I'll make an exception here."*

Leaning back in his sofa, Avinash put his feet up on the coffee table. "How's the weather down in Houston?"

"I wouldn't know. I'm actually in New York City—Manhattan to be more exact."

"What makes a self-proclaimed cowboy like you grace us New Yorkers with your presence?

"Business, believe it or not."

"Medical business?"

"Well nobody's going to be sending a doctor on accounting business, now are they?"

Avinash lightly laughed. "I would have thought that Memorial Herman would have wised up and fired you by now."

"Yeah…they still haven't figured out what a sham I am. It's not like I'm making headlines like my oh-so-great former roommate is."

As Avinash spoke to his old friend, every memory they shared in medical school flashed through his mind. "You did graduate in second place, didn't you? Maybe that's why you're not as great as me?"

Mirza chuckled on the other end. *"You'll never let me live that down will you?"*

"Not for all the gold in the world."

"I don't doubt that." Mirza was silent for a moment. *"The reason I am calling is to see if you have some free time tomorrow to grab some coffee."*

"For you, I'll make time. How about lunch? I have a surgery early morning, but it's a simple one. I can grab a late bite with you around 1:30 if you can come to the cafeteria. I'm sure you know where my hospital is."

"Perfect and yes, I do. Talk more tomorrow."

"Goodnight."

The line went dead, and Avinash rose to his feet. Seeing that, Taxi followed him out of the living room and towards his bedroom. A slight smile had come to his face upon hearing his friend's voice after all these years.

As he made his way, the entire conversation replayed back through his mind. Although Mirza tried to hide it, something seemed off. On the surface, Mirza's voice sounded as normal and jovial as ever. But he called Avinash after all these years for a reason. He would not have called this late just to schedule a lunch.

Avinash did not know what it was, but as he went to bed, he knew that he would certainly find out soon enough.

CHAPTER 11
CROSSROADS

When Avinash saw his friend, he let out joyous laughter and embraced him like anyone would embrace a long-lost brother. He had changed out of his scrubs and now wore his white coat over his kakis and cerulean polo shirt. Mirza was dressed in a pair of stylish jeans, a tucked in white-collared shirt, and a black sports coat. Like the picture in Dr. Singh's office illustrated, Mirza was not nearly the size of Avinash, but his strong posture made him look taller than he actually was.

"You're stylish as ever, my friend!"

Mirza nodded in appreciation as they firmly shook hands. His free hand patted the side of Avinash's shoulder. "I learned from the best. You're taller than I remember."

"All the good press must be going to my head."

"Wouldn't surprise me."

Avinash lightly chuckled as he looked over at the cafeteria's kitchen. "Hope you're hungry."

"Is the food here any good?"

"It's better than that damn food we ate every day for four years."

"Hey, we were broke med students. Don't judge."

There was no line in the cafeteria since the lunch rush had ended almost half an hour prior. Throughout the sitting area, only a handful of people were seen, leaving countless tables and chairs unoccupied. The cleaning crew was in the midst of their routine, wiping off the tables and sweeping the floor.

144

Coming up to the ordering counter, they were met by a round, middle-aged, African-American lady on the opposite side. The rest of the staff was on their lunch break, leaving her alone to hold down the fort. She was dressed in starched white clothes and a tainted apron. She was tired and a little sweaty having been overworked during the lunch hour. But seeing the friendly face of the nice doctor, she smiled at him, and her voice showed her happiness.

"Docta' Singh!"

"Afternoon Cathy." Avinash motioned to Mirza. "This is my friend from med school, Mirza. He's visiting from Houston."

Cathy nodded in the guest's direction. "Hiya. You from Texas?"

"The *nation* of Texas as we Texans like to call it."

Avinash lightly scoffed. "Ignore him, Cathy. He's not even a real Texan. He was born in Florida."

"Our hearts make us Texan," Mirza countered.

The cook smiled and dramatically shook her head. "You Texas folk are all the same." She looked back at Avinash. "The usual salad with an unsweetened iced tea?"

"Why start a new habit?"

"Yessuh." Her eyes came onto Mirza. "And for you, suh?"

"A cheeseburger, save the onions. And a water bottle."

"Coming right up."

As the lady turned around to start putting the orders together, Mirza lightly elbowed his friend in the ribs. "A salad? Since when have you started eating salads?"

"It's a new habit. I'm trying to cut back on my meat."

"Don't tell me you're becoming a vegetarian. You couldn't survive a day without meat back in med school."

"No harm in trying, is there?"

Mirza slightly shook his head. "I guess not."

A few minutes later, the two of them were seated in the nearly empty cafeteria. With their food-filled trays, they sat at a small circular table. It had been wiped off moments ago, leaving its silver surface shining and reflecting the high ceiling lights. They were well out of ear shot from any of the other patrons.

The aroma of Mirza's sizzling burger filled both of their nostrils. The cheese and meat could be heard as they melted into one another, creating the perfect mix for anyone's taste buds. But the smells and sounds did not make Avinash regret his choice of a meatless salad.

"I can only imagine the offers you must be getting." Mirza took a bite of his burger and his expression showed how much the taste satisfied him.

"There have been plenty...including one very alluring offer that came yesterday from the New York Medical Center."

The self-proclaimed Texan swallowed his mouthful. "Have you taken it?"

Avinash shook his head as he chewed on a small bite.

For a moment, Avinash thought he saw a short-lived flash of relief in his friend's eyes before Mirza continued, "Why not?"

"...I really don't know. Something told me to wait."

"Maybe it's not what you want."

Avinash shook his head. "That can't be it. It's an offer that every man dreams of."

"But is it what *you* dreamt of having?"

He did not answer.

Mirza waited a long time before speaking. "And speaking of offers...that brings me to what I wanted to talk to you about."

Avinash's voice showed his surprise. "You have one? Don't tell me it's from Memorial Herman."

"I do have one…but it's not from that hospital." Mirza was silent for a moment. "I'm actually no longer with them. It's been six months since we parted ways."

Avinash's eyes widened. "Did they let you go?"

"No…I actually left them."

Without thinking, the fork dropped from Avinash's hand and fell onto the cafeteria's grey-tiled floor. The metal utensil sounded off loudly as it crashed onto the ground. It's soft echo resonated throughout the empty cafeteria. "…Why? I thought you loved it there."

"I did…but I wasn't content. The pay was good, the people were good, but something was missing."

"…What?"

"I became a doctor to help people. I wanted to make a difference."

Dr. Singh reached down and put his fork back onto the table. "You were. I mean as a surgeon—"

"Sure, I was patching people up. But I was not—I don't know how to explain this—but I was not complete. Working at the hospital, I was not doing something that any other surgeon could not do. I wasn't making a *real* difference. At least not in my mind."

Avinash was silent. All the jovial happiness that had been on Mirza's face when he walked into the cafeteria was gone. It was replaced with a seriousness that Avinash had hardly ever seen on his friend's face in their time together.

"I want more than to just be a doctor. I'm a man, Avinash. And like any real man, I want my life to have purpose. I want to be somewhere that requires courage. I want to do something that others don't have the courage to do. That—that hospital felt like a cage to me. And with each passing day there, I felt more like a prisoner of my own ambition."

"…And what are you doing now?"

"Have you ever heard of Jonathan Daniels?"

"Who hasn't? He's one of the world's biggest philanthropists. He's definitely living up to his brother's reputation."

Mirza nodded. "Well, one of the missions of Jonathan's organization is to help those who can't help themselves…to be a guardian to them. He sends medical aid groups and relief groups into many hot spots and war zones that are not receiving any international help from organizations like the UN or UNICEF. He's even gone so far as to hire a small army of mercenaries that he uses to protect his camps when needed."

"I've heard of his group's efforts." Avinash did not like where this was headed.

"I've was oversees in Amaristan. For the past five months, I've been with them."

Avinash did not believe his ears. He blankly stared at his friend, shock forcing him to remain quiet. The country Mirza mentioned had been all over the news for the past few months. Rebel forces had declared an all-out war against the local regime along with anyone who did not stand with them. Hundreds of thousands had been killed. Millions brutally injured. And tens of millions had been displaced. The nation had descended into savagery. Murder, pillaging, and kidnapping ran rampant throughout the nation.

Mirza leaned forward as he spat out his next sentences like a rapid fire machine gun. "Avinash, you know the situation there. The people there are being massacred. The government is on the run, leaving the rebels in charge. The rebel's leader has gone on a rampage, instilling himself into power by fear. No aid is going into the country because the rebels have already killed countless doctors and relief workers that were sent in by the UN or any other aid group. Everybody is too scared to send in any more aid workers. They don't think that the country is worth the risk because it was never an advantageous nation to begin with. The only entity doing anything is the organization I'm with." Mirza took a deep breath. "This...this is what I wanted to see you about, Avinash."

Avinash took a breath before replying, "...What exactly are you saying, Mirza?"

"That I want you to come with me."

Avinash was silent for a few long moments as he digested his friend's words. He should have expected that request, but hearing those words come out of Mirza's mouth sounded so unbelievable. "You want me...to...go with you...to Amaristan?"

Mirza silently nodded. He glanced down before looking back up at his friend. "Avinash, we need people like you—unconventional thinkers. People who value human life...people who are warriors."

"Were you asked to come recruit me? Did your boss send you?" As he spoke, Avinash crossed his arms. A part of him was angry that his friend had come only to throw another offer at him. But another side hung on every word that Mirza said. "Or was this your own idea?"

"No, I'm here as a friend. I've heard you talk about honoring your forefathers and battling until the end. Well, this is a fight that's worth fighting. And this is a battle that needs real warriors."

Avinash was silent for a long time. "A part of me wants to believe you. But another part of me thinks that your organization wants me to join because my present popularity will give them more coverage in the press."

"You know me better than that. I've never used you before, have I?"

Dr. Singh was silent, immediately regretting his words.

"I have been there for the past five months...you would not believe the things that are happening there. The media is not doing it justice. They're not telling the whole story. People are dying from the simplest wounds. Simple things that are no problem for you and me to patch up are killing people because there are not enough doctors and nurses to go around. The revolutionaries are killing aid workers in an effort to keep outsiders too scared to come in. And the worst part of it is that their intimidation is working. It's—it's an international disaster. The genocide that the revolutionaries are committing will be remembered as the Holocaust of this century."

Dr. Singh's gaze fell down onto his lap. Silence was his response for what felt like a long time. The lunch had gone anything other than as planned. His mind was still trying to digest everything that he was hearing. This whole thing came out of left field.

His heart was pounding faster and faster with each moment as it realized what was happening here. Finally, his gaze came back to Mirza. He spoke without thinking. "Mirza, my friend, thank you for coming to me. I want to help you—I really do."

Knowing what was coming, Mirza leaned back in his seat and looked down at the table.

"But I can't just go with you right now. I...I have things I need to do *here*. The offer that came to me is one that I just can't turn down. Not right now. The difference that I can make here through continuing my research is going to impact generations. This...this cause is your calling, not mine."

Mirza drew a deep breath before he let his eyes lock back with Avinash's. "Remember what Dr. Stone used to always say?"

Avinash knew what their former medical professor's saying was, but he remained silent.

"Research can wait until tomorrow...but the human life cannot." Mirza got up out of his chair. "And it's not this offer from New York Medical Center that is holding you back. Even if you didn't have it, you still wouldn't come with me. We both know that."

The cardiothoracic surgeon said nothing.

"It's fear, Avinash. Fear. I never thought you'd be one to let that hold you back. Not when the lives of the innocent are at stake.

150

But I must have been wrong. The Avinash I know is not the one I'm looking at."

And before Avinash knew it, he was alone.

***

"Dr. Singh?"

Avinash suddenly looked up and came back to reality. Fiza was staring at him from the other side of his desk. Her light skin and green eyes showed her Syrian heritage. In her hands were a clipboard and a pen.

Avinash realized that she had been standing there and speaking to him, but he had not heard a word. He had probably greeted her on auto-pilot. Finally realizing that she was there, Avinash quickly came back to reality.

"Fiza…sorry." He wiped his palm over his face as he tried to come back to the present. "My mind was somewhere else."

"I thought so. I just wanted to let you know that your 3:30 appointment had to reschedule. Said it was a family emergency."

He nodded. "That's the one with William Adams, isn't it?"

"Yes."

"Okay." He quickly looked down at his silver wristwatch. "Looks like I have some time to burn."

The nurse was silent for a few moments. "…Are you okay doctor?"

His eyes focused back on her. "Is it that obvious?"

"Whenever you're not speaking quicker than the person can listen, it usually means something is bothering you."

A light smile quickly flashed upon the doctor's face before disappearing. "Sorry about that." He glanced down at his desk for a quick moment. "It's just that my visit with my friend did not go as expected."

"The one from med school you were telling us about?"

He nodded. "He's not like I remembered? That…or maybe I'm not."

"Change is not always a bad thing. Sometimes it is what needs to happen."

"Yeah…but sometimes the question is what kind of change do we need." Avinash slowly rose to his feet. "I'm going to take a walk around the block. If anyone needs me, they can call me."

"Yes, Dr. Singh."

"I should know this, but when is Alice coming back for her follow-up?"

"Tomorrow."

For a moment, his eyes lit up.

***

A little after dinner, Avinash's phone rang. Having just washed the two dishes he had eaten on, he wiped his hands on a towel. He looked down at the ringing phone and saw his parent's number displayed on the caller ID. Avinash quickly glanced at the clock and saw that dawn was just breaking in Bihar. It was a couple hours earlier than when his parents usually called. And they almost never called back-to-back days unless it was an emergency.

He quickly answered the call. *"Namaste pita ji."*

"Namaste, *Avinash.*" His father's voice sounded softer than normal. Avinash knew what that meant. *"Are you still at the hospital?"*

"No, I just ate dinner. How are you feeling?"

"My knee is still bothering me, the joints in my fingers still hurt a bit— that rascal doctor has no idea what he's doing—nothing he gives me fixes the problem…"

Avinash blocked out the rest of the complaints as his father rattled them off. They were always the same things.

152

"But I didn't call you to talk about this."

"What is it?"

"Last night when we spoke, you hid something from me."

Avinash's eyes slightly widened. "Hid something from you?"

"I know…and your mother knows."

"Why would I hide something from you?"

"We brought you into this world, Avinash. And we know when there is something you're not telling us."

There was no arguing with that one.

His father's normal, military-like voice came back. *"Tell us what it is."*

Avinash let out a quiet sigh. He would have to tell them sooner or later so there was no point in hiding it. "I received an offer…two actually."

"What are they?"

"The first was from the New York City Medical Center."

There was quiet on the other end for several seconds. But then there was a sudden outburst that Avinash sensed was coming. *"New York City Medical Center!"* The father's voice was brimming with shock and excitement.

"Yes…and the second was from my friend, Mirza—my roommate from med school."

"That Muslim boy?" The excitement had been replaced with distaste.

Avinash took a deep breath not wanting to argue with his father. "He had an offer from a humanitarian organization…one that operates in war zones for relief."

"Is that man mad? Why does he think that you would even consider an offer like that?"

Avinash was about to say something, but he stopped himself.

"I mean, at a time like this where the world is at your feet, is that boy foolish enough to even think that you would bat an eye at a thing like that? I

always knew he would be trouble for you." His father was silent for a moment. "*Have you taken up the hospital on their offer yet?*"

"…Not yet."

"*Why not?*"

"Because…I don't know if it's the right fit for me. I don't know if it's what I really want."

"*What do you mean, 'The right fit?' It's what you have always dreamed of…it's what you wanted—to work at such a prestigious place. It's the only choice you can make. Do not tell me that that other man's offer has clouded your mind.*"

The son did not answer.

His father's voice changed to be more forceful than ever. He said each word with an ocean of command behind it. "*Listen to me…tomorrow you are going to call the hospital and take them up on the offer.*"

Avinash took a deep breath. "…I understand."

***

Not this nightmare again.

Avinash couldn't breathe.

Avinash flailed his arms trying to keep himself afloat. But he sunk like a rock, swallowing a gulp of pool water in the process. His heart rate spiked as the water engulfed him.

All around the edge of the pool, his schoolmates watched. They were the same ones who tormented him every day. Now, they had pushed him in knowing he couldn't swim. They pointed and mockingly laughed. Their taunts echoed through the room. Even if he could have heard them, Avinash would not know what they were saying. And he did not know why they did this to him.

As more water filled his lungs, Avinash felt his toes lightly touch the bottom of the pool. His heart was going crazy, and his senses were a wreck. His mind screamed for one thing: air. He could feel his fingers and toes starting to become numb as his head became light.

Through the water, he could see the blurred vision of the boys that had pushed him in. They were in an uproar as they continued jeering him. His thoughts focused on one thing. With a last heave, he pushed up with his legs and moved his arms in a way to pull himself up like he had seen done before.

It worked.

With another heave, he came closer to the surface. And with the third, his head burst through the surface of the water. He immediately reached over and grabbed the nearest ledge before his head sunk back in. Luckily, he ended up on the opposite side of the pool from the boys who would have kicked him back in.

Seeing as their entertainment was over the boys turned and left, mocking him as they did. He couldn't understand their words, but Avinash could understand their cruel intentions. He understood that here in this foreign land called America, he was different. He didn't belong. This was not his home.

And he certainly had no place here and would never be one of them.

***

Avinash was drenched in his own sweat when he suddenly woke up in the middle of the night. It took him a few moments to realize that it was all over. He wasn't in that forsaken pool. He wasn't the victim of his schoolmates. Once again, he was the respected Dr. Singh.

It was no accident that this nightmare reoccurred tonight. His mind was reminding him of the last time that he had gone to a foreign place. Decades ago, he came to the foreign land of America with the intention of making it his new home. But instead, what he found was misery. His mind was asking him if he really wanted to put himself through that once more?

And he didn't know the answer.

***

"So everything is looking good, Mr. Richards. Alice's recovery is coming along very nicely." Making a few notes on his clipboard, Avinash looked back up at his young patient's father. He handed the clipboard to the smiling Martha next to him.

"Thank you doctor," Mr. Richards said with a smile.

"Just make sure that she doesn't do anything that will raise her heart rate too much. Keep exercising limited to walking; no horror movies, roller coasters, or things that would get her overly excited."

"You think something like that could be detrimental to the procedure?"

"I'm not sure. It's more of a precaution. I would advise you to keep her home from school until our next check-up. By then if everything checks out, she will be able to do everything that a kid can do."

Alice's father nodded. "Okay."

Avinash smiled and then looked over at his patient. The young girl was sitting up on the bench dressed in a yellow and white, sleeveless dress that ran from her shoulders to her knees. "You hear that, Alice? No school for two more weeks!"

She grinned back at him and let out a short-lived, "Yipee."

Dr. Singh looked back at Mr. Richards. "Any more questions?"

"Nope." He glanced down at Alice for a moment. As the man's eyes fell upon his happy daughter, his own grin grew. "It still seems so…like a miracle…doesn't it?"

Avinash's gaze came onto the little girl as a smile slowly spread across his face.

"Sometimes I fear that this is all a dream," Mr. Richards continued. "And that I will wake up at any moment to come back to the horrendous reality that we were trapped in for so long. You…you were the blessing that my family needed."

"It was a blessing from above that saved your daughter, Mr. Richards, not me."

"I can never thank you enough, Dr. Singh."

Avinash's eyes met with the father's. "And you should never thank me. I'm not the one who gives and takes life."

Mr. Richards smiled without a word as the two men shook hands.

The doctor looked back at the girl. Her long auburn locks were held back from her face by a headband. There was so much joy in her. So much potential. So much life. Life that may not have been there if he had not shown the courage to do what he felt was his duty. The young girl's light brown eyes were looking down at her feet, which did not even come within a foot of touching the ground. They slowly swung back and forth, back and forth, back and forth. A baby could have been put to sleep watching them.

He was not sure how long he kept his eyes on the girl. It could not have been more than a few long moments. But that short time was enough.

Without a word, she told him what he needed to hear.

Less than a minute later, Avinash walked out of the room and into the hospital's hallway. He slowly made his way down the crowded corridor, past all of the people in scrubs and all of the visitors. They all went about their business, and he went about his. Their voices filled the hallway as they spoke to one another, and his voice filled his head. The slight smile that had come upon his face was still painted there.

"Dr. Singh!"

Avinash discreetly looked behind him as Martha caught up to walk alongside him.

"What happened to you in there? You were in some sort of trance."

He did not answer as he looked straight ahead.

"Something came to your mind? What is it?"

"I...I think I know what I need to do."

"*Need to do?*"

"There's something I haven't told you, Martha. I got an offer—from New York City Medical Center. The man who came to visit me two days ago—Nate Hopkins—he was from there."

Her eyes widened in surprise as they turned the corner. Her voice mirrored the same excitement that his father's had. "...*New York City Medical Center?*"

He nodded.

"Have—have you taken it?"

"No...and I don't know if I will. I received another offer...this one from my friend who came by yesterday."

"Which hospital is it for?"

"None."

"A school?"

He shook his head.

"Then what?"

His eyes finally came back to her. "A warzone."

Complete awe and confusion kept her speechless.

"He wants me to come with him. Those people there—the refugees who are fleeing for their lives—they need all the help they can get." Once again, his eyes left her and focused straight ahead. "I'm on the verge of making my decision—one that will certainly not bode well with my parents. But I'm only missing one thing."

"Wh—what's that?"

"Confirmation."

"Confirmation?"

He knowingly nodded. "And I think I know where I'll find it."

***

When Avinash got back to his apartment, he skipped dinner. He did not even feel any hunger. All he could see was the image of Alice sitting on that bench. The only thing on his mind was the eight-year-old girl who was alive and well because he had possessed the courage to do his best without worrying about the consequences.

And that was the courage that he would need once again.

Coming into his bedroom, Avinash slung off his coat and threw it over the chair as he switched on the lights. Walking directly to a small, green chest with golden straps that was in an empty corner of the room, he crouched down next to it. On top of the chest was a small, bronze key which the doctor quickly took into his hands before unlocking the trunk. Inside the chest were a few old letters, but he was not interested in them.

What he focused on was the journal.

Taking it into his hands, he ran his fingers over the brown, leather cover. He could feel its rough surface and worn out edges while his nose picked up the smell of his grandfather. It all immediately took him back to the first time he had been given the journal.

He needed to find his courage. He needed to find the inspiration to not let the fear of death or loss keep him from making his decision. Avinash knew that it had to be in here. He had not picked up the journal since Alice's surgery. After the surgery, he once again locked the journal away and let its words guide him in his mission. And in the weeks that ensued, Avinash did not have the heart to open the journal. He had been waiting for the right time to read the next entry.

And this was it.

CHAPTER 12
THE PRISONER

A time comes in every man's life when he faces death. Either it has come to him or he arrives at its doorstep. And at that moment, there is a choice. Will he go quietly into that good night, or will his final cry be in heat of battle? Will his legacy echo through eternity and be something that is remembered in history?

A man must find his courage. He must find what gives him his courage. Faith, purpose, and love! These are the integral parts of a man. What can one man do in a world where evil overpowers good? What can man do against such hate?

Face it with courage. He can walk with his head held high and with the fire of bravery burning in his veins. He can show the world what one man can do.

One man's worth. One man's defiance. One man's valor.

On the first page, there was a note that Avinash quickly read. It said that although the entry was about his ancestor, it had not been written by his own hand. Instead, a man named Henry Ducard had written it. The man claimed to have witnessed most of the event's occurrence. The parts that he did not witness were relayed to him by Avinash's ancestor, Veeresh, or a man named Amir.

With a deep breath, Avinash continued.

***

India. Winter of 1857.

For months now, the nation had been at war, but not with a neighbor or a distant land. It was a war that was fought between the rulers and the indigenous people. British rulers, under the banner of the East India Company, had ruled this land for over 100 years. They came in as traders before taking power from the waning Mughul Dynasties. And over the centuries, the land and people of India gave them mountains of wealth.

But the foreign rulers finally pushed their luck. They had gone too far, and war was now upon them. The Company stopped seeing India as a land and began viewing it as an asset. They began to exact as many riches as they could without considering the people who lived there. Decades of misrule caused poverty throughout certain regions of India. Tensions became high, but the final straw came when the Company tricked Muslims and Hindu soldiers into breaking their religions' codes.

When the Enfield Rifle came into circulation, there were rumors that the gun's paper cartridges were greased with pork and beef. However, The Company denied such rumors and commanded their Muslim and Hindu soldiers to use the rifles and bite into the cartridges. But the truth soon came to light. And it was then that the people of India realized that the Company was no longer just a ruler. It was now a cruel oppressor.

The British called it a revolt, but the people of India called it a revolution. The British called their adversaries terrorists, but the people of India called them freedom fighters. But both sides could agree on one thing.

They all knew that this war would change the Company and the land forever.

***

Death was not worse than this.

161

A part of Veeresh wished that he had been killed on that fateful day instead of being taken prisoner. There was nothing worse than living in this endless hell. Nothing worse than living in this prison of inescapable torture.

Not only the prison of the body, but the prison of the mind. The prison of not having seen her for the past four months and knowing that he would never quench his thirst to see her ever again. The prison of knowing that she was now nothing more than a distant memory from another life.

His eyes slowly opened. Veeresh looked at the rough stone walls he had stared at for the past few months. The eight-feet by eight-feet cell was his home now. And until his upcoming hanging, it would be his last abode. There was no light down here below the ground, but Veeresh could see everything perfectly in his mind. He had memorized every crack and crevice. He had memorized every inch of its surface. He could feel the jagged and uneven walls of the cell as he leaned his back against them. They were covered in dirt, but it did not bother Veeresh in the slightest. At three of the top corners, spiders had built their intricate webs. On the ground, many dead bugs lay upturned.

In the four months he had been here, much had changed in the outside world. The revolution continued to engulf the nation. Thousands were dead. The climate of the country was changing day by day. Nothing was the same.

Hearing footsteps coming down the corridor, Veeresh kept his eyes on the wall. Wearing the same clothes he had worn since the day he was imprisoned, he could feel the dirty hair that covered his face. When he was thrown in here, he had been a handsome and well-groomed man. But now, he looked like nothing more than a street beggar. His hair was growing out. His cheeks and chin, which had been cleanly shaven all his life, was now covered in an unkempt beard. Having not been fed a decent diet, he was not as strong as he

162

was before. After months of living in here, much of his strength was gone.

The cell door swung open with a loud creak. The torch light that illuminated the dungeon-like hallways flooded the dark cell. Veeresh looked at three men standing in the doorway. One was the English guard who had worked here since the day Veeresh was imprisoned, Edward. The other British man was a guard named Henry. Between the two of them, the guards held the third man, a prisoner, by his arms. Edward held him roughly while Henry tried to hold him with some decency.

"Damn *sepoys*," Edward said in disgust, "God knows how you were ever of any use to us."

With a quick shove, Edward sent the prisoner sprawling into his shared cell. The inmate, Amir, roughly and painfully landed on the hard floor. But he did not let out any grunt of pain. He would not give the guard that pleasure.

"We should have known that your kind would turn on us. This is what happens when you employ so many devil worshipers."

As Edward's words ended, the door loudly closed. The room was once again thrown into darkness. As the loud echo momentarily consumed the room, Amir's gaze slowly came onto his fellow prisoner.

But Veeresh quickly looked away from his cellmate's bruised face.

Slowly, Amir made his way over to his counterpart and collapsed right beside him with a grunt. As he leaned against the wall, Amir looked over at his colleague and spoke. "It's the same every day with these dogs."

"It wouldn't be if you held your tongue."

Amir quietly laughed, but no amusement came onto Veeresh's face. "If I am to die by my enemy's hands, I will die defiantly. What else can a man do when he has nothing left to lose?"

"A man always has something left to lose even in the face of death: his pride." Veeresh looked over at his friend. "...and his dreams."

***

Colonel James Smith had been summoned to his commander's office. Wearing his red military uniform, he walked through the crisp, clean hallways of the fort. Situated at the edge of the building, large windows were lined up on the left side of the corridor allowing the sun's light to remove the need for candles during the day.

Outside of the general's office, one of the prison's guards was stationed. The man, Henry Ducard, had been here as long as James. But the colonel did not pay him any heed as he marched straight past him. He entered through the heavy and polished wooden doors to find his superior officer at his auburn desk.

The floor was wooden, but a red and white carpet led from the entrance to the desk. On the other side of the desk was a large window. Its blinds were pulled back, allowing rivers of sunlight to enter and bounce off of the room's walls, floor, and ceiling. On one side of the room was a bookshelf that went from one end of the wall to the midway point. It was full of books neatly lined up. Most were books of war that the general had studied throughout his youth and years of service. On the same wall was a golden-framed portrait of Queen Victoria. And not far from it was a portrait of Sir Frederick Currie, director of the Company, and Mr. Ross Donnelly Mangles, chairman of the Company. Hanging on the opposite wall were swords and ceremonial rifles that had been collected over the general's career.

164

The colonel stood at attention and saluted his commanding officer.

The general nodded at the colonel. "At ease, colonel."

Coming to ease, James noticed a third man in the room.

On a chair opposite of his commander was a man dressed in dark clothing. A black dinner jacket with silk facings and two buttons on the front was worn over everything else. Underneath them, he wore a matching waistcoat over a white shirt. Like the style of the day, his shirt collars were pressed into 'wings' and had a stiff front. Around his collar was the newly fashionable Ascot tie. He wore a pair of dark trousers over his legs and narrow-toed shoes on his feet. With a black bowler hat covering his perfectly combed hair, a walking stick that the man carried purely for style was leaning against the desk. His face was cleanly shaven except for a subtle, light brown mustache. The fabric of his attire along with his posture evidenced the man's wealth and pride.

"Colonel Smith," the general began, "This is Mr. Wilkinson. He works directly under Mr. Mangles and has been sent down from the Company."

James came forward to greet Mr. Wilkinson, but the representative did not get up. Coming all the way to the desk, James shook hands with Mr. Wilkinson. However, the suited man still did not even give the colonel the courtesy of rising out of his chair.

"I was telling Mr. Wilkinson about how you are the best interrogator in the region. The information you were able to pull out of the captured insurgents was instrumental in our victory at the Siege of Delhi."

"Just doing my duty, sir."

Mr. Wilkinson finally spoke. "The general tells me that your methods of interrogation are...shall we say, *persuasive*."

"Enemies of the Company and Crown deserve whatever I do to them. Especially enemies that call that damned traitor, Mangal

Panday, a hero. Had I been his executioner, I would not have hung him. I would have used my methods on him publically to show all these savages just how brutal the Company will be when it comes to making sure that order is followed."

The gentleman nodded in agreement. "How long have you been here, colonel?"

"I arrived a month before the hanging of Panday."

Mr. Wilkinson slightly leaned back in his seat. "And just what is your opinion of the natives that surround you?"

"One Englishman is worth the entire lot. There's a reason God gave us a prosperous land like England and gave these savages such a hell to live and die in. And there's a reason that he put them under us. They're savages—as bad as dogs. They have no loyalty— no ability to think for themselves. They'd stab each other in the back if they had the chance."

A small but short-lived smirk flashed upon Mr. Wilkinson's face. "How familiar are you with the state of the Company?"

"I stay focused on my duties, sir. I leave the health of the Company to more qualified men like yourself."

"A dutiful man. I like that. Men like you are what keeps the Company alive and have made it into the greatest company the world has ever seen."

James nodded in appreciation.

"And I have come here looking for a man willing to carry out a duty. One that will bring this revolt to its knees." Mr. Wilkinson glanced at the general. "And I have been told that you are best man for it."

"I would be honored, sir."

"The state of the Company before this revolt was not one to be boasted. Flawed decisions by our former chairman and directors brought us to this state." Mr. Wilkinson looked in the direction of the portraits. "Our current leaders, in all their wisdom, have created

166

a strategy to bring us back to glory." His gaze came back onto the soldier. "However, this revolt has been a grave expense, hindering such plans. It has brought the Company down even further. It is well known that since the Battle of Dehli, the revolution is no longer unified. Each region is carrying out their own strategies. The revolt will be put down within the next year. However, if it is not put out quickly enough, the Company may very well be facing its end. And a loss of that caliber will be a loss to the people and the Crown of England."

James was speechless. The end of the Company? After being the crown jewel for England for hundreds of years, how could it end?

"I understand you have a certain person of interest in your prison here. A man named Veeresh Singh?"

"I do not know the prisoners by name—"

"I looked at the records."

"Yes, sir. I am sure that the records are accurate."

"Do you know who he is? Or should I say, who he *was*?"

"I am not familiar with the prisoner."

"We do not know if he ever participated in any insurgent strategies against the Company. However, we do know that he verbally endorsed the revolt before his capture."

"We have many like him here—"

"No you don't, colonel. He is the most vicious man in this prison. He may be the most dangerous man in the entire revolt. In one instance alone, he murdered six British soldiers."

The colonel was silent, unable to imagine what he heard. One savage killed six honorable soldiers of England?

"And he is respected by the people. His defection caused thousands of others in this very region to become sympathetic to the revolt's so-called cause. Although he is young, no older than twenty-four from our records, his word carries weight with the locals."

James nodded. "I understand, sir."

"I have with me a task to be commissioned. If you are willing to take it and carry it out successfully, your name will be heard in the ears and spoken on the lips of the director himself. If not, then your career with the Company may not go as well as you have hoped."

"...Yes, sir."

"Singh is scheduled to be hung for his crimes against the Company and the Crown in two weeks' time. Being that the date has already been announced to the public, it cannot be changed lest we wish to give off an image of indecisiveness. That would be detrimental in a time of war."

"Of course."

Mr. Wilkinson took a deep breath. "What you must do is get this Singh to publically denounce the revolt. Make him denounce its leaders, followers, and purpose. Make him publically say that he was wrong for fighting against the Company and turning his back to it after it has given him and his people so much."

Colonel Smith kept his eyes locked with the eyes of Mr. Wilkinson. The gentleman's eyes were the eyes of an animal. An animal that was willing to do whatever it needed to survive. *Whatever it needed.* Finally, the soldier nodded. "I will do it."

"Good. I will stay here until you do. The general has graciously allowed me to take his office after he removes his personal belongings."

The general's eyes showed the truth, but he remained silent.

Wilkinson slowly rose to his feet and walked towards the large window with his hands clasped behind his back. "This war had shown us something. It has shown us that India is a lion waiting to be awaken. The power that this land possesses is enormous when the people are united."

James watched the gentleman look back at him.

"The age of colonialism will soon come to an end. Whether it is this year or in the next century, sooner or later India will leave the empire. When that day comes, we must ensure that the people are separated and divided. When this war ends, the Company and the Crown will take measures to begin to divide the people along the lines of religion so that when India does break away, it will not remain one nation. There are many people here, but education is yet to be widespread. And we will use that against them."

"...I understand."

"However, that is not our assignment today. Our assignment is to break the spirit of the revolt. I will tell you that this particular assignment is never to go on record. None will ever hear of it."

James nodded.

"In every region, men like you are being tasked to persuade their most influential prisoners to denounce the revolution. In doing so, we will break the spirit of the people. And to do your part, you will need to break this man..." There was a quick flash in Wilkinson's eyes. "By any means necessary."

***

The door to the prison cell quietly opened. Being a light sleeper, Veeresh's eyes shot open to see Henry entering the cell. The torchlight from the hallway dimly illuminated the dark cell. Veeresh instinctively elbowed his comrade, waking him up.

A rifle was strapped to the guard's back. In Henry's hand was three-quarters of a loaf of recently baked bread and on his face was an empathetic smile. Veeresh rose to his feet along with Amir.

169

"The officers just finished eating. This was the best thing left." Henry handed the bread to Veeresh.

Veeresh instinctively broke it in half and tried giving the larger portion to Amir. However, Amir took the smaller piece instead.

"Thank you, my friend," Veeresh said to Henry. "If it wasn't for your kindness, I would think that we were trapped in Hell."

"Hell is what many of my so-called honorable comrades will receive for what they have done." Henry motioned towards the bread. "I didn't see any other guards in the corridor, but make sure you eat it quickly all the same."

Amir nodded. "Of course."

"It's inhumane the lack of food they provide the prisoners here. For men who call themselves Christian, they certainly do not act like it."

"Few men who proclaim themselves pious truly are."

Henry's eyes agreed.

"However, when I do think of Christians, you are the face that comes to my mind."

The guard smiled before patting his friend on the shoulder.

And a few moments later, Henry left the cell and locked the door behind him. Once again, the cell was shrouded in darkness. But it did not bother the prisoners. After their months in captivity, their eyes were trained for the darkness and had been molded by it.

They made quick work of the bread, and did not leave a single crumb. As he swallowed his last bit, Amir glanced over at his friend. "If there is one thing that the British learned in India, it is how to cook decent bread."

Veeresh softly chuckled but did not say anything in return. Not long after, the two of them again retired in the darkness. They had no way to see if it was night or day outside, but their internal clocks convinced them that the moon was still out.

As he closed his eyes, Veeresh knew who he would dream of. It was the same person he dreamt of every night. The woman he had sworn to protect until his dying breath. The one who had brought him more happiness than any other person.

His wife...

CHAPTER 13
THE PROPOSAL

The first time Veeresh saw her, he learned what a true heartbeat felt like. It was more than two years before he would find himself in a prison. The son of the city's wealthiest man was getting married to a girl from a highly respected family, and nearly every townsperson was in attendance. Dressed in their finest garments, men wore bright-colored *sherwanis*. The heavy fabrics had the presence of a lining and were a cross between the British frock coat and Indian *kameez*. Alongside their male companions, women were covered in vibrant *shalwar kameezes* or *saris*. Their garments came in many colors and sizes. Some were heavy while others were lightweight .

The groom's family owned a large three-story complex where the entire family from the great-grandfather to the great-grandchildren lived. It was the largest home within a hundred mile radius of Bhagwanpur. The red-bricked building could be seen for miles around, and its architecture was something to marvel. It reminded many of the palaces of old.

The festivities were held in an open field next to the complex. Red, green, and gold tents and canopies were set up throughout the grounds, protecting the wedding's guests from the evening sun. The largest canopy, a red and gold patterned one, was set up in the center of the field. The last marriage ceremony, the *Saptapadi*, had been performed under it only hours ago. The fire that the groom and bride circled seven times still burned, and its thin line of smoke continued to rise into the heavens.

172

A professional band played joyous music in the field using a variety of instruments ranging from stringed instruments to aerophones to drums. But the two most prominent were the drum-like *dholka* and *tabla*. The musicians expertly beat upon them, and their sounds could be heard in every corner of the field.

Children could be seen running around the tents and dodging the adults as they chased one another. To them, this was the highlight of the wedding. Their laughter filled the air as they played their games. Their jubilant voices were so loud that they rivaled the music.

Women wore the decorative *henna* on their hands, and the younger ladies took every opportunity to compare their temporary body art with one another. After all, whomever had the better design would have bragging rights until the next occasion. Older women all spoke of the new couple and surmised what their thoughts were. They guessed whether the first child would be a son or a daughter. And as they did at every wedding, they tried to predict which eligible singles would be next in line for marriage.

Men spoke of politics with one another. Tensions had been escalating between the Company and the people of India. Some spoke of revolution, but most did not believe it would come to that. At least not in their lifetimes.

Over the last century, blissful occasions like this had become rarer and rarer. People could not afford lavish ceremonies such as this, and the ones that could were not willing to do so. After all, it had not been long ago that countless Biharis were forced to migrate to the West Indian islands as indentured servants. And at the root of all the chaos was the misrule of the Company and Crown.

But today, that was on nobody's mind.

Veeresh was well-groomed for the function. His cheeks and chin was cleanly shaven. The only facial hair he wore was the traditional Brahmin mustache. He wore a light brown outfit with

173

loose, white trousers that covered him to his ankles. After witnessing the ceremony, he chose to go to the complex like many of the men. He was not one who enjoyed being in the middle of a celebration. Instead, he preferred to be outside-looking-in. With his hands behind his back, the handsome and well-spoken man walked along the balcony of the third floor as he looked down at the function below. He could see the entire thing in one glance from his high vantage point. Although he was a man of eloquence, he was not one to start a conversation. He was an observer. Many described him as a man of quiet strength.

As he passed by numerous people, they all spoke their greetings to him, and he returned them with respect. Every person in the town recognized Veeresh, but it was not just because he was one of the strongest and tallest men in the city. Instead, it was because he was a man who many youth aspired to be and a person who many elders even looked at with reverence.

His eyes came back onto the scene on the ground floor. It seemed that the excitement was building as the day went on. Men mingled with men and women mingled with women. Outside of the children, there was not traditionally much interaction between opposite genders.

And it was here, at this point, that he saw her beautiful face.

When he first laid eyes on her, she was smiling and laughing. Dressed in a vibrant, yellow outfit that covered her slender figure, each lock of her long black hair seemed to fall perfectly into place. Her face was fairer and lighter than any other person's just as his was. She appeared to be a few years younger than he.

She was surrounded by other girls her age and younger. Their laughter filled the air and drowned out the music at times. However, he could make out her pretty laughter above the rest. Its sweet sound filled every inch of his heart and he felt his heart rate start to accelerate.

But what captivated him most were her eyes.

They were the eyes of beauty and innocence. Almond shaped, the brown eyes had a hint of yellow in them. It was seeing them that Avinash knew what perfection really was.

His gaze remained on her as she moved her hands through the air in excitement and spoke to her peers. As she turned her head to look from one companion to the next, her hair moved flawlessly. Her eyes held so much excitement and happiness. Veeresh was not sure how long he spent looking down and marveling at her beauty and perfection. It may have been minutes. A slight smile formed at the corners of his lips without his knowing. He became lost in her. Lost in her movements. Lost in her voice. Lost in the sight of her.

Another girl began to speak and they all looked at her, including the girl he had been watching. But her eyes did not stay there for long. Feeling his gaze, she slowly looked up and saw him high above her.

And for the first time, their eyes met.

***

By the end of the night, Veeresh learned her name: Pari. It was the perfect name for her. After all, the moment he saw her, she became a beautiful fairy to him. She was from a neighboring village only five miles away from Veeresh's ancestral lands.

The next day, Veeresh informed his parents of who he wished for them to send a proposal to. Seeing that he had chosen a respectable girl, they had no objections to his choice. And by the week's end, they took the proposal to Pari's parents through a mutual friend.

It was not long after that his parents sat down with hers. After only two days, the proposal was accepted, and their marriage was arranged within the next two days. It was not a difficult decision for Pari's parents to make. They were Brahmin as was Veeresh. Furthermore, the two families were respected and belonged to the upper tier of the village. But to Pari's parents, the most important thing was that the man they were marrying their daughter to was from a widely respected, land-owning family.

Within hours, word had spread throughout Bhagwanpur that their most eligible bachelor had found his bride in the neighboring village. Veeresh kept his composure upon hearing the news and calmly nodded when his father informed him. However, that night, Veeresh could not get a wink of sleep. He was afraid that he would wake up from this beautiful dream.

From that day forward, Veeresh had an added duty in his day's schedule. An hour before every sunrise, he left the land he farmed to go to the top of a hill several miles away. He arrived there just as the sun came half-way over the horizon. The journey was not an easy one to make every day and would take its toll on him, but he did not care about the cost.

From the top of the hill, he could see the house of Pari's family. The house was at the far outskirts of their village. Like Veeresh, Pari came from a family of farmers, and every day the men in her family went out to tend their fields. Every time Veeresh arrived, Pari would be in the walled courtyard as she washed dirty clothes before hanging them out to dry.

There was no cover on that hill, leaving him at the mercy of the hot and unforgiving sun. But at the first sight of her, he lost all the weariness from his journey.

The first day he was on the hill, she did not notice him right away. As she entered the courtyard, she was singing a beautiful song to herself. He could not make out the words, but the faint whisper of her voice reached his ears. As she started to wash the clothes, she saw him standing at the top of the hill. He was too far away to speak to, but close enough to observe in detail. Pari looked at him for only a split-second before turning away and going about her duties. But she made sure not to make a mistake in her chores.

On the first day, she was dressed in an outfit that was far from her best. It was dull-colored and nothing to brag about. But on the second day and every day thereafter, she wore more colorful outfits that made her stand out. She even took the time to make her hair casually presentable. As the first week passed, she never looked up at him except for a split moment to see if he was there when she entered the courtyard.

The entire time that Veeresh watched her, the edges of his lips would be curled into a joyful and loving smile. She seemed so perfect in every way imaginable. During the second week, she was halfway through her chores when she did something out-of-the ordinary. She looked up at him with a friendly smile on her lips and love in her eyes. It was not a long gaze, but in that moment Veeresh felt as tall as a giant.

And from that day, Pari cast that same look his way every now and then as she went about her chores. Each one seemed to warm his heart even more than the previous.

As their parents arranged the details of their wedding and became more acquainted with one another, the bride to-be and groom learned of each other through only their eyes.

And without speaking a word to each other, they began to fall in love.

***

They were married the next month. The wedding was a simple one. On the auspicious day, the sky was clear except for a few clouds which provided them cool shade on this hot, summer day.

During the ceremony, tears ran freely on both sides. The bride's family was letting go of a daughter that they had raised like a flower. The groom's family was gaining the responsibility and honor to look after the coming bride. Pari cast a few tears as she and her husband made seven rounds around the holy fire during the *Saptapadi* ceremony. Veeresh was never a man to wear his emotions on his sleeve, but even he encountered difficulty containing them today.

After three days of wedding ceremonies, Veeresh brought her back to his home just as the sun disappeared over the horizon. His abode was next to his parent's home and rested on their expansive lands just outside of Bhagwanpur's borders. Not long after arriving, the two of them were seated on the bed next to one another. They had changed out of their wedding garments and into simpler clothes. Still a little hesitant, Veeresh had done so in private and gave his new bride the same courtesy.

His eyes were on her as they sat next to one another, but her gaze was aimed down at her lap. He had never been this close to her before today, and she looked even prettier right now than the day he first saw her. But he was not sure what to say. It finally occurred to him that he had yet to speak to her directly. He had carried out so many conversations with her in his mind and dreams that he never realized the fact that they had yet to speak in person.

Veeresh's eyes glanced down at the bed for a quick moment before he finally broke the silence. "...When your parents received the proposal, did they ask your opinion?"

She slightly nodded without looking at him.

"And did you agree to it?"

Her eyes finally met his. "I did."

His heart smiled upon hearing those words, but his expression did not change. "Why?"

"Any girl in the province would be honored to marry a respected man like you. People look up to you...they admire you and your family. You are known as a kind man and are the person that any girl would want to marry."

"But why did *you* agree?"

She looked at his chest for a few moments before her pretty eyes came back onto his face. "...Because of the way you were looking at me when I first saw you."

A subtle smile came onto Veeresh's face.

"It was a way that nobody had ever looked at me before. I had heard of love in stories such as *Layla and Majnun*, but had never seen it before. I never knew what it would be like or how it would seem. But when I looked into your eyes, I saw it. I knew what it was."

The next words rolled right off of his heart. "And I promise you that the look you saw will never leave my eyes. *Bhagwan* has entrusted me with you. He has placed you in my care and in my protection. I have since thanked Him for it more times that I could bear to count. You are the rose that I will water and nurture with every ounce of energy that I have."

As he spoke, a gleam of happiness and love filled Pari's eyes.

"I cannot promise you a future, for only *Bhagwan* knows what lies ahead. But I dedicate every breath of mine to you. I dedicate everything I have: my wealth, my body, my spirit, my mind...and my love! It's for you. All of it." There was a short pause. "That...that I can promise you."

Pari smiled as her soft hand came onto his.

***

The memories ended.

Veeresh's eyes shot open, and he was back in his cell. The door swung open and the torchlight spilled into the room. The first thing he saw was a uniformed soldier standing above him. Without a word, he was roughly grabbed by his arm and brought to his feet. Three more guards were in the room, including Edward and Henry. The latter was carrying a lit torch in his hand.

Veeresh looked to his right and saw Amir was awake and standing in a corner of the cell. Edward shackled Veeresh's hands with a rusty metal chain. In the next instant, the guard who had brought Veeresh up to his feet forcefully grabbed him by his shoulder and began to shove him out of the cell.

"Move, you!"

He was led through the narrow corridors of the prison between the lamps that lit the way. The stone walls of this place were reminiscent of a dungeon. They were old and made uneven by the years. Bugs could be seen running up and down the floor and countless cobwebs dangled from the walls and ceilings. He was moved so quickly by his captors that he did not have a chance to see any of the rooms and corridors he went by. If he slowed down even a step, he was shoved in the back by the large guard. The prisoner shortly arrived to a part of the fortress that was foreign to him.

Coming to a remote room, Veeresh was led through the open entrance. Henry and another guard remained outside, but the rest entered with the prisoner. As Veeresh saw his friend stay out of the room, he caught the grimace on Henry's face. It was a worried expression that Veeresh had never seen his friend wear.

The room would have been dark, except for a small window at the top of a far wall, allowing streams of sunlight to bounce off of the stone walls and dimly illuminate the chamber. The walls of this place reminded him of his cell, except they were more run-down.

At the center of the room was a wooden chair. Time had taken a toll on it, but it was still plenty sturdy. Veeresh was forced into it and within seconds, his ankles and wrists were securely shackled to its armrests and legs.

Without another word, the guards left him. His eyes went from one corner of the room to the next. But much of the room was shrouded in darkness.

"Prisoner Singh."

Veeresh swiftly turned his head toward the open doorway and saw a man standing who had not been there before. There, in his full military uniform, he took a few steps into the chamber, and a guard closed the door behind him. After the thick door was closed, Veeresh heard it being locked from the outside. Wearing a colonel's uniform, his hands were clasped behind his back. But he slowly brought his hands into view, revealing a metal rod in one.

"How has your time here been?"

Veeresh was silent.

The colonel stopped in front of the prisoner as Veeresh continued to look him in the eyes. A sinister smile formed on the captor's face as he gazed down at the man who was chained to the chair. "From what I've been told, you have been the ideal prisoner. Well...as ideal as your kind can be expected to behave."

The prisoner took a deep, silent breath.

"And I've learned that you were a respectable man before being brought here." The colonel began to circle around his prey. As he did, he tauntingly swung the rod back and forth. "You should know, men like you have options. Selecting the right choices can bring you freedom."

Veeresh kept his eyes straight ahead and sat up straight in his chair. If he had any fear, he did not show it.

"There are two types of men in a crisis. Those who can make the right choices, and those who make the wrong ones. The

181

right choices can lead to happiness. The wrong ones...not so much." Stopping in front of him, the colonel put his hands on the armrests and leaned in close, his face only inches from the prisoner. "So...I only need to know one thing from you, Prisoner Singh. Are you willing to make the right choices?"

Veeresh stared right into the whites of the colonel's eyes. "What are you asking of me?"

The colonel stood back up as his gaze rose to the small opening that allowed the sunlight in. "All I want for you to do is one act. Then you will be free to go back to your village." He looked back at the prisoner. "Denounce the terrorists fighting against the Company and Crown. Publically say that you were wrong to ever have endorsed them."

Silence was his response. There was no change in emotion— not even a subtle one. It was as if he had expected this to be the request.

"Prisoner Singh?"

Again, there was no reply or reaction.

After a few moments, the colonel glanced down for a second and slowly nodded in understanding. "Do you know who I am?"

"James Smith."

"*Colonel* James Smith. I am sure you have heard of my persuasive abilities."

"I know the kind of man you are."

"And I know the kind of man *you* are, *Prisoner Singh.* You're the kind that killed six British soldiers. Six honorable British soldiers that were making this wretched land a safe place for people like you."

"I didn't kill six soldiers. I killed six criminals! Six dogs—"

Without warning, Smith's rod powerfully smashed against Veeresh's face, making him spit out blood. The sound of the strike was heard by the guards in the corridor.

Reaching down, James roughly grabbed Veeresh by his long hair. "I would rip out your tongue, *prisoner*, if I did not need it."

Veeresh defiantly looked at his captor. The strike had formed a cut across his left cheek and blood slowly seeped out of it before being soaked into his beard. His expression held no pain, and his eyes showed no fear. He did not utter a sound. He knew men like James Smith. They lived off of the pain of others, and Veeresh would not give him any pleasure.

The captor let go of his prisoner's hair and resumed his previous position. "There are many theories on the best way to break a man. Some believe in physical pain while other believe in psychological. As for me? I believe in doing whatever it takes. *Whatever. It. Takes!*"

There was a short silence.

"I have been commissioned to make you denounce these terrorists. And I have been given the privilege of doing so by any means that I deem prudent. I would like to make this easy for both of us. I offer you your freedom if you are willing to make this public statement. I offer you the chance to walk out of here as a man with long and fruitful years ahead of him."

The prisoner said nothing.

"Think for a moment. Are you going to be the man who makes the right choice in a crisis or the one who makes the wrong one?"

"I am thinking. And I know what you are trying to do. Do you take me for a fool?"

Now Colonel Smith was silent.

"The Company is about to be ruined because of the revolution. And your final effort is to break the spirit of the people. My denouncement would be a part of that. So, *colonel*, I know what choice I am making."

James blankly stared at his prisoner's face. But after a long moment, he took a deep breath. He slowly nodded before looking down at the rod in his hands. "Well...if that's the case..."

***

The cell door opened with a loud creak. When it was half-open, Veeresh was thrown in and collapsed like a rag doll. Edward's snickering voice was heard as the door was slammed shut, and the room was thrown into darkness. "Be ready for a nice bath tomorrow."

Amir had been sitting on his knees in a corner of the cell. During the time his friend was gone, he had been praying that a hedge of protection would be kept around him. As the guards left, he heard the echo of the guard's footsteps slowly get softer and softer until they were too far to hear. But Amir's eyes stayed on the immobile body of his friend.

Suddenly, he got up and ran to his friend's side.

"Veeresh!?"

The bloodied man let out a soft groan. It was the first sound of pain he had uttered all day.

Amir gently took Veeresh's head and placed it in his lap. He lightly ran his hand over his friend's face and could feel the cuts that the darkness prevented his eyes from seeing. He felt warm blood on his fingers, but it did not bother him.

All he felt was rage. They had beaten his friend like a stray dog. But this rage was soon overridden by a foreboding feeling of worry. If they had done this to his friend on the first day, then what would be in store for him the next? And why were they doing this to him?

Reaching to his right, Amir felt for a small bowl that was half-full of water. He quickly brought it to his friend's lips and let him drink the bowl dry before putting it aside. "...Why do they do this to you?"

"They...w...want me..."

Amir leaned his ears in closer to his friend.

"...To denounce...the freedom fighters."

As he held his friend's broken body in his hands, Amir fell silent. It all made sense. There were rumors that the Company's back was against the wall. This just confirmed them. In their final effort to end the war early enough for the Company to survive, they were going to beat respected men like Veeresh into submission.

"...But...but...I won't."

Amir looked down at his friend.

"I won't...give in." There was a silence. "They've already... taken enough from me....they won't take this."

***

It seemed that as soon as sleep overcame the pain Veeresh felt, he was roughly awaken. Edward was crouched down over him while another large guard that Veeresh did not recognize towered over him as well. Behind them were two more guards. On all their faces were wicked smiles.

"Time for your morning bath."

Before he had a chance to digest what was happening, he was grabbed by his collar and forced to his feet. The two guards came on either side of him and coarsely led him out of the dark cell and into the torch-lit hall. Amir leapt to his feet upon seeing the intruders, but was knocked down by a guard and swiftly kicked by another.

As Veeresh was roughly taken away, he heard Amir's voice come from behind. His friend spoke in a language that their captors would not understand. "Be strong, my brother. Don't give these devils what they want."

Pulled into the corridor, he collapsed almost immediately, but the guards kept him from falling as the cell door was closed behind him by a third guard.

"Don't pass out on us now," Edward taunted. "The fun has only begun."

He was roughly forced—almost dragged—down the corridor. He could barely keep up with the guards as they quickly moved him along the stone floor giving him sharp shoves every few steps. For much of the way, his bare feet were lugged across the coarse stone floor.

As they turned another corner, Veeresh almost collapsed yet again. He could hardly feel his legs. But the guards continued to hold him upright.

"Looks like the bugger might die before we even get there," Edward said to the other guard before the two of them let out a snicker. Edward's eyes came onto his prisoner. "You wouldn't do that to us, would you? Not after we spent all night preparing for your day's festivities."

Once again, they dragged him through the corridor. Every inch and every corner of his body rang with pain. Even though Veeresh's mind was still catching up to reality and he was just digesting what was happening, he did not show any emotion on his face.

No fear. No worry. No pain. He did not show any of it.

He was finally brought to the torture chamber. Outside, Henry stood watch. His eyes came onto Veeresh as the prisoner arrived. Their gazes locked for only a moment. But in that moment, Henry's eyes told him to be strong.

The set-up of the chamber was different. The chair was no longer there. Instead, in its place was a rusting tub of water—dirty water.

Nearby were several buckets of water that would be used to refill the tub if necessary. Colonel Smith was standing next to the tub looking into it. Feeling a presence behind him, he slowly turned around and devilishly smiled at his prisoner.

"When's the last time you had a bath, Prisoner Singh?"

Veeresh stoically stared at his captor.

"We think it's long overdue, don't we boys?"

CHAPTER 14
RULER OF THE SPIRIT

Veeresh's head hovered inches above the dirty water. The water was filled with so much filth that he could not see the bottom of the tub, but he smelt the odor of urine and feces coming from it.

Edward held one side of him while another guard held the other. His wrists were tied together behind his back as were his ankles, forcing him to balance on his knees. Two other guards were standing behind him with their hands pressing down on his shoulders, keeping him in place. Standing on the other side of the tub was James Smith. His arms were locked behind his back as he looked down at his prisoner.

Veeresh raised his eyes to look up defiantly at the colonel. A sinister smile formed on the corner of James' lips. After a brief moment, he gave his order. "Dunk him."

With a loud splash, Veeresh's head was plunged into the water. Edward's hand held his neck down. Every instinct told him to struggle for air. It told him to fight his captors for his life, but he fought back the urges. With his eyes shut, he could feel the dirty water all around his head. It filled his nose and ears. He could feel his lungs screaming for air. His heart beat so fast that he thought it would burst out of his chest.

But he did not fight.

Nor did he give his captors any sign of weakness. He would not give them that pleasure even as he began to grow more desperate. Finally, as consciousness started to leave him, he was pulled back up. He immediately began to violently cough and gasp for air. He heard two of the guards taunt him, but he did not hear their words.

As the water spilled out, Veeresh's defiant eyes set back onto his torturer. With his hair and beard completely drenched by the filthy water, he took another deep breath to calm down his rapidly-beating heart. He kept his expression as stoic as possible as his eyes stayed locked with his captor.

After a long moment, Veeresh spoke with all the courage he had. "I don't think that was quite long enough."

"Dunk him."

Veeresh's head was forced back into the tub. Right before he went in, he took a quick breath and held it in his lungs. With a loud splash, the prisoner's head was again surrounded by the murky water. He shut his eyes and sealed his lips tight. His chest was forcefully pressed against the tub's edge, making it difficult for him to hold his breath. But he did so.

The seconds passed. With each one, he could hear his own heart beat louder and louder as his body screamed for air. But all he thought of were two things. One was his God. The name of his Lord echoed in his head as he prayed to Him with his thoughts. But in the other corner of his mind, he could see Pari's beautiful eyes. The love of his life.

He began to feel the clutches of death. It started at his fingers and toes and began to slowly work towards his heart. Suddenly, he was ripped out of the murky water. Soaked in filth, he inhaled another gasp of air and again violently coughed. He took a few deep breaths as his eyes again locked with his captor's. Veeresh hid all his emotions behind his defiant gaze.

Smith's smirk began to fade. Behind his back, one of his hands tightly curled into a fist.

The prisoner's head was throbbing and he could barely see straight, but he kept his composure. "After an entire night of

189

planning, *this* was the method you concocted? I'm disappointed in you."

"Dunk. Him."

The prisoner took a deep breath. Once again, Veeresh's head was shoved into the water, and his chest was pressing against the tub's edge. Edward's grip on the back of his neck was tighter now. Veeresh's eyes and lips were tightly shut. He knew that this time, he would be kept in longer.

And once again, he thought of her eyes.

***

Veeresh and Pari's marriage was a blissful one. A day of married life held more happiness than the entirety of Veeresh's unmarried life. Every day seemed like a dream—one that would never end.

The days always began with him waking up to tend the fields along with his father and younger brothers. Throughout the year, almost every crop capable of being grown in Bihar could be found on their land: rice, corn, wheat, sweet potatoes, onions, sugar cane, mangoes, and more. But during these summer months, rice was the main crop. Along with it were the long stems of sugar cane that were just beginning to enter their harvesting season.

Every morning, Veeresh woke up to his sleeping wife beside him. It would take a moment for him to realize that their marriage was no dream. By the time Veeresh was ready to depart for the fields just before sunrise, Pari would have prepared his breakfast. Even though just the sight of her took his hunger away, he ate every bite of the prepared meal.

He worked the fields with his tools in his hands and his wife at the forefront of his mind. Because the field was so large, each man in the family had their section to tend to. Veeresh's was a quarter mile from his abode. Every day as the sun reached its peak, she came out to meet him. He always knew when she was approaching because he would hear his younger brother greet her as she passed by.

"*Namaste, bhabi,*" his brother would say.

And in her sweet voice, Pari would return the cultural greeting, "*Namaste.*"

Pari always seemed to arrive when the sun was at its highest point, bringing their lunch in hand. They would both sit under the shade of a massive Bodhi tree in one another's company. Soon after their marriage, Veeresh discovered that a love for sugar cane was another thing that they both took pleasure in. As they finished their meals, Veeresh plucked two stems of sugar cane that were ripe enough to enjoy. Without a knife or any tool, they skillfully bit into it and sucked its sweet juice dry.

The first day that she came out to see him, Veeresh was nervous, not knowing what to say to his new bride. But his heart was so full that the two never had a dull moment. They spoke of their life. Their hopes. Their dreams.

Their bright future.

She always stayed longer than either of them intended. There were times when the sun was halfway to the horizon by the time she left. But neither of them cared in the least. Veeresh was willing to work twice as hard during the day's remaining hours to make up for any lost time.

He would return home as the sun was nearing the horizon. Before seeing what Pari had prepared for that evening, he would bathe himself and change into a fresh set of clothes.

Pari seemed to be able to make the simplest meals into a feast. Veeresh did not know if she was that skilled of a cook or if he was so in love that everything she made was a masterpiece. But either way, he was always happy at dinner.

He learned after marriage that Pari had a passion for music that equaled his own. But unlike his talent in playing the *Sitar*, her talent resided in her voice. After dinner, the two of them would sit on the floor next to one another. He would have his stringed, wooden instrument in his lap. The *Sitar* had a distinct timbre from any other instrument Veeresh had ever come across. It received this unique resonance from is sympathetic strings, long hollow neck, bridge design, and gourd-like resonating chamber. One of Pari's hands would rest in her lap and the other would be on Veeresh's shoulder or on his arm.

And together, they made beautiful music.

It could be heard throughout their abode and at times, it could be heard faintly by his father and mother. His parents never mentioned it except once when Veeresh's mother complimented Pari's voice. She described Pari's voice as the loveliest in Bhagwanpur.

Often times as the two of them made music together, Veeresh would find himself looking at his wife. And almost every time, her eyes would be locked with his as well. He would let every note and syllable sink into his heart. Her voice was absolutely perfect, just like she was.

And it was at those times that Veeresh believed he was in Paradise.

***

Veeresh's head was yanked out of the dirty water. Like clockwork, he coughed out a storm and took a few deep breaths to bring life back into his beaten body. He was nearly unconscious. At the moment that he nearly blacked out, the face that consumed his mind was Pari's.

But now he was back in reality. Smith's cruel features replaced Pari's smiling face.

His head and hair was drenched, dripping, and heavy with the foul water. Much of his clothes were soaked in it as well. Puddles had formed all around him from the water that splashed out of the tub when he was forced in and out of it repeatedly. How many times had he been nearly drowned today? Veeresh had stopped counting. It may have been hours. A part of Veeresh believed that by now the sun was almost at the horizon. The angle of the light coming into the chamber added to his belief.

He took a few more gasps. His vision was completely blurred when he was pulled out of the tub, but it slowly began to return and focus on his interrogator each time. But his body remained completely exhausted, and he barely had the strength to stand. He wanted to collapse on the ground and lay there for days. However, the guards holding him up prevented him from doing so.

Smith's sadistic smile had now been replaced by a straight face. Veeresh wondered how long his captor expected him to last before breaking. From the expression on Smith's face, Veeresh assumed he had long passed that mark.

"Prisoner Singh, it is only going to get worse. You know this."

Veeresh took a few deep breaths as he kept his eyes locked with Smith's. His head felt like it would burst from all the pain. His insides were trembling. But he did not utter a word.

"Dunk him."

He went back into the water again.

And again.

And again.

As he was roughly brought out and regained his breath, he heard the colonel's demeaning, taunting voice. "Of all the dogs I've beaten into submission, you are proving to be the most difficult to tame."

Again there was silence.

"You people are dirt. Just like this land is. It's a nation of dirt."

"If..." Hardly able to breath, let alone speak, Veeresh somehow managed to muster the strength to do so. His words were filled with nothing but conviction. "If it is dirt, then why have you people occupied it for so long? And why are you fighting so hard to keep it?"

Anger suddenly filled James' expressions. His hands left his back, and in one of them was a rod. The same rod that had beat Veeresh the day before. He looked at the guards, and every syllable of his voice was filled with anger. "Drop him."

The guards on either side of Veeresh let go of him, and he collapsed onto the ground on his side. They all backed away as James came upon him. He raised his rod and brought it down onto Veeresh's defenseless body. It powerfully collided with his ribs.

But he did not make a sound.

"Who do you think you are!?"

He hit him again. The strikes echo shook the very room.

"You dare talk to an Englishman like this?"

Again, the rod collided with the defenseless man, leaving a long cut on his back.

"As if you are *even worthy* of looking us in the eyes."

James' boot crashed into Veeresh's stomach, making him cough out more water.

"Today...today, I will teach you how a dog is beaten."

And with those words, James was upon him.

***

It was well into the night when the door to the cell opened. But this time, it was no fiend that came in. The visitor came only to find Veeresh lying on his back with Amir sitting next to him. The flames of the torches broke the darkness of the cell as Henry entered. His eyes were full of worry, and in his hands were two containers.

As he saw the state of his friend, the guard's eyes widened. "...Those bastards!"

"He was completely exhausted when he was brought back." Amir looked away from Henry and back at Veeresh. "I gave him all the water we had. But they've cut our rations down as well."

"I know. I was outside the door the entire time. I...I heard it all." Henry came to them as he handed a full water canteen to Amir. "I brought some things."

Amir took it and quickly removed its top before having Veeresh drink from it.

Henry came to Veeresh's side as he took off the top of his other container, revealing a bowl full of rice. He looked up at Amir. "He needs to keep up his strength.

Amir watched the Englishman feed the weak prisoner. "...What would happen if they found you here?"

"No other guard is on duty in these halls. They're all resting after having spent their strength on Veeresh today."

Amir watched the man in awe. "You're a good man, Henry."

"I am not. If I was a man I would stop these bloody animals from doing what they do to him. This is the least I can do."

"It's more than a normal man would do. Your actions could very well cost you your life."

"Then so be it." Henry looked back down at the beaten prisoner. "But our friend has won the first two days. Veeresh did more to James than was done to him today. For all the physical torture that he has endured, he has given James tenfold the mental torment."

"...What do you mean?"

Henry continued to feed Veeresh. "No man has ever stood so defiantly against the colonel. It is slowly grinding on him and may even break him."

Veeresh suddenly broke his silence as he swallowed a bite of the rice. His eyes were weakly open and focused on Henry. "...Henry?"

"Yes?"

Veeresh's voice was so soft that Henry barely heard it. "...My wife...is...is she okay?"

He was silent.

"...I...I need to know."

Slowly Henry looked up at Amir. "Is his wife still in Bhagwanpur?"

Amir nodded.

Henry looked back down. "I will see to it that she is well."

"...They will hang me...soon they will hang...me. I won't...break." Veeresh closed his eyes as he recited an ancient proverb. "One man with courage...he can change the world."

"I swear to you, Veeresh, I will make sure that no harm comes to your wife. My family is wealthy. I will send her enough so that she is never in need. I promise you that."

Veeresh's eyes showed his thanks.

The guard looked back at Amir. "It will only get worse from here on out. A man from the Company is pressuring John Smith to break Veeresh. Even as we speak, Smith is in that man's company and being humiliated so that he will take his anger out on Veeresh. I heard some of the conversation myself."

"Veeresh will not break. I know it."

"How?"

196

"He is a lion. And one thing that a lion never loses, even in the face of death, is his courage."

***

"Colonel James Smith, I was told that you were the Company's best interrogator. Perhaps there has been some mistake in this claim." From behind his desk, Mr. Wilkinson looked at the soldier.

Three candles provided the large room's only lighting at this late hour, dimly reflecting off the bookshelves, desks, and walls. The curtains blocked out the moonlight and stars. Colonel Smith stood at attention on the other side of the desk as he listened on.

"It's been two days. That leaves twelve for you to break him before his hanging in thirteen days. If he has not broken by then...well, you don't need me to remind you what is at stake, do you?"

"Sir, I am limited in my options because of the situation. When he does make his statement, it is not in our best interest to have Prisoner Singh wearing any marks of my persuasion. If somebody was to see any visible physical or bodily injury, they would know that his statement had been coerced. This limits my options—"

Wilkinson's fist slammed onto his desk. "Do not give me excuses, colonel! I gave you a mission, and I gave you its parameters. You are a soldier, are you not?"

James was silent.

"Your task is to complete the assignment, not give me a list of reasons as to why it is difficult. If it was simple, I would have brought on any man to do the job. But I was told you were the best. Was this a false claim?"

Again, there was no response.

Wilkinson glanced down at his desk before his eyes came back onto the soldier. "Perhaps...perhaps this is my fault. Maybe I did not give you the proper motivation required."

"...Sir?"

"Listen closely. If the Company goes down, it is not just your career that will be done with." He leaned forward a bit. "I know what you did in London during the fall of 1853. I have the evidence to prove it."

James was silent, but his eyes showed that it was not respect that stopped him from speaking. It was fear. His gaze reeked of it as he heard his superior utter those words.

"Listen closely, Smith. If you fail, I will destroy your family's reputation. People will look at you as a leper, and no respectable person will ever be in your company again."

***

Veeresh was again roughly taken to the chamber just as the sun was coming up over the horizon. The tub was there again as was the chair. But along with them were a few new apparatuses. His shirt was stripped off, and he was strapped to a wooden cross with his back facing out. His wrists and ankles were tied to it with leather belts, immobilizing him. His torso and arms were covered in bruises and splotches of dried blood.

Colonel Smith held his infamous rod. He came up to Veeresh's left shoulder as the prisoner turned his head defiantly so that he could see him.

"Don't you realize that you are fighting a losing battle? You are alone."

"I am not in the minority, colonel. For one man with courage *makes* a majority."

"Ancient proverbs of courage will not do you any good." James paused for a moment. "You have a family, don't you, Prisoner Singh?"

He did not respond.

"A wife from what I understand."

Veeresh continued to look defiantly at his captor's eyes.

"I wonder how much good your talks of courage and honor will do when I come upon her? How much comfort will they give her?"

Silence was again the response.

"Heed my words, prisoner. If you do not give in, you will bring unimaginable harm unto her. *I* will personally go to her. I will hurt her in *every* way possible. Then...I will kill her." James took a step closer. "Is this the kind of man you are? One that would let his wife suffer needlessly for the sake of pride?"

There was a long moment of silence. The prisoner's eyes stayed locked with his tormentor's. For a moment, James thought that his words put a dent in his victim's courage. Maybe he had found his prisoner's weak point. But then Veeresh slightly smiled. "My wife is not defenseless. She would kill a coward like you before you could even lay a finger on her."

In an angry rage, James violently grabbed Veeresh by his hair. "You believe that what you are doing is honorable? All that you will accomplish if you succeed is prolonging a war that will take even more of your people's lives. And the outcome will be just the same."

"That is where you are wrong. Your vile Company will be in ashes."

Smith looked down at his rod and then back at his prisoner. "No, Veeresh...you will."

CHAPTER 15
EYES OF A LION

Some say that there is only so much a man can take before breaking. Others say that the sign of a worthy man is one who can take any amount of beating without breaking. That is what Veeresh believed.

And that was what he demonstrated.

James Smith had no lack of experience in his field. He always bent men to his will. His vile techniques turned the strongest men into sheep. He had broken every kind of man: young, old, rich, and poor. And after years of mastering his art, the colonel believed that he had seen it all. However, the man he now faced was one whose willpower was the stuff of legends.

The third day ended with Veeresh unconscious. Every time James tried to punish his captive, all he got in return was a taunt either by the tongue or eyes. Hours into their session, the colonel lost his temper and struck Veeresh's head hard enough to knock him out.

On the fourth day, they were back at the tub. The fifth, sixth, seventh, and eighth day went by so fast that James could not remember what he had put his prisoner through. Each day, he gave Veeresh a torture and torment that no other had taken without breaking.

But not this man.

Every day, Henry waited outside the door. He heard the sounds of the torture. He heard the threats and taunts. But the one thing he never heard were Veeresh's screams. The man did not

200

utter a sound of pain. And the more he endured, the more that he did not show pain, the more it hurt James Smith.

When the merciful nights came, Henry would go to Veeresh's and Amir's cell when possible. He brought anything he could to ease his friend's suffering. Henry was powerless to physically aid his friend during the day. But Henry did whatever he could to prepare the warrior for the next day's battle.

On the ninth and tenth day, James displayed more anger in him than all the previous days put together. Veeresh's courage took its toll on the torturer. And he took his rage out on his prisoner, beating him down to a pulp with his bare hands. Curses rang from the colonel's mouth and echoed throughout the catacombs. But Veeresh did not yield. Veeresh was bloodied, but his head remained unbowed. Those treacherous eyes continued to stare defiantly at the colonel, mocking him. Taunting him. Telling him that even with all his strength, he was nothing.

And those eyes began to haunt James during every waking moment.

He could not sleep. He could not eat. He could not think. Every time he closed his eyes, he saw Veeresh Singh's defiant gaze. They were the eyes of a lion who was ready to die for what he believed in.

James had never imagined that men like this existed. He had always believed that they were just the creations of ancient tales. But he was now facing one every single day.

On the eleventh day, he tried to break Veeresh's mind. He sat him down on a chair and tried to make the prisoner imagine things. Horrible things. Things that James promised to do to Veeresh's family if he did not submit.

But again, Veeresh did not yield. He did not utter a word. Throughout the entire day, all he did was stare deep into his captor's eyes. Instead of James torturing Veeresh, James was

201

tormented. And as the day slowly came to an end, he began to feel fear. Fear that he had met his match. Fear that now his family would suffer the consequences of the Company's wrath.

The twelfth day they were back at the tub. James did not keep count of how many times Veeresh came to the edge of death. But Henry did. But even Henry lost count hours into it, unable to bear the sound of Veeresh's near drowning again and again and again.

James could not bear to see Veeresh's eyes grow even more defiant each time he was put into the tub. By the end of the thirteenth day, James Smith again resorted to beating his prisoner with his bare hands. He had not slept in days. The thought of his foe's eyes slowly drove him mad. He let out all his rage. All his hate. All his anger.

But Veeresh did not break.

Day after day, Veeresh's beaten and broken body was thrown back into his cell. Had it not been for Henry's kindness and Amir's care, he surely would have died of dehydration. It was only then, in the darkness where no one but his friend could see him, that he showed any weakness or pain.

Veeresh's tormentors did not know this. They did not know the source of this man's strength. The truth was this: every time pain and torment descended upon Veeresh, he focused on his Lord and Pari's eyes. The image of her beautiful soul filled his mind so completely that he did not even realize when he came to the brink of death. All he did was think of her, and he felt peace.

Veeresh's nights passed with dreams of Pari. Dreams of what life had been with her and of where he should be right now. He could hear her voice, see her face, and yearned to touch her skin. It was so real that a part of him began to believe that this entire ordeal was nothing but a nightmare.

But then he would wake up and find himself back in his reality. He would remember that those warm and love-filled days were gone. Like his forefathers who had battled against the forces of outside invaders in the name of protecting their lands and people, he was fighting for...

The future of the same land.

***

The last night that Veeresh spent with Pari, the two of them were lying in their bed. He lay on his back with his eyes gazing up at the ceiling while her head rested on his strong, bare chest. His legs were covered with a pair of loose trousers while a plain yellow and white *shalwar kameez* covered his wife. Today's harvest had been tough, and the scorching sun had not helped. But even after well over a year of marriage to Pari, just the sight of her smiling at him made him forget any discomfort.

As they lay there quietly, there was not a sound to be heard. The night was peaceful and their home was quiet. He found himself in a state of serenity as he often did. Feeling her head against his chest brought an immeasurable amount of tranquility.

Lying like this against his large, well-built frame made her feel as though she were wrapped in an armor of protection. As she lay there, she felt as if nothing could ever harm her as long as he was near.

Their heart rates were in sync with one another. Reaching over, she took one of his hands in hers and their fingers interlocked. She slowly looked up at him with a smile on her face.

He returned the gesture. Behind her eyes, he could see something. "What thoughts are on your mind?"

"I had a dream last night, Veeresh." Her grasp tightened. "A beautiful dream."

"What did you see?"

"A man appeared...my *Babaji*."

Hearing her mention her late grandfather caught Veeresh's attention. She had never mentioned seeing him in a dream before.

"He came to me, sat down beside me in this very room, and told me something wonderful."

"...What?" His tone showed his anticipation.

"That I am to bear a child soon."

Upon hearing those words, Veeresh's smile only grew warmer. Her words echoed in his ears and reached every corner of his heart. Without thinking, he suddenly embraced her tightly and took her from his left side to his right. The two of them let out joyous laughs that rang through every corner of their abode and could be heard outside.

"It must be so!" he proclaimed. "If your *Babaji* came, it must be so! I sensed there was something from the time I saw your eyes this morning. I knew it!"

"I didn't know how to tell you—I wanted to make it special."

Veeresh kissed his wife.

There was a long silence as the two of them looked at one another.

"I made you a promise the night we were married. Do you remember?"

Still smiling, she nodded.

"And I make the same promise now...I make it to our child. Whether it be a son or a daughter, I will lay my life down before I let any harm come near you or our child. From now until the day I die, I will do what any man should to keep his family safe, happy, and content."

Her soft hand reached out and touched his cheek. "You have never given me a reason to doubt your promise...and I know you never will."

***

On the fourteenth day of the captive's torment, Veeresh found himself in the center of the torture chamber sitting upright on the floor. His hands were tied behind his back, and his ankles were bound together by a heavy metal chain. Around his neck was a thick rope that ran up high to a wooden apparatus. Two large guards stood next to it as they held the other end of the rope.

The rope had left deep bruises on his neck. He desperately struggled to regain his breath as James looked down on him. The British man's eyes were red with weariness while his cheeks and chin were unkempt.

"Tomorrow, you will not be shown mercy, Prisoner Singh." James leaned in closer. "Tomorrow, you will be hung until death without any mercy?"

"Without...without any mercy?" Veeresh slowly began. "You are mistaken."

James was silent.

"I will be shown mercy...in the afterlife."

The captor took a step back. "Again."

The two men pulled down on the rope. By his neck, Veeresh was painfully hauled up into the air until his legs were three feet off the ground. Suspended in the air with the heavy chain around his ankles weighing him down, Veeresh felt pain radiate from his head all the way to his feet. His lungs begged for air, and his neck felt like it would snap at any moment. The rope seemed to set his neck on fire while his body felt like it would rip in half. With his gaze stuck on the stone ceiling, his hands were clenched into tight fists as he did all he could to sustain his composure.

Growing numb, his vision began to go black. It started at the periphery and worked its way in until all he could see was darkness.

He could not feel anything except his throbbing head. Was this what dying felt like? With his eyes shut, he focused everything he had on his wife's face.

Suddenly, he landed roughly on his side. He gasped for air, coughing violently. After a few long moments, his vision slowly returned along with his complete awareness of his pain. His head throbbed, and his heart beat like a madman.

James was towering over him. With his hands on his knees, he crouched down. "Tomorrow will be worse, Prisoner Singh. Tomorrow you *will* die."

Veeresh let out a cough. Then another. "...It's...it's not death I fear...it's facing my Lord in the form of a coward."

The prisoner was hauled back up. James watched the man helplessly hang in the air. He witnessed the color quickly leave his face as he came closer and closer to death. How could he take it? How could all this torture have no effect on his resolve? What was driving this man?

Once again, he was brought to the brink of death. Seeing their commander's signal, the two guards dropped the rope and Veeresh loudly crashed onto the ground, collapsing on his side as before. But as he regained consciousness, his eyes focused on his foe.

James came down to one knee beside his fallen prisoner. "Don't put yourself through this. Give in now. There is still time for you, Prisoner Singh. There is still time for you to choose life over death."

"I...I would have thought that...on the fourteenth day your torture would have been beyond hell." Veeresh looked defiantly at his captor. "I am disappointed."

"Again!"

He was nearly suffocated once more.

"Why do you resist me?"

206

"Because...a man should never yield to a dog's will."

"Again!"

He was lifted and brought down again, seconds from death.

"You people...you people are like stray dogs. No amount of beating can tame you."

"...If tame is the word that you use to describe yourself...then I would pray to remain a stray dog."

James gave his prisoner a swift kick in the stomach. "Choke this bastard!"

Veeresh was hauled back into the air. This time, he was sure that death would take him. He did not know how he could go any closer to it without finally embracing it. He knew this would be the end. It had to be. For a moment, he could not feel anything, not even the throbbing in his head. The image of Pari faded away and was replaced by an abyss. Everything went black.

But this was not his day of death.

He landed on the ground without feeling anything. James imposingly stood over him, holding him by his collar. His face was full of anger and hate. He quivered with it. He did not know what more he could do. "Prisoner Singh! Why!? Why do you do this!?"

Suddenly, all of Veeresh's pain disappeared as something came over him. A breath of newfound life came out of his heart and blew through his body. He shot upright, knocking his captor off of him and onto the floor. Somehow, he slowly rose to his feet without the chain around his ankle tripping him.

With the captor lying on the ground, Veeresh Singh stood tall, and his shadow was cast over his torturer. His eyes looked down at James. And when he spoke, his voice had more power than any king. "My name is Veeresh Singh. And my name means the 'king of all warriors.' I am the descendent of the Lion of Bihar. Even with all your strength, even with all your power, even will all your devices, you cannot harm me. Because only one owns my soul.

Only one is the master of my fate. And that man is me. And my belief in my Lord has made that so. I have beaten you, *James*. This lowly prisoner whose name you did not even know has beaten you. You...you have been disgraced. You have lost and so has your vile Company."

James was completely silent. Every man was silent. They could say nothing but look at the man they had beaten and tortured mercilessly for the last two weeks. But they had done nothing to his spirit. Nothing but make his resolve to die honorably increase a hundredfold.

All the anger and arrogance in James' eyes was gone. It had been replaced by something else. As he lay in the shadow of Veeresh, he could not move a muscle. Finally, James spoke. "Why...why did you kill those men? The six soldiers? Why did you bring this on yourself?"

"Those men, they were no soldiers. They were criminals." Veeresh took a deep breath. "They tried to attack my wife. They tried to dishonor her. And I did what any man should do. I sent them to their maker. If death be the consequence for that, then I embrace it with open arms."

Not a man said a word. All they could do was stare at this lion. The measure of his resolve could be seen in his eyes. It was unbreakable.

As was his spirit.

***

"He...he was unlike any man I have ever seen." When nightfall came, James stood before Wilkinson in the latter's office. "Everything I could do, I did. Physical torture...mental pain...humiliation. Nothing phased him. All it did was make him stronger."

208

"So you failed...against this—this lowly prisoner."

"I did not fail. He..." James looked away from the dark-suited man. "He defeated me."

"Nonetheless, in the eyes of the Company, you will be seen as a disgrace. An embarrassment...a man who has fallen out of glory and could not fulfill a task when the Company direly needed it. Tomorrow when the prisoner is hung, you will wish that it was you. You will be arrested and brought back to England to be tried for your past crimes." Wilkinson paused for a moment and leaned in a little closer. "Unless you are willing to take an alternative route."

James took a deep breath and nodded. "...I understand."

***

The next day came. A little after sunrise, the cell door opened and Henry stood on the other side of it. He found Amir and Veeresh in prayer side-by-side. One prayed as a Muslim and the other as a Hindu. But both as brothers.

"It's time."

Veeresh rose and so did his friend. They shared one last embrace before Amir said a final prayer over him. The two men said their goodbyes without uttering a single word. The guard noticed the streaks of dried tears on Amir's face.

A few moments later, Henry escorted the limping Veeresh down the corridor. He held one side of his friend, ensuring that the journey was not too difficult on his injured body.

"You arrived earlier than expected, Henry."

The guard nodded. "There is someone here to see you."

They went up a flight of stairs and entered a new hallway. But unlike the one below, this one was not reminiscent of a catacomb. There were no cobwebs or roaches. Instead of torches

209

lighting the way, there were rays of sunlight. Veeresh had not seen this hallway since the day he was first brought here.

Outside of the two of them, there was nobody else to be seen. Arriving at a closed door, Henry came to a stop, and Veeresh followed suit. The guard quickly unlocked the door before pushing it open. He looked over at Veeresh and put his hand on his friend's shoulder. "Go on. I'll give you a few moments...as many as can be spared."

Veeresh hesitated for a moment before following his friend's instructions. He heard Henry gently close the door behind him. The room was empty except for a bench. But unlike the prisons below, this room had been cleaned only days ago. Even the walls were smooth and did not threaten to cut into a person's back. A window near the top of one wall filled the entire chamber with morning sunlight.

But Veeresh saw none of that. What he saw was the one other person who was in the room: Pari.

There was a long silence as his eyes fell onto her and she looked at him. For a long moment, he thought he was dreaming. But as he watched her eyes look at his beaten face, he knew that they were too real to be from a dream.

Suddenly, she rushed forward and embraced him.

The two of them held on to each other tighter than they ever had before. Realizing what was happening, his heart suddenly began to run wild as did his emotions. Pari's body trembled in his arms. He could hear her crying as tears streamed down her soft cheeks.

He was not sure how long he held her in his arms. But just one second of it was worth everything he had endured. He forgot all the pain, all the heartbreak, and all the loneliness.

Even his impending death.

After some time, his heart began to calm down like it always did in her presence. Just as it had been on their last night together,

210

their hearts became one. But as he held her, he suddenly felt something. They were not alone. He looked down at her as her eyes met his. Between the two of them, in her belly, there was life.

He saw the streams of tears running out of her beautiful eyes. "You...you're with child."

She nodded as a smile finally came to her face. "For four months now."

The smile that was on her face came onto his. He lovingly wiped away his wife's tears.

"The day after you were taken away, I realized that the dream's prediction came true."

His hand gently touched her stomach. He fell to a knee as he looked at it in complete awe. He came back to his feet and tightly embraced her. Lifting her off of her feet, he swung her around before putting her back down. As she flew through the air, joyous laughter escaped her—the same laughter that rang in his dreams and kept him sane while buried in this dark pit for so long. And for a moment, they forgot about everything else.

For a moment, there was nothing but happiness.

Without thinking, he leaned in and kissed his wife. "Today...today, *Bhagwan* has accepted all of my prayers. And he has fulfilled them all...all except for one. And that will be fulfilled in the next life."

"Which one is it?"

"That you, I, and our child will live in eternity together."

Her soft hand reached out and touched his cheek like it had that night long ago. "I know, Veeresh...I know."

He watched her smile slowly disappear.

"But...but why must you do this. Your friend told me what is happening. There is still time. If you say what they are asking, then—then you will be there to hold your child."

211

"I...I cannot do that, Pari. As much as it pains me...I must face my death. I will have no honor if I turn back now."

"Your honor does not mean anything to me, Veeresh. Even if you lost it all, I would still be with you."

"My honor means nothing to me either, Pari. But...but it means everything to our child." He looked down at her stomach. "How can I tell my child that he is the descendent of lions when I am a coward? How can I, as a man, allow my child to be born of a father who sold their respect to dogs?"

Pari was silent.

"I have lived more in my life than most men would in ten lifetimes. I have been at the brink of death more times than most. I was on the brink of breaking more times that any one of my captor's could have possibly imagined...but I never fell into it. You kept me going. You gave me my strength to keep living when every fiber of me wanted to let go and give in to them."

In her husband's eyes, Pari saw the gleam of a warrior.

"I...I wanted to show my enemies that the descendent of the lion and the husband of the honorable Pari is a man...a man who does not even fear death. A man who did what he needed to do to protect his family and faced whatever consequences came his way. And now I must show it. Now I must face death one last time. And this time—this time I will embrace it with open arms. I will finally go into the abode of my eternal friend who has been beckoning me. And there...there I will wait until I see you again."

There were no more tears in Pari's eyes. Hearing him speak made them all disappear. "I...I will tell our child who his father was. I will tell them that he was the King of Warriors. He was a man who would not submit even to death except on his own terms...and he was the bravest man I have ever set my eyes on." Her soft hand came onto his rough and beaten cheek. "I love you, Veeresh. You will have my love in this life and in every other one to come."

212

For the last time, Veeresh and Pari embraced.

***

A crowd of men, women, and children formed around the gallows. It was the largest crowd that had ever gathered for a hanging outside of the prison. People came from miles away to see the honorable Veeresh take his last breath. They could not free him from the clutches of his captors, but they could at least show him respect. A row of guards made sure that they kept their distance. The executioner removed the test dummy after ensuring that there would be no errors today.

Henry first escorted Pari safely out of the prison before he came to get Veeresh, taking him on his final journey. As Henry escorted Veeresh to the courtyard's entrance, he informed Veeresh that he would personally see Pari safely to Veeresh's family's land. Even though Veeresh's parents would continue to treat her like their own daughter, Henry promised to help as much as he could.

Veeresh's response was that of a brotherly embrace.

Hearing the loud prison door open, all eyes went there. A small path led from the door to the stage. And along the lane was a line of evenly spaced guards.

The crowd fell silent as Veeresh made his way by them. There were no chains on him. Henry did not hold him by his arm, leading him like an animal. Instead, Veeresh walked like a free man. His eyes did not look at the crowd. Nor did they fall onto any of the guards, even the ones who had beaten him the day before. Instead, they focused on the noose.

As he passed each uniformed guard, they felt a shiver run up their spines as they saw his eyes. There was no fear or hesitation.

There was only life.

He came onto the stage and took his place. The executioner wrapped the noose around his neck as an officer read off his crimes. He gave Veeresh an opportunity to repent, but there was no repentance to ask for. He gave Veeresh the opportunity to say any final words, but Veeresh's eyes told the crowd everything he wanted to say.

Neither James nor Wilkinson watched the hanging. Wilkinson could not bear watching the death of the Company happen right before his eyes. He had left an hour before, intending to go back to London.

James would be found an hour later by Edward, sitting at his desk. But his body would be limp from the poison that had been mixed in his tea by his own hand.

As Veeresh stared straight into the crowd, he saw the one person that he wished to see. Pari was standing in the middle of the crowd. Her eyes locked with his. She was not trembling with fear. As they looked at one another, the courage in Veeresh flowed through his wife's veins.

And through his eyes, he told her one last time how much he loved her.

As the executioner pulled the lever, the last thought Veeresh had was that they would be together again. This was not the end of their tale. It was only the beginning. And in time, the next chapter of their love story would begin. They had not been given the chance to grow old together in this life. He never got to see his son. But he knew that one day, either in this world or the next, he would embrace his family once more.

Veeresh Singh died with a smile.

***

Memories Of My Future

A time comes in every man's life when he faces death. Either it has come to him or he arrives at its doorstep. And at that moment, there is a choice. Will he go quietly into that good night, or will his final cry be in heat of battle? Will his legacy echo through eternity and be something that is remembered?

A man must find his courage. He must find what gives him his courage. Faith, purpose, and love! These are the integral parts of a man. What can one man do in a world where evil overpowers good? What can man do against such hate?

Face it with courage. He can walk with his head held high and with the fire of bravery burning in his veins. He can show the world what one man can do.

One man's worth. One man's defiance. One man's valor.

CHAPTER 16
THE PHONE CALL

The stars were out in their full glory tonight. The skies were clear, and the air was cool. Large planes could be seen and loudly heard as they made their descent towards LaGuardia not far from the hotel.

Dinner had taken longer than expected. The long lines and slow service turned a half-hour meal into a two hour ordeal. But what else could Mirza have expected in Time Square on a Friday night? And the taxi ride back to his hotel was a long one. He would have been better off if he had followed his gut and just stayed in to order room service. Now he would only have a few hours to rest before his early morning flight tomorrow.

Feeling for his room key in his jacket's inside pocket, the doctor finally found it beneath his wallet. He inserted it into the door's silver lock. As he pulled it out quickly, the green light indicated success.

He wanted nothing more than to sleep. This trip had been far from fruitful. He had expected Avinash to show no hesitation in joining him. The Avinash from med school certainly would have done so. But people change.

And so had his friend.

The gleam that had always been in Avinash's eyes was no longer as bright. It was still there, buried deep inside. Somewhere, the Avinash that feared nothing, not even death, was still alive. But Mirza could see that time had taken its toll on Avinash's spirit.

As he came into the room and closed the door behind him, he heard his phone ring. Mirza pulled it out of his pocket and looked at the illuminated screen as he shut the door behind him. Seeing the name on the Caller ID, he thought that his weariness was making him see things. The phone continued to ring as Mirza blankly stared at the name while approaching his bed. He gently put his backpack onto the mattress before finally answering the phone.

"…Avi?"

"Hey pal."

"Hey yourself…I wasn't expecting to hear from you."

"I wouldn't have either after the way we ended things today."

"…Sorry about that…I shouldn't have been so rude. We all have our places in life and yours is here."

"You might have that wrong."

Mirza was silent, thinking that his ears were deceiving him as he sat down on the bed.

"You still there?"

"…Ye—yeah I'm here. Just couldn't believe what you just said. I mean—you sounded pretty adamant today."

"It's been a long day."

"…What happened?"

"It's a long story. Literally."

"Is that why you're calling me?"

"…Yes. I've done some thinking—actually, I've done a lot of thinking about our discussion. I found something that allowed me to do some soul-searching as to who I am, where I come from, and what I stand for."

"And what have your thoughts led you to?"

Mirza could hear Avinash smiling as the renowned surgeon said his next words. *"You'll be buying two tickets on your next journey overseas."*

For a long moment, Mirza did and said nothing. He simply stared at the opposite wall as he digested his friend's words. Over the next few seconds, they seemed to echo over a hundred times in every corner of his mind. Finally, a smile crept onto his face. "Now, that sounds like the Avinash I know."

"Seems like I was starting to let my success go to my head."

"I'll—I'll inform Mr. Daniels. He'll call you tomorrow for sure. I know he was really excited about the prospect of having you onboard. He really admires you." Mirza was silent for a long moment. "How much do you have to take care of before you'd be ready to go?"

"Not much. I have a few things to take care of before we go—namely just some goodbyes…but…"

"…Yes?"

"There is one in particular that I'll have to take care of tomorrow night."

Mirza knew what his friend meant. He had met Avinash's father once before at their graduation. And with just one look, the man had stricken him with more fear than anyone had ever done before. "I definitely wouldn't want to be there when you tell your folks."

"Good thing it's over the phone."

Mirza laughed.

"So how is this going to work?"

"Umm…like I said, Mr. Daniels will be giving you a call shortly with all the details. I know he won't believe it when I tell him that you want to come. He'll probably fly you out to his office and will do all the paperwork with you there—maybe even do a photo op since you're such a celebrity."

Avinash lightly chuckled. *"Seems like he'll squeeze out every ounce of publicity he can get from me."*

"Maybe…but trust me, he's a good man. He cares a lot for humanity. And he's a good friend to have." Mirza was quiet for a long moment. "But honestly Avi, I cannot tell you how ecstatic I am to be getting this call from you."

"Me too. Let's change the world one life at a time."

Memories Of My Future

***

Avinash called Martha to his office the following Monday. The window curtains were pulled back and the blinds were raised up, allowing endless sunlight to flood the room. His desk had been cleaned, and for the first time in his entire career, all of his papers were filed away in their proper places. The only things resting on the polished surface were his desktop computer, nametag, family photos, and jar of pens.

The nurse came in through the open door to see him staring at a photo. The doctor himself was dressed in his usual attire. His face was cleanly shaven, and he looked as fresh as ever. Hearing her enter, he looked up at the seasoned nurse with a lighthearted smile. "Martha, good morning."

"Hi, Avi."

"Close the door please."

She did so before coming to his desk and sitting across from him. Looking behind his eyes, she could see something there that she had not seen before. "…What's on your mind?"

"I need a favor from you."

"Tell me."

"Take care of Taxi while I'm gone."

The nurse was silent for a long moment. For a second, she thought that her ears had deceived her. "…What?"

"I'm leaving, Martha."

She did not say a word at first. "…Leaving?"

He nodded. "In about a month."

"…A…a *month*?" Looking into Avinash's eyes, Martha knew what was taking him away. She looked down at her lap for what seemed like a long time before looking back up at him. His gaze stayed on her the entire time. "You're taking your friend's offer, aren't you?"

Avinash slowly nodded.

She took a deep breath. "I knew this day would come. I just did not think that it would come so quickly. This place...this hospital...it has never had a doctor like you—a man like you. It will always have a place for you, but your place is not here. I don't know if it ever really was. You must follow your heart."

"It was for a time. You made it so. There were times where I forgot how alone I was here. Times where I nearly forgot that my family was on the other side of the planet. And it was because I found a family here in you."

As Avinash spoke, a warm smile spread across Martha's face.

Without looking at it, he slid the picture he had been observing across the table to Martha. "Can you do me a favor?"

She took the photo of Isabel into her hands. "Get rid of the picture?"

He nodded. "I'm starting a new chapter...and it's time to cut off the ties of the past."

Martha slightly smiled.

He looked directly into the nurse's eyes. "The only things I would like to take with me are the memories of the good people who made my life all that it is."

Avinash could not believe it, but tears formed in Martha's eyes. Her smile slowly grew. "When you came into these doors for the first time...I never thought you'd be the one to fill the shoes of the son that I lost...you'd be the one to take away the pain I felt when I lost him."

She had only ever mentioned her son once before. Her child, David, had been in his final year of medical school when a drunk driver ended his life. After he died, she nearly took her own. But three months after David died, Avinash walked through the hospital's doors.

220

"But you did…" Tears began to run down her cheeks. "You were the one who lessened the pain and made me feel like…like a mother again."

Rising to his feet, Avinash came around his desk and embraced Martha in a way only a child could hug a mother. He could feel tears beginning to form in his own eyes. "I would not be here if it was not for you, Martha. My entire family was on the other side of the world, but you were always here for me. You were the mother that I needed—the one who kept me going. Without you here, every day would have been difficult. But you turned some of my darkest days into my brightest."

And in that embrace, Martha said goodbye to her son.

***

Avinash drew a deep breath. His goat curry from *Brick Lane Curry House* was warming up on the stove and its fresh, mouthwatering aroma slowly filled the entire kitchen and spilled into the living room. It would still be a while before it was ready. That would allow him enough time to finally do this. But as he stared at the phone in his hands, food was the last thing on his mind. The phone felt heavier than ever before. His palms were sweating as his gaze stayed on the device. He knew it would be tough, but he had never imagined that his heart would be racing this fast.

Without speaking a word out loud, he reminded himself that the hardest part would be dialing the number. Once he broke through that wall, it would be too late to turn back. But even that reassurance was not enough.

He took another deep breath. Avinash closed his eyes. The image of Khau battling the Mongols and Veeresh's unbreakable spirit flashed in his mind. He could see both scenes clear as day. He could see Khau's warrior eyes and his powerful figure. And he could see Veeresh's broken but unbowed body.

If those things were what his ancestors had gone through, then surely he could do this.

Without waiting another moment, he slowly dialed in the number. First, it was the country code for India. The same country that Khau had courageously fought for when India was combined with Pakistan and Bangladesh. Then, it was the area code of his family's land. The same land that Khau had received hundreds of years ago for his heroism. Finally, it was the number for his home and family. The same family that Veeresh died for so that they would be free from oppression.

Putting the phone to his ear, there was silence. This was his last chance to hang up, but he did not. Within moments, he could hear the phone ringing. It rang once. Then again. And again. For a moment, Avinash thought that nobody would answer.

But then he heard his father's voice.

"Hello?"

Avinash spoke as calmly as ever. *"Namaste, pita ji."*

"Avinash! How are you?"

"I'm fine…did I wake you?

"No, I was just waking up before you called. I had a feeling that you would call."

From his father's voice, Avinash could tell that the man was expecting Avinash to say what he had commanded him to do in their previous conversation. Avinash was silent for a long time. Fear was keeping the words on his mind from going to his tongue.

"Avinash?"

He took a deep breath. It was time. Time to change the course of his life.

CHAPTER 17
FLAMES OF WAR

Two months later:

Amaristan's name meant "the land of love." But these days, it was anything but that. War had engulfed the entire nation for nearly a year. Almost every single one of its 150 million inhabitants fell victim to it. The only ones who had not witnessed it firsthand were those who could afford to flee across the borders, but within the nation's boundaries there was only chaos.

Cities were burning. Homes were destroyed. Lives were lost.

The rebels were taking control of the nation over a mountain of corpses. Their leader had proclaimed himself a god, and his followers were mad enough to believe him. He gave eloquent speeches detailing how he would change the world, and his followers cheered as they let his words fuel their fire. Nobody truly knew what his true goals were. Many believed that he had no true plan and was just a madman intent on slaughtering all that opposed him.

The military, already weak and corrupt, tried to fight the rebels. At first the army was winning. However, two months after the war began, the rebels captured a military base near the capital. With the newly acquired weapons, they turned the tide and sent the military fleeing to the south.

The army's general pulled all his soldiers back to the southern part of the nation. He had carved it out as the military's domain and left the rest of the nation at the rebels' mercy.

The president himself fled the nation along with many of its richest citizens. Now, they were safe in England while the people he had sworn to protect suffered. Nobody had heard from him since he left. He stayed within the walls of his fortress-like manor. And if history was any indicator, nobody expected him to ever set foot in Amaristan again.

Although the country was well-populated, it held no real power before the rebellion started. It gave no political or strategic advantage to its allies and did not possess any highly-demanded resources. For that reason, almost no outside entity even considered coming to its aid. However, there were some brave souls who came here to make a difference. Jonathan Daniels made that possible.

And amongst those individuals who came was Avinash.

***

The refugee camp was set up a few miles from the nation's largest city, which was still not controlled by the rebels. The city became a battleground a few months after the revolution began. Thousands of the citizens fled, but most could not. Rotting corpses littered the streets. Some were riddled with bullets while others had been cut down by machetes. Some neighborhoods had formed vigilante groups to protect themselves, but most were not strong enough to stop the rebels' advances.

Even here at the camp, the sound of gunfire and explosions could be faintly heard during the quiet hours of the night. It was a constant memento that countless were dying only a few miles away.

The grounds were walled off by thick, ten-foot tall barriers with barbed wire lining their tops. There were only two gates. One was on the wall which faced the city. The other was at the opposite end of the camp. The former remained open for a large part of the day as floods of injured refugees poured through, while the latter was usually kept shut.

There were nearly fifty armed guards watching for any rebels that came too close. They hardly ever had to fire a shot because just the sight of the trained soldiers with their modernized weapons was enough to intimidate the rebels.

The compound itself was massive. And its hospital's size rivaled the largest hospitals in New York City. But unlike any hospital Avinash had ever seen, there were more patients than space here. Millions of dollars had been spent in building this facility, and millions more were used to sustain it.

But it was still not enough.

There was not an hour where refugees did not come flooding through the gate. Most came in wearing dirty rags. Some came limping while others were carried by loved ones or strangers with good hearts. Some were conscious, screaming in pain, and covered in their own blood while others were unconscious and numb to the pain. However, many were dead by the time they got to the gate. As they arrived, the guards checked them for weapons and confiscated any that they found. This delay caused some patients to die before they had a chance to be seen by a doctor, but it was a necessary precaution.

Doctors, nurses, and aid workers had come from every corner of the globe. From America to Brazil. From England to Germany. From Egypt to Spain. From Israel to Pakistan. From China to Nepal. From France to Russia. Fair-skinned to dark-skinned and everything in-between. Christian, Muslim, Hindu, Buddhist, Jew, and atheist. Some were doctors and nurses while others were people with no formal education. But they were all here for the same reason. They had not come bearing the banner of *their* people. They bore the banner of *one* people.

Children, women, and men poured into the camp with no other place to go. Within these walls was the last haven from the

225

rebels and the only place where the refugees could get medical aid. The doctors and aid workers did everything possible, but equipment was stretched thin and so were the facilities. However, their courage and passion for humanity were not.

Patients could not stay here long. They were kept until their wounds were treated or until their bed needed to be used by a more critical patient. Most patients never stayed for more than two weeks. Avinash saw many patients forced to leave when they were still far from being fully recovered.

But every day many also died.

Avinash would find his hands covered in blood. Some was from the living while some was from the dead. His scrubs began each day cleanly washed. But by the end, they were drenched by the blood of his patients. He had more patients before him in a day than he saw in a week back at the hospital.

The patients under his care were brought into one large room, measuring 50 yards by 40 yards. It had a high ceiling, almost thirty feet high, with some windows on the east wall. There were over a hundred people in this room at any given time. The wounded would be lying almost next to one other, leaving a little space between them to allow the workers to walk by.

At any one moment in the compound, there were more surgeries occurring than operating rooms available. But Avinash did not even bother to check if a room was available. He performed most of his minor surgeries in this very room. He knew that in the time it took to wheel a patient into an operating room, five more patients would die waiting on him.

Of all the inflictions he saw, the most common were bullet wounds. It seemed that the rebels just fired upon anyone they saw not wearing their symbols. The oldest victim Avinash saw was a ninety-eight-year-old man. The youngest was a newborn girl.

Both died.

226

But the thing that caused the most deaths in the camp was not the mistakes or inabilities of the doctors and nurses. It was the fact that no matter how quickly they worked or how well they maximized their efforts, there was not personnel enough to go around. Avinash was the fastest and most effective doctor in the compound, but it always seemed that by the time he treated one soul, more died waiting for him.

Every day, truckloads of the dead were driven off. Avinash did not know where the corpses of the innocent were taken. He never had the heart to ask.

Sometimes he worked for sixteen hours without a break. Even when his day was over and another surgeon came to relieve him, he kept on working. Many times, he would forget to eat. His mind was filled with two things. The first were the eyes of his dead patients. The second were those vile murderers.

Within hours of his work beginning each day, his fingers would almost become sore. His feet started hurting, and fatigue would settle in. His mind was consumed by weariness. His eyes were as red as his blood-drenched hands and blood-soaked clothes.

But he did not care.

He was not here for himself. He would not have made the choice to be here if he was of the weak. This was not a place for the cowardly who would cave in after a little discomfort.

When night came, he spent much of his time listening to the sounds of distant gunfire in the city. With each shot, he found more anger in his soul—anger aimed at those who were killing their own people for nothing more than greed and sport. He saw the eyes of dead children. He heard the last words of all the woman who died. He saw the color leave the faces of all the men who lost their lives.

How could he sleep peacefully when so much was happening around him?

There were many days when he made himself forget that this was reality. He tricked his mind into thinking that it was all a game to see how many patients he could save. This was sometimes the only way he could keep his sanity and not let the sight of endless death have any effect on his ability to help the next patient.

But there were other days where he was once again confronted with the harsh reality. He fully realized that all the injured flooding into the camp were the products of merciless massacres.

It was on those days that he was one step away from completely losing his mind.

***

During his time at the camp, Avinash became close to many of the other aid workers. Mirza had been here for several months before Avinash joined the cause. Not a single person here had a bad word to say about Mirza.

A husband and wife from Pakistan, Sikhandar and Nasim, became like family to Avinash. The two were general surgeons and had come here as soon as they finished their training. Since medical education in Pakistan was far quicker than it was in the states, the two of them were a bit younger than him.

Another man, Eric, was also stationed close to Avinash. The two shared a bedroom as well. Being that Eric was from Israel, Avi was curious to learn more about his culture. But they had become incredibly close even though days would pass without them seeing much of each other because of their opposite work schedules.

There was also Christina and Huang. The two were fiancés who hailed from California. Huang was born and raised in China before moving to America in his late teens. It was in nursing school that Huang met Christina. Huang now worked as Avinash's main assistant while Christina assisted Nasim with her patients.

228

Everyone in this camp that Avinash came across was capable at their job, but they were even better human beings. Each were here for their own reasons. Sikhandar and Nasim had lost their first child. Eric's wife had been murdered in cold blood. Huang and Christina were overcoming the loss of his parents. Mirza found a cause that he was willing to die for.

But Avinash…he was here for one simple reason. He was here because it was what Khau or Veeresh would have done. He was here to honor his forefathers and carry on their legacy. He was here because he wanted to serve humanity with his gift and become what his forefathers were…

***

Today was a day where Avinash was playing mind games with himself. He was making his mind think of this all as a game so the deaths he witnessed would not slow him down. He was working quickly and moving from patient to patient without giving his mind any time to really digest all that he was seeing.

In a room full of patients, Avinash was the only doctor. There were about eight other workers who each had at least some sort of nursing training. Of them, Huang was the most capable and experienced nurse. Ten more workers had no formal medical training. Their duties were to keep the families in the room calm and to make sure the patients with the severest wounds received priority. At least a hundred patients were in the large room. And along with the patients, there were countless family members and strangers who had come in with the wounded.

This room was always too hot. The air conditioner was working fine and so were the fans. Avinash did not know if it was all the body heat or the emotions that made it feel sweltering. Along with the unbearable heat was the odor.

It was the smell of the wounded, the dying…and the dead.

The illuminated lights on the high ceiling shined their light down on the floor. Had the floor been clean, the reflection would have been blinding. However, the floor was covered with blood. Two women were constantly cleaning the floor, but it seemed to get dirty as quickly as they cleaned it.

The deafening cries of patients consumed the room. Some cried out for God while others cried out to their loved ones. The families of the patients did all that they could to sooth them, but nothing they did could take away the pain.

However, Avinash did not let the voices of the wounded or the efforts of their caretakers break his concentration. He blocked it out and made sure to speak above it all as he directed the efforts of his staff.

Avinash's gloved fingers were covered in blood as he held a scalpel in his hands. A skinny child sat on the bed in front of him. The girl's mother sat next to her and held the child's uninjured arm. In New York City, Avinash never let anyone other than nurses and medical students in surgery with him. But in the months spent here, he became accustomed to having the loved ones of his patients in the same room with him during minor procedures.

As the mother said prayers in their native tongue with her eyes tightly shut and head bowed, Avinash studied the angle that the bullet had cut through the child's left arm and lodged itself near the bone.

He ran his fingers over the girl's arm and figured out where the bullet had planted itself. Blood still streamed out of the wound. Luckily, the girl was nowhere near the point of bleeding out.

Avinash turned to the mother and spoke in her native language as she opened her eyes. "It will be a simple procedure. I'll clean the wound first. Then I'll cut into the wound and control the bleeding before patching her up. Gala has sterilized the wound and injected it with Lidocaine to numb her arm. She'll barely feel a thing."

He looked back at the girl. "This will hurt a little. I want you to keep your eyes on your mother, understand?"

The girl nodded.

Avinash looked at the nurse that stood behind the girl before speaking in English. "Hold her steady, Gala."

The African nurse nodded and placed her hands firmly on either shoulder of the girl as the doctor prepared to cut into the girl's arm.

As he expertly cut into the girl's skin, he heard her wince. He wished he could have given her more anesthesia, but they needed to use it sparingly. The girl's mother held her opposite hand tightly as she ran her fingers through her daughter's hair and tried to console her. The girl's wincing did not bother him since he had become accustomed to it, but it did appeal to his humanity.

Blood seeped out of the knife wound as Avinash dug a little deeper. It behaved the same way that a ripe plum would pump out its juices when cut into. He wanted to cut as little as possible to limit the girl's pain, but still needed to cut deep enough so that he could see all the damage that the bullet had caused. The bullet had stopped a centimeter from the bone and that caused a sigh of relief from Gala, who was looking over his shoulder.

Avinash wasted no time in assessing what damage had been done by the path of the bullet. Nothing major was damaged except for a small vessel, and he quickly stopped the bleeding with a clamp.

Soon, the wound was patched up. The entire procedure took no more than ten minutes and could not have been done any better.

The doctor looked at the mother and quickly spoke to her. "The wound is clean and she's fine now. She won't be staying here. But if you see any puss, redness, or tenderness in the area, bring her back. Gala will give you some antibiotics for your daughter to take and will answer any questions you have."

The mother nodded.

Avinash looked at the girl. "Thank you for being brave."

The young girl smiled weakly at him as she wiped away the tears that had streamed down her face during the surgery.

Without another word, Avinash turned away from the patient. Huang had already prepped the next patient and had done all he could. It was another simple wound. The woman had been shot twice in the shoulder and once in the arm. Two of the bullets had gone straight through her while the third had broken her humerus. When she entered the room, Huang quickly put pressure on the bleeding and stabilized her so that she would not bleed out.

"Dr. Singh!" A voice called out.

Swiftly turning around, Avinash saw a worker wheel in another patient. The young male victim was lying on a bed. He was no older than eighteen. Less than an hour ago, he had been a young, fit man.

But now his right leg had been blown clean off from just below the knee.

The boy screamed in agony. He called out to God. He called out for his mother. His cries could be heard down the corridor; just one syllable of them brought a wretched feeling into every person's heart. His own blood was splattered all over his body, and blood continued to seep out of the open wound. One look at him told Avinash that he didn't have long.

"Sophie, with me!"

As the doctor and Russian nurse came to the dying patient, Avinash laid his hands on the boy's chest as he looked deep into his eyes. The gurney was covered and drenched in the boy's blood. A couple of streams were running off of the stretcher and onto the floor. There were only minutes left before he would bleed out.

"He doesn't have long. I need to put a clamp on the bleeder to stop the bleeding."

Sophie quickly handed Avinash a tourniquet. This apparatus was a smaller version of the type he used in New York City. It was

232

called a Combat Application Tourniquet, similar to the ones used by military forces. Avinash quickly applied it above the bleeder. Avinash's gloves were quickly covered in his patient's blood, but he didn't give it a second thought. He efficiently placed the clamp on the bleeder.

"Check his vital signs."

Sophie put her index and middle fingers on the boy's neck.

Wrapping the tourniquet above the patent's bloodied and bleeding knee, Avinash locked it into place before giving the tourniquet's stick a few quick turns. With each rotation, the device put more and more pressure on the patient's femoral artery in an effort to stop the bleeding. And within a matter of moments, the seeping blood became a trickle before it came to an end.

"His pulse is starting to slow down," Sophie commented.

"What is it?"

"160…150…140…" Her eyes came back onto Avinash. "It's dropping towards normal."

He nodded as he tied the bleeder off. "Good. Stay with him and dress the wound…I'll have Huang come over when he finishes with his patient to prepare him for surgery."

The nurse nodded.

As Avinash turned back to go to his previous patient with the wounded shoulder and arm, another voice called for him. And just as before, one second of hearing the tone of the voice evidenced its dire need.

"Dr. Singh! Come quick!"

***

That night, Eric came back to the room to find Avinash awake and at his desk with the lamp illuminated. The top of his desk held a few photos of people close to him. Some were of his family. Others were of friends back in New York City.

He had brought a few other pieces of memorabilia with him, including his Taekwondo black belt. Even with no equipment, Avinash had practiced his forms in the little free time he had here. Like always, it helped him relieve his stress and made him feel closer to his forefathers.

But outside of the pictures and the memorabilia, the desk was mostly populated with documents, sketches, and notes. Working hard on a drawing, Avinash glanced at the doorway as his roommate and friend entered.

Eric had taken a shower before entering and wore a pair of athletic shorts and shirt. He smiled at his friend. "You're still awake?"

"Are you surprised?"

"I guess not." Eric closed the door behind him. Looking over his friend's shoulder, he could see that Avinash was drawing out designs for some sort of device. And next to that was a hand-written essay he was working on. "You going to tell me what it is?"

"You know the answer to that." Avinash looked back at his screen.

"Ah yes, your secret project." Making his way over to the bed on his side of the room, Eric took a seat.

"When it's ready, you'll be among the first to know."

He took a deep breath as he readied himself for sleep. "Fair enough."

CHAPTER 18
BEAUTIFUL RESCUER

Several mornings later, Avinash awoke early as he always did. It was still another two hours before the first rays would make their appearance across the horizon. Sitting up, Avinash looked to the other side of the room and saw Eric sound asleep. The man had returned to the room around midnight after his day's work had ended. Again, he had found Avinash hard at work on his project.

Knowing Eric, he would sleep for the majority of his break before starting again around noon. Avinash threw off his covers and took a few soundless steps to the window. He quietly pulled back the curtains and looked outside. The stars brightly burned in the dark sky. It was so peaceful. In New York City, the sky was never this clear. Never this beautiful.

However, had he been at the opposite end of the building, he would have witnessed the burning city only miles away. Unlike the peaceful night here, the city would soon hold more corpses than living souls.

But from here, all he could see was a peaceful forest and stars. His gaze drifted up to the heavens, and he studied the remaining stars that lingered before dawn. Those stars had seen so much. From the beginning of the earth to now, they had watched this planet's surface and seen everything. The good and the bad. The wars and the peaceful times. The sorrows and the joys. They had seen the best, and they had witnessed the worst. What wisdom did they have for the human race?

Closing his eyes, Avinash lowered his head and whispered the same prayer he offered every day. "God...give me the strength, give me the abilities to be the best I can be today. Bless me with courage, and bless me with strength. Bless me with the abilities to be an example for everyone else. Let nobody see my fear or my weakness. I do my work in your name. Let me use the gifts you gave me to make this world a better place by the time the sun sets tonight."

***

None of the workers ever stepped foot outside of the camp. In fact, except for the guards, none had ever even walked out to the compound's wall. The workers were ordered to stay at least fifty yards away from it at all times.

At least, that was the official policy.

But the times that Avinash left the camp, he did not go to the city. Instead, he travelled in the opposite direction. A woman he saved told him about a sight he would see there. And she had not exaggerated when promising that it would be the most beautiful sight he had ever laid eyes on.

When aid workers first came to the camp, they were flown in by helicopter, and supplies were regularly flown in the same way. The only way they knew what happened in the city was through the television set or through the eyes and words of their patients.

Avinash was never one to rely on news reports and received his information firsthand through the refugees who filtered through the camp. As each day passed, the situation seemed to be getting worse. The death toll was in the tens of thousands although some estimated that the number was inaccurate, citing that the international media was downplaying the actual casualties to lessen the pressure on other nations to help. The numbers of displaced refugees were now in the millions, and those figures were growing every day.

Every rebel seemed to be a brainwashed animal. They would yell their chants and war cries without giving thought to their words.

With their machetes and guns raised above their heads, they promised death to all who opposed them. Along with killing their own people, they had slain countless relief workers and promised to kill any who assisted their so-called enemies.

With their guns and their numbers, the rebels acted as if they were warriors. But take that away, and Avinash knew that they would beg for their lives. They were all hyenas who would flee at the first sight of a lion. There were times that Avinash imagined what he would do to the rebels if he ever came face-to-face with them. He imagined looking them in their cowardly eyes and showing them what real courage was—the courage of Khau and Veeresh.

But the opportunity never came.

For the rebels hardly every came close to the compound. Rumors were always circulating that the rebels would mount an attack on the compound. One time, a pack of them came close in an effort to intimidate the guards. But they were all shot dead by the trained sharpshooters. Since then, they kept their distance from all relief camps under Jonathan Daniels' banner.

However, the victims of the rebels never ceased to enter.

***

"Dr. Singh!"

Every now and then, Avinash experienced a day that reminded him just how real the situation was. On these days, the illusion that his self-imposed mind games provided vanished.

And today would be one of those days.

It had been nearly twelve hours since Avinash came on duty. His day was nearing its end, but he still had a healthy hour left. The room was like it always was at this time of day: hot, loud, and consumed by the stench of the wounded, dying, and dead.

Hearing his name, Avinash whirled his head around to see four patients wheeled into the large room. Their agony-filled groans drowned out everything else. Just by one syllable, he knew that they were all at the brink of death. He had been wrapping up a patient whose ear had been shot clean off. After sanitizing and disinfected the boy's wound, he was in the process of bandaging it up, but he immediately turned away when he heard his nurse.

"Abdi, finish wrapping him up! Huang, with me."

Avinash rushed over to the patients, running between countless other wounded as he did. He quickly analyzed all four of them. At first, his mind could not fathom what he was seeing, but it quickly registered everything. A young man had been shot several times in the left side of his chest. The second male was shot in the stomach by at least four rounds. A third person, a woman no older than twenty-one, had been shot in her upper back with the bullets now lodged in her chest. And the fourth man had been shot near his heart as well.

But he was already dead.

Avinash looked away from the patient who died and back at the other three. With a quick move, he motioned to the second and third patients while speaking to his nurses and the workers who had wheeled them in. "Stabilize those two! Do what you can on them!"

The doctor ripped off the first patient's shirt before throwing it to the ground. None of the bullets had gone through him, instead lodging themselves in his body. Huang came to Avinash's side and took a quick X-Ray with a portable machine. The X-Ray showed that five bullets were lodged in his left side and blood was filling up his left chest. Looking up, Avinash saw the patient gasping for air. "His chest is filling up with blood. We need to drain it with a chest tube."

"On it." Huang quickly grabbed what they needed.

Looking even further up, the doctor's eyes met with the patient's. He could see life leaving them. After all the instances

Avinash had seen this happen over the past months, he knew that time was running out.

"Give me the scalpel," Avinash ordered.

Avinash worked efficiently. He was an artist, and this was his canvass. Quickly, he inserted the chest tube with perfect expertise having done so hundreds of times before. Huang watched as always. It took somebody with a high level of skill and training to insert the tube with such precision. Positioning it perfectly, Avinash nodded and the drainage of the excess blood began.

The task did not take long. As the tube continued to drain the blood, Avinash saw life coming back into the young man's eyes. He secured the tube to the chest wall with a suture and asked Huang to put a sterile occlusive dressing around the tube.

Avinash looked up at Huang. Avinash knew that the nurse had the ability to take it from here. "Keep watching his vitals and the output from the tube. I need to see the other two patients, and then I'll come back."

Huang nodded as Avinash turned around to see the next victim. But he suddenly froze.

The woman was dead. And so was the other man.

The doctor stared blankly at the two patients. The two of them died only minutes ago while Avinash was treating the first patient. He had been so focused that he did not hear their moans come to an end or the nurses confirming their deaths.

His gaze went from the woman's lifeless eyes to the man's and then back to the woman's. For a moment, he was in disbelief. But then reality finally set in, and Avinash's hands fell to his sides in defeat.

He had not been fast enough. He had done the procedure as quickly as humanly possible, but it was not enough. Stripping his gaze away from the lifeless eyes, he looked at the wounds of the dead. He knew beyond a shadow of a doubt that he could have given them both a fighting chance if he had only been given more time. Had he somehow been able to save the other patient in half the time, these two may not have joined the list of this wretched war's victims.

But fate had not granted him any favors.

As he stared at the corpses, he could hear endless cries echoing all around him. Some were from other patients waiting for him and others were from severely injured patients being rushed down the corridor into various rooms. All around him, nurses were frantically working. Some were calling for him while others were calling to one another, but their voices were all a blur. For as he stared at the dead corpses, he felt his stomach turn over on itself. His head began to spin and pound as hard as ever. The lights became a blur. His knees began to wobble. The eyes of all the corpses he had seen flashed through his mind like rapid fire: the men, women, children, young, and old. He saw each and every one of their eyes.

These were just two more corpses to add to the list. Just like so many before, he would have been able to save them had he gotten to them in time. He felt like collapsing, but did not. He felt like letting out his rage, but did not. All he could do was what he always did—the only thing any soldier could do.

Keep on fighting.

***

Moments after he was relieved by another doctor, Avinash shoved open the hospital's heavy door and staggered out onto the grounds. His legs trembled. His vision was blurred as he stumbled onto the grass. The scorching sun was nearing the horizon, but still mercilessly beat down on his face and blinded him. The air was still and the humidity was like hell.

In the distance, he could see the camp's walls. His face was drenched in sweat. His stomach was tossing and turning on itself. Had he not been relieved less than an hour after those two patients died, he surely would have collapsed or lost his self-control.

Losing all strength, he roughly fell to his knees, sending a jolt through his body. Suddenly, what he was feeling in his stomach went into his throat. Avinash keeled over before loudly coughing and letting loose his breakfast without any warning. The chunky liquid violently spilled out of his mouth and onto the ground. The doctor forcefully coughed as the puke endlessly came out. His throat felt like it was on fire, and the stench of his vomit consumed his nostrils. The sweat running down his face doubled. His head was pounding worse than ever. Tears swelled in his eyes and streamed down his dirty cheeks. His weary body gave out on him.

With a final heave, it was all out of his system.

He took a few deep breaths as he stared down at the vomit soaking into the ground. Its vile taste was left in his mouth. Its odor was all around him. On his knees, he did not bother to wipe any of the sweat or tears from his face. As he kept his eyes downcast, all he could see were the faces of the dead.

It was all too much. How could there be so much hate in the world? Didn't those rebels realize what they were doing? What type of animals were they to kill their own brethren?

A presence came from behind him.

At that moment, the merciless sun no longer beat against his back. Somebody's shadow now covered him. Feeling a soft hand come onto his shoulder, Avinash slowly turned his head around as he wiped his mouth with his sleeve.

The first thing he saw was her hand. The skin was a light brown—almost fawn—shade. His weary gaze travelled from her hand up to her face. His exhausted and almost broken eyes met with her caring ones. At first, the sun's glare made her nothing more than a dark figure. But his eyes slowly focused themselves.

His first thought was that she was an angel sent down from heaven to rescue him. Her beautiful green eyes had a hint of yellow around the pupils. They were so captivating, and her smile was so gentle. For a moment, his heart stopped. The entire world stopped. He forgot what was happening all around him: the war, his state, the killings.

Everything.

Without a word, her free hand offered him a wet cloth. As his eyes stayed locked with hers, he took it and wiped the sweat and tears off of his face. Her hand left his shoulder.

"…You must be Dr. Singh."

Her voice was as beautiful as her eyes. And it was as gentle as her smile. He immediately picked up the Spanish accent. But Avinash did not answer as he kept his eyes on hers. She had taken his breath, and he could not say a word even if he wanted to.

"…Are…are you okay?"

"…Y—y—yes." Avinash finally brought himself back to reality. His mind was finally convinced that this was no dream. He slowly looked away from her and back at the cloth. It was now drenched with his sweat. "…Sorry. I think I ruined this."

But when he looked back up, she was gone.

CHAPTER 19
SUNRISE

The night passed with little sleep. But it was not nightmares that kept Avinash awake. Instead, it was her eyes. They were drowning him in happiness. They were filling him with joy. The more he thought of them, the more he experienced an emotion that he had not felt since coming here: hope.

When his next shift ended, Avinash broke away from his usual schedule. He went around the compound in search of those eyes. He went to each and every corner looking for her. He did not know what he would say. He did not know why he was searching for her when he was so fatigued. But it was to no avail because she was nowhere to be found.

***

Avinash finally saw her again the next morning.

Making his way to the operating room to relieve Dr. Phillips, he hurried down the corridor not minding his surroundings. His heart was still depressed on not seeing her again, but his mind focused on his present day's work. Coming to the intersection of two hallways, he saw her arriving at the crossing at the last moment. As his eyes came upon her, his first thought was that he was still dreaming.

But he quickly realized what was happening. Not stopping himself in time, the two lightly ran into one another. His jaw collided with her forehead at the last minute.

The collision was not enough to knock down a well-built man like Avinash, but it made his counterpart fall softly onto her backside. The doctor's face turned red as embarrassment flooded through his veins. He quickly crouched down to help her to her feet. As he picked her up gently by her arm, she rubbed the top of her forehead.

"I'm—I'm so sorry." He brought her back up.

"It's my fault. I wasn't looking where I was going."

"No, it's mine. My mind was somewhere else."

Finally looking up at him, she recognized the doctor. "Oh! It's you."

He slightly nodded. "Yeah…it's me. Hope I didn't hurt you too bad."

"I've been hurt worse."

There was an awkward silence between the two as their eyes remained locked. Her voice was just as it had been before. Perfect. She was as beautiful as she had been under the hot sun. Her eyes gave him the same feeling they had at their last encounter, except much more.

Avinash finally broke the stillness. "I never got a chance to thank you."

She slightly smiled. "Thank me for what?"

"Coming to my rescue yesterday. I'm—I'm not entirely sure what came over me. It wasn't my finest moment."

"Everyone needs a hand every now and then."

Avinash smiled. "Seems like we were going in the same direction. Mind if I walk with you?"

"Of course not."

The two began to make their way down the corridor. This part of the compound was the living quarters of the aid workers. Given that the ones not on duty were asleep in their rooms, it was empty except for the two of them.

244

Avinash spoke again as he noticed her uniform. "You're a nurse?"

She slyly smiled. "No, I'm a taxi driver. They just gave me the uniform for fun."

Avinash grinned without laughing. "How long have you been here?"

"Two days."

He turned to look at her in surprise. "Two days? You must still be taking all this in."

"I was at the camp near the northern border before this."

"Was it as bad?"

She slightly shook her head. "Seems like this region got the worst of it."

There was another silence as the two continued to make their way down the hallway. Avinash could not believe it, but the lady walking beside him seemed even more beautiful today than before. Yesterday when he first saw her, his eyes had been so focused on her face. But today, he was able to take in the entire sight of her. Her light brown skin tone almost made her look like a fair-skinned north Indian. Her long black locks had a bit of a natural curl to them. Underneath her nurses uniform was a slender figure. She was pretty— prettier than anyone Avinash had ever come across. He estimated her age to be no older than twenty-five.

"I never got your name."

"It's Lia."

"Lia…" Avinash repeated the name to himself with a smile. "Doesn't the name mean 'bringer of good news'?"

Her eyes lit up. "Seems like you know your Spanish, Dr. Singh."

"I'm fluent in it actually."

"I'm impressed. Can you speak any other languages?"

"Five in all. And please just call me Avi. The only people I let call me Dr. Singh are people I don't like."

Lia lightly laughed. "This may surprise you, but I know the meaning of your name too."

"Really?"

She nodded. "A warrior with an indestructible spirit who brings happiness to those around him."

"Don't tell me you speak Hindi."

"Not yet at least. I just read about it in an article after you had your breakthrough. I think the name fits you perfectly."

Avinash's heart smiled upon hearing those words. There was some more silence as they turned the corner and came closer to the operating rooms in the compound's west wing. The echo of their footsteps travelled down the empty corridors.

"You're from Spain?"

Lia nodded. "I'm from the countryside there."

"Which doctor have you been assigned to?"

"You."

His voice showed his surprise. "...Me?"

"I was given the option and chose you."

"...Really? Why?"

"I think you'll find out soon enough."

***

From that day on, there was a bright spot in the operating room that had not been there before.

Lia proved to be the best nurse Avinash had ever worked with. Her efforts in the operating room mirrored his own. Like him, something drove her to give everything she had to every patient she came across. She was not the most experienced or the most educated nurse. By all measures, Huang had much more experience and education than her. But on her worst days, she was just as good as him. And on her best days, she surpassed him.

It was not her skill or experience that made her such a capable nurse. It was something in her soul that drove her. Avinash did not know what it was. He could not put his finger on it. But whatever it was, it made her into something more than just a good nurse.

It turned Lia into a passionate woman who treated all her patients like her own family.

The next weeks passed with Avinash and Lia working side-by-side. The days went by with hundreds of people coming before the two of them. Patients upon patients were brought in. Scores upon scores poured in every hour in an endless procession. Many came with death only moments away.

There was no end to it all. Avinash constantly had at least one patient in front of him. But there were times when he worked on three patients at once. No other doctor could do that. They relied too much on machines to help them diagnose and treat their patients. Avinash was of the opinion that most of the time, just asking the patient what was wrong and doing a quick examination would tell a doctor everything they needed to know to treat them.

The first two weeks working with Lia, Avinash never had to wait more than a few seconds for Lia to complete any command. He never had to double-check her work or correct her. She could stitch up a patient with ease and precision. She even took care of some of the smaller injuries herself. Avinash found that her greatest gift was her ability to keep a patient calm as they felt the pains of a procedure. Avinash could not imagine how she could be a better nurse or how their chemistry could get any better.

But it did.

After the first two weeks, the two of them were on the same wavelength. She knew what he would say before even he did. When a patient came in, she would hand him his tools exactly as he needed them. As soon as he reached out, whatever he needed would be in his hand. She did what was required without being asked. Everything between the two of them was timed perfectly, and in an hour, they went through as many patients as other doctors and nurses took half a day to go through.

Hardly any words would be exchanged between the two during their work. They became one in the operating room. She was always at his side unless she was tending to another patient alone. Nobody at the base had ever seen a doctor and nurse be so in sync. Everyone who saw them working together marveled at their perfect chemistry. Even with Martha, Avinash never experienced such a powerful connection in surgery.

Having her by his side, Avinash felt like he need not carry this burden on his own. The pain of seeing men, women, and children die right before his eyes and in his arms did not hurt as badly. No matter how dark it became in the operating room, there was always one bright light beside him. They both saw all the lives that were lost. They faced it together.

But they also saw the lives that were saved. They saw the children who were returned to their parents. They saw the wives returned to their husbands. They saw the husbands returned to their families. They saw the lovers reunited.

And most of all, they could feel the spirits of the living return.

During the times that they were not in surgery, their friendship blossomed as well. The two spent their evenings together when they were not on duty. If Avinash was not working on his private project, he passed his time with her. She witnessed him working on his documents and drawings, but never asked him about them.

Avinash did not know why the two of them opened up to one another so quickly. But around her, he wore no armor. They spoke from their hearts. As time passed, everything that was on their hearts came out as words. The future. Fate. Duty. Honor. Making their lives matter.

He learned much about Lia. From her favorite insect being a butterfly to her greatest fear being regret, he slowly learned every part of her. She had seen much of the world considering her young age. She was born and raised in Spain, but spent a good deal of time in places like Germany, America, Brazil, China, and South Africa. Like Avinash, she had lost her brother. But her brother had died in adulthood on the field of battle. He had been a Special Forces soldier in the Spanish Military and had given his life so his fellow men could return home.

Unlike almost every worker in the camp, she was not here for any worldly reason. Like Avinash, she had come to this war zone because she believed that it was the right thing to do. She believed that it was her duty to be here and help her fellow human beings.

Avinash began to appreciate her more for her soul than for her beauty and her abilities. He began to learn of her desire to continue to travel the world. He learned of her dreams. He learned of everything she wished to see before her time of death came.

And the more he got to know her, the more he began to love her…

***

Four months passed since the day that Avinash had first lay eyes on Lia.

One night, Avinash was next to Lia like so many times before. But although they had spent countless hours together, it always felt like a new experience.

The two of them were standing on a balcony on the compound's second floor. From here, all they could see was the hill country's forest. He was dressed in a pair of blue jeans and a black, short-sleeved collared shirt, allowing his powerful figure to show from under his clothing. Lia was covered in a short-sleeved, yellow tunic that went halfway to her knees. Over her legs, she wore a pair of white pants while her long hair hung freely.

The sun had gone over the horizon some time ago, and its last beams of orange and red light were long gone. Stars were slowly beginning to dot the sky, and the full moon was bright.

The two of them looked at the heavens as Lia spoke. "Beautiful night, isn't it?"

From the corner of his eye, Avinash discreetly looked at her. "Yeah...beautiful."

With a quiet, but deep breath she took in the sight as she turned her head to face him. "There's something I've wanted to ask you for some time now."

His eyes met with hers. "Yes?"

"What is it you're always working on?"

"...What?"

"In your room, I've seen the files. You've been working on the drawings for something. Whenever you're not with me, you're working on it."

"Who told you that?"

"Let me think..." Wearing a slight smirk, her gaze looked up in playful thoughtfulness before it came back to him. "Everybody."

Avinash smiled.

"What is it?"

Avinash thought for a moment. "Let me ask you something, Lia: how many patients do we see die every day?"

Her smile disappeared. "I don't keep count."

"Nor do I. Anyone who did would go mad with grief. But I do keep count on how many die because we cannot get to them quickly. It's probably why about half of the patients in this camp die. There is simply not a large enough staff to get to them all. Many of those who

250

die are dying of the simplest wounds. They could easily be saved if a doctor or capable nurse could get to them in time. He took a deep breath. "What I'm working on is something that could drastically cut down the time it takes to treat somebody wounded in the chest area."

Her eyes showed her amazement at his words as she softly spoke. "…Tell me."

"To put it simply, the device allows complications of chest wounds—caused by guns, knives, and almost any other weapon—to be treated easily, quickly, and by anyone with minimal training. The device is equipped with a camera, ultrasound device, pressure differential detector, precise tissue cutting abilities, and robotics. It diagnoses the problem and treats it as well. All the operator needs to know is simple anatomy and how to follow robotic instructions.

"Imagine, Lia, what a device like this would be able to do. Any person with little training could use it. And by cutting the time down on those procedures, many more will walk out of this camp alive."

Seeing the excitement in his eyes, her eyes began to light up.

He looked out at the forest. "And…and if we could get it widely distributed around the globe, it would change the world as we know it. Wounded patients who can't get to a doctor in time could be saved by paramedical personnel. Imagine if every school, mall, and public place had a device like this. How many people would live?"

Lia could not believe what she was hearing. She had imagined that whatever Avinash was working on would be of significance. But she never could have envisioned this. "That's…that's amazing, Avinash. Have you started on a prototype?"

He nodded. "Once it's done, I'll be showing it to Jonathan Daniels. I've spoken to him about it, and he will use his organizations and influence to get it approved once tested."

Lia's hand landed softly on his.

Feeling it, Avinash looked down at her small hand as it rested atop of his own. His eyes drifted back up and locked with Lia's gaze.

"You'll change the world, Avi…more than you already have."
Avinash smiled.

***

The next hour of the night passed in silence. Neither of them really knew what to say next. But they did not want to retire for the night. Everything was so beautiful: the forest, each other's company…everything. As Avinash shared his night with her, half of his mind forgot that he was in a warzone and started to think that he was in Paradise.

Avinash's words finally tore through the silence. "…Why do you do it, Lia?"

Her eyes again met with his. "Do what?"

"What drives you? You could do anything in the world. You're smart, capable, and beautiful. Why come here to this place? What makes you want to help people so much?"

Lia was silent for a while as she kept her eyes with his. And from her gaze, he knew that what she would say next had never been said to another soul in this camp. Slowly, she looked out at the forest and finally spoke with Avinash's gaze still on her. "Five years ago, I was diagnosed with an illness. A rare disease that the doctors could not cure."

Avinash was speechless. It was the last thing he expected to hear. All he could do was digest words and let them echo in every part of his soul. As they did, his heart was drowned in a sudden flood of sorrow. "…What was it?"

"Melanoma. Stage 4."

"…*Stage 4?*"

She slightly nodded. "I was given an experimental treatment. It was based on Dr. Rosenberg's research. They said that if I made it to

252

five years after the treatment, I had a 90% chance of survival." Lia smiled. "It's been five and a half."

Hearing those words, a wave of relief descended upon Avinash.

"When we think about it, none of us know how long we have to live. It could be an hour…it could be a century. But what I do know is how precious life is. I learned a valuable lesson the day I became ill. I learned that I was not living the life I wanted. Fear is what was holding me back. It's what holds most people back from becoming who they were meant to be. From doing what they were created to do." She took a deep breath. "And I now know just how I want to live my life. I want to live every day to the fullest. I wanted to seize every day—to see everything there is to see in the world. To make a difference. To see the world for just how beautiful it really is. And when I meet my Lord in the afterlife, I want to meet Him with a smile and no regrets."

Avinash was silent. As his eyes stayed with hers, he tried to take in everything that she was saying. In all this time he had known her, he could never have imagined this. Of all the people he had met, nobody held a brighter soul than she. Was it because she no longer feared death? Was it because she had learned to live every day as her last? "…What brought you here?"

"My list. Something I wanted to see was here."

"A place?"

She shook her head. "No. A person…"

"I think you may have come to the wrong place."

Lia slightly smiled. "I came to the right place. I'm standing in his gaze."

He was at a loss for words. On the surface, he remained unchanged, but his heart and soul lit up as he heard her words.

"When I heard about what you did, how you found a way to save the lives of the people, I was as impressed as anybody. But then I saw your interview. I saw the way you spoke. I saw the look in your eyes. Even through the glass, I could feel your presence…your spirit. I thought that it was too good to be true. You had the same look as my brother. He was a soldier, and the last time I saw him, he had the same gleam in his eyes. Only, you had it more.

"Then I heard about what you did next. You turned down the riches of the world that were yours for the taking. And in return, you came to this place. You turned down a palace full of gold for a shack full of misery. When I was at the northern camp, I heard about you day and night. Everyone talked about you. By joining this cause, you brought international spotlight to what is going on here, and others are starting to take notice.

"But not only that. You have proven to be the most capable and bravest man at this base. You've taken on more burden than any other person. You've saved more lives and seen more die than anyone else in the time that you've been here. You do the work with honor."

There was a long silence. Listening to her sweet voice speak of him as such, seeing her caring eyes look at him the way they were, Avinash felt taller than Goliath.

Reaching out, he took her hands into his. "I don't know what to say."

"Then don't say anything."

Under the stars and for the first time, they kissed.

CHAPTER 20
BUTTERFLIES

Three mornings later, Lia met him in the camp's grounds an hour before sunrise. The last stars of the night were starting to make their exit, and the moon was already back in hiding. A nice breeze was blowing through the region to welcome everyone into the new day. The last part of the night was peaceful as nothing but the whisper of the soft wind could be heard.

She saw him by the southwest corner of the compound. Leaning against the wall, he had been waiting for her and smiled upon seeing her come into view. Slung across his back was a beige backpack. He was dressed in a pair of rugged jeans and a short-sleeved shirt while she wore cargo pants and a yellow sleeveless top. A headscarf kept her long locks at bay.

A few early birds soared above them and swooped in to pick insects. Aside from them, the only ones to be seen were the several guards. Some watched over the area on the other side of the walls while others patrolled the grounds. Avinash asked other doctors and nurses to cover his and Lia's work for the day. Neither of them had taken a day off in a while, so it was not hard to find somebody willing to help them.

When she was close enough to hear him, Avinash spoke. "Hope you brought plenty of water."

"I did." She reached back and patted the backpack that she wore. It was not nearly as full as Avinash's. "Are you going to tell me what's going on here?"

"I'm going to be helping you with your list."

255

Her eyes suddenly lit up upon hearing that.

"On your list, you wanted to see the most beautiful sight in the world, right?"

She nodded.

"There's a pretty good candidate for that not too far from here."

"You mean...*outside* of the camp?"

"I don't suppose you've ever been in the forest."

"Nobody has."

"How sure are you of that?" He playfully winked at her.

After a long moment, she smiled. "How?"

"It helps to be friends with the guards."

***

Leaving the camp, Lia felt as if she was entering a whole new world. She had been so consumed with her work here, never noticing the beautiful forest that rested in the opposite direction of the city. She had failed to realize that not far from death was life.

The forest began not too far outside of the camp's walls. With each step they took, they went further and further away from everything they had known these past months: the camp, the war, the misery. The deeper they travelled into the forest, the more they left their burdens behind. They forgot the dark days they had seen and all the deaths they had witnessed.

Out here, they were free.

Stepping over fallen logs and branches while making their way between the ancient trees, the two of them embarked on their journey. All around them was ripe and blossoming vegetation. Many of the trees were covered in greenery and surrounded by long vines. Even from their branches, thick patches of vines hung down and almost touched the forest's floor. The entire floor was covered by their thick and endless shade.

Soon, the sun appeared over the horizon. And the longer that their journey lasted, the higher it ascended into the heavens. It sent down its merciless heat onto the world below. However, the two travelers could hardly feel the sun's rays or even noticed it as they made their way. The shade's merciful coolness made it so. The breeze that had been blowing through the camp in the early morning still went through the forest. The leaves quietly rustled in the breeze. Its soft wind kissed Avinash and Lia. But the wind was a welcome relief for the two travelers; it was fresh breath for their muscles and seemed to pour its energy into them.

They could hear the calls of birds as the animals soared from branch to branch. The voices of the hatchlings calling out to their mothers were constantly heard. Small birds plucked out insects from the ground while others picked out their meals from the trees. But the appetites of the larger birds could not be as easily subdued. They captured smaller snakes and critters from the trees and ground before taking them back to their nests.

Bright yellow and orange flowers could be seen everywhere. As the wind blew between the trees, the flora gently swayed with it. Standing proudly, they added color to the otherwise green forest. Patches of flowers went from the base of a tree all the way to the base of the next one. It was almost impossible to avoid stepping on them.

Smaller animals could be seen coming out as the sun continued to climb into the heavens. They poked their heads out of the trees or ground to examine their surroundings before making their way. Several snakes came into sight. Some slithered through the grass while others climbed up trees and wrapped themselves around the branches. A few turned their heads to look at the two travelers and sent out a short hiss. But Avinash knew that they were all harmless. They would go their way while Avinash and Lia went theirs. A handful of times, he saw Lia cast a worried glance, but he tightly squeezed her hand in reassurance.

It was so peaceful here.

Outside of nature's reassuring voice, the only thing that could be heard were the footsteps of Avinash and his companion. As they moved along, the two of them pointed out sights to one another: beautiful flowers, motherly animals caring for their young, birds gracefully soaring through the air.

There was no path here. Out in this forest, there was no sign of man's contamination of nature's poetry. There was simply harmony, balance, and beauty. The longer they were out here, the more they began to lose themselves to it. The happiness on their faces and in their hearts continued to climb higher along with the sun.

Whenever they stopped for a quick break, the two of them sat with their backs against the moss-covered tree trunks. They soaked in the beautiful sights all around them. Next to one another, the two of them ate whatever snacks Avinash had prepared.

On one occasion, Avinash pulled out a container full of *samosas*. The small fried pastries were stuffed and nearly bursting from potatoes and peas found inside. He opened the steel container, and their aroma filled into the air. Looking at the pastries, both of their mouths began to water as they thought of the delicious and fulfilling taste that each pastry held. Avinash gave her one before taking one out for himself. Smiling, they clinked their snacks together before digging in. But as they took their bites, Avinash and Lia tasted anything but perfection.

The pastries were completely soggy.

Avinash immediately spit his out, and Lia swallowed it whole without taking another bite. Realizing his error, he slowly looked over at her with a sheepish smile. "I now know why you're supposed to let them cool off before putting them in a sealed container."

She laughed.

258

Twice, they crossed a small creak. It was not very large, but a few fish could be seen traveling along with the current. Avinash stepped across it with ease and without touching the water before making sure that Lia could hop across it. Taking a step back, she leapt across, and her feet landed on the other side. But just as she landed, she almost lost her footing and fell into the creek. She let out a quick shriek as she fell backwards, but Avinash instinctively caught her forearm.

"Got'cha!" He pulled her to him.

As she suddenly came upon him, Lia instinctively grabbed ahold of him and stayed like that for several moments before she realized that she was safe. Her eyes looked up at his with slight embarrassment. "I don't think me falling in the creek was how you envisioned this trip."

His gaze stayed with hers. "Not in the slightest...but I'm not complaining."

At the second crossing, the stream was much larger and measured nearly three feet deep and twenty-five feet across. Stopping at its bank, Avinash looked down and saw several small orange fish swimming along with the current. His gaze then went to his companion and saw Lia contemplating how to cross it without getting wet. A slight smile came onto his face.

Without thinking, he reached down and effortlessly scooped her up into his arms. Before she even realized what was happening, he waded into the stream, carrying her with ease. Her joyous laughter cut into the air as her arms clasped tightly around his shoulders. The water crashed against his powerful legs, but it did not bother him in the least. Feeling her embrace and hearing her laughter, he looked down at her blissful face and saw the loving gleam in her eyes. It was another beautiful moment that he would take with him to his grave.

The three times that they came to fallen trees they could not go around, Avinash stepped onto the trees before turning back

259

around. Reaching down, he helped pull her over the trees before joining her on the other side. She seemed as light as a feather in his strong arms, and there was no hint of strain on his face as he did so.

The third time they did this, she made a lighthearted comment about it. "Was the purpose of this trip to make me feel bad for being shorter than you?"

He let out a quick laugh. "No…but it's starting to seem that way, isn't it?"

"Hopefully the endgame is all worth it."

"Trust me, it is."

Lia did not know how long they had journeyed. She could not believe it when she saw the sun nearing its peak. It felt like mere minutes since they had started. If there was ever a day she wished not to end, this was it. The joy she felt with Avinash was nothing she had ever experienced before.

Finally, Avinash came to a halt. In front of him was a thick wall of vines that were hanging from a high branch. He slowly turned to look at Lia, and their eyes met. She thought that she could faintly hear a waterfall nearby but was not sure. He slyly smiled at her and she returned the gesture.

His eyes were bursting with excitement. "Are you ready?"

She nodded.

Pushing the vines aside, he grabbed a hold of Lia's hand before leading her through.

***

Lia's breath was taken away.

As she witnessed the sight that lay before her, her free hand came to her heart as her eyes widened. For a moment, her mind was certain that this was all a dream. Her heart was flooded with awe, and she was paralyzed by it.

The warm sun shined down at the entire scene. Not far away, at the bottom of the hill, was a lake. Its cerulean waters were crystal clear. Even from where they stood, Lia could see the bottom of the lake's cool waters. She could even make out the orange and yellow fish that were swimming in it. The sun's rays beautifully reflected off of the water. From the lake, several creeks and streams ran into the forest in different directions. And about forty feet above the lake was a waterfall whose mix of periwinkle blue and white waters fell right into the lake. The waterfall's steady stream fell off of the low cliff and rolled atop of the rocky ridge before peacefully splashing into the lake below. Its waters were just as clear and beautiful as the lakes. But it seemed too quiet to be a real waterfall as the falling water hardly made a sound as it mixed with the lake. As it splashed into the lake, a white mist seemed to rise up.

But that was not what had taken her breath away at first sight. It was what surrounded them. The creatures that were hovering all around the lake as if they were dancing to the waterfall's soft tune.

Butterflies.

Seemingly hundreds if not thousands of them were everywhere. Orange. Yellow. Royal blue. Bright red. Chartreuse green. They were dancing all around her. Some were fluttering only inches away from her eyes unthreatened by the presence of a stranger. If she listened closely enough, she could hear the soft fluttering of their wings. She could see the patterns on their wings in the most intricate detail. They were all unique. Nature had not created a single one the same.

She was completely speechless as she watched it all with a child's heart. At the edges of the lake and streams were flowers of all colors. They were even more beautiful than the ones found throughout the forest. Every shade of the rainbow could be seen in the flora from red to yellow to violet. They were all so bright and colorful that Lia first thought them to be painted. But they were truly a gift of nature. They gently swayed with the light breeze that blew through this paradise. Many of the butterflies that were not in the air were resting upon the colorful vegetation.

Lia felt Avinash's grip around her hand gently tighten as he led her down to the edge of the lake below. She followed as her gaze continued to wander all around her. Within a few steps, they left the shade of the trees and were under the sun's rays once again. But here, the sun's rays were not hot. They were perfect.

Just like this place was.

The closer she came to the lake, the more butterflies surrounded her. She could not believe how close they were coming to her. It was as if they were studying this newcomer. They were as amazed with her as she was with them. Never in all her travels had she seen the creatures come so close to humans.

Avinash stopped when they were at the edge of the lake. If Lia had stretched out her foot, her toes would have felt the cool waters. But she did not wish to disturb its perfection. Turning around, Avinash faced her as his gaze locked with hers. The two of them were smiling. Hers was of utter disbelief while his was of happiness.

He came behind her and his hand softly went onto her forearm. Gently, he guided her to stretch out her arm while keeping her hand open at eye level. She willingly complied and kept her gaze on her open palm. Within a matter of moments, an orange and black butterfly lightly landed on her hand. She could hardly feel its weight and could barely feel its touch. But there it was, right in the palm of her hand.

The butterfly's eyes were locked with hers. Lia did not dare move a muscle in her hand or arm. At that moment, her heart went to the moon and back with happiness. She slowly looked back at Avinash, eyes wide open as part of her thought this to be a hallucination. He nodded reassuring her that this was in fact happening before Lia looked back at the beautiful creature that she

262

held. Avinash's hand stayed on her arm to hold it steady. But slowly, he reeled her arm back in so that her hand came closer to her eyes. When he stopped, the butterfly was only inches away from her face. Her smile was larger than it had ever been before. If it was not for Avinash holding her arm steady, she would have been trembling with excitement.

She did not know how long the butterfly stayed on her hand. It may have been nearly a minute. But at last, the creature flew off to rejoin its comrades in the air all around the lake. Lia was motionless as she watched it take off and leave her. Her heart was still racing, and her mind was still trying to take in everything.

Slowly, she turned around to face Avinash once again. His hand stayed on her arm as their gazes met. After a long moment, he broke the silence.

"Quite a place, isn't it?"

Her smile gave him his answer. She leaned in and lightly kissed him on the cheek.

"Would you call it the most beautiful sight in the world?" Avinash asked.

"…Wouldn't you?"

He slightly shook his head. "No…but what I'm looking at right now *is*."

***

They journeyed back to the camp well after the sun's descent had begun. They stayed in their secret paradise for some time, but it only felt like mere moments. By the time they could see the camp, the sun was halfway finished with its descent. The day had been filled with smiles, overflowing with laughter, and ripe with love.

Lia became numb to the fatigue of the journey. Just one moment in that secluded dreamland took all of the weariness away from her. As for Avinash, seeing her so elated gave him joy. Her laughter and smile was worth it all.

The hike back was a quiet one. There was nothing that needed to be said. Lia tried to digest everything she had seen and done at the lake. Although she had left that paradise behind, her heart was still soaking it all in.

However, this was indeed reality.

She followed Avinash on their way back, not knowing the way herself. Half the time she was only two steps behind him. The other half, they travelled hand-in-hand. They did not need to say a thing for their hearts did all the talking. The feeling of peace stayed over them the entire way back.

But that feeling immediately disappeared when they saw the camp.

The first thing they saw was smoke. The kind of smoke that could only be formed by bombs. Black smog rose from various parts of the grounds. Countless uniformed guards surrounded the compound's western wing. They were lined up fifty yards away from the wall. Weapons raised, they had the wing completely surrounded. And on the roof of the western wing, Avinash and Lia saw one thing perched at the top of the highest point.

The rebels' black flag.

CHAPTER 21
HERO

The cool breeze was gone. The air was still. The sun's rays were once again unbearably hot. They ran down to the bottom of the hill, and within minutes, they were at the camp's walls. The guard's recognized them and let them through. Avinash kept his eyes on the rebel flag, hoping and praying that this was all just a nightmare.

The closer Avinash came to the perimeter, the more his mind registered the situation. His heart began to race faster as sweat began to pour down his face. None of the guards who had their rifles aimed at the west wing paid the two newcomers any attention. They all kept their gazes glued onto the compound's west wing waiting for any sign of movement. Reaching the perimeter, Avinash quickly found the head guard. The man was speaking into his radio but immediately stopped when he saw the duo come up from behind him.

"Zach!" Avinash's voice showed his fatigue as he tried to catch his breath.

The British man breathed a sigh of relief as he put his radio back onto his belt. "Dr. Singh…" He looked over at the nurse. "Lia…thank God you were both gone."

Avinash could see something in Zach's eyes. "What's happening?"

"The rebels…they've taken control of the western wing."

There was a silence between the trio. Before asking that question, Avinash's knew that Zach would say those words, but hearing them stabbed a dagger through his heart. "…How?"

"Two hours after sunrise, there was an attack on the eastern and northern walls. Nearly seventy-five rebels in all were making a move, and I sent all available units there. We quickly took care of them without taking any casualties on our side." Zach sadly shook his head as his gaze fell to Avinash's feet. "But it was a distraction. While we fought them off, around thirty rebels came over the western wall. There were only a handful of guards left at that position. There was a gunfight. Every guard was killed or wounded along with majority of the rebels. But at least six made it inside the compound armed with automatic rifles and machetes. They took hostages—"

"How many?" Avinash kept his unwavering eyes on the captain.

Zach looked back up at the doctor. "...Including the wounded...hundreds. After taking control of the western part of the compound, they said that if we did not remove all guards from the western part of the building, they'd kill the hostages. You know these animals, Dr. Singh—you've seen what they are capable of doing. I had no choice at the moment but to comply. And once I complied, they held up their agreement and let most of the hostages go. They also have five aid workers holed up in one of the large operating rooms."

"Do you know which workers?"

He nodded "Huang, Sikhandar, Jeremy, Patrick...and Mirza."

Avinash's eyes widened. Hearing the name of his close friend, a heavy burden fell upon his heart. The dagger that stabbed his heart moments ago was driven straight through it. The thought of Mirza at the hands of those animals was unbearable. He felt Lia's hand grab a tight hold of his. "...Mirza?"

Zach nodded.

"But—but the wounded refugees? They're still coming in. Are they still being treated?"

Again, Zach nodded. "We have the eastern part along with most of the southern and northern wings of the compound still operating at full capacity. I have guards posted in all the hallways leading into the western wing. They're doing all they can with what they have. But without the western part of the compound, everything is limited."

"But you're going to move in, aren't you? What's the plan?"

"As of right now, it's in development."

"So you don't have one."

"They've taken out all of our cameras. We don't know what the situation right now. If we move in, we risk the lives of all the hostages. Our priority is to get the cameras back up; then we'll assess the situation and make a move." Zach took a deep breath as he put his hand on Avinash's strong shoulder. "We're doing what we can, Dr. Singh."

"What—what do they want?"

Zach paused for a long moment as he stared directly into Avinash's eyes. "…You."

***

"…Me?"

Zach nodded. "Of everyone here, you offer the most leverage as a hostage. They attacked to capture you. That's why they went directly into the west wing—because they thought you would be there like always."

Lia and Avinash simply stared at the captain as they registered his words.

"When they took your operating room hostage, they realized that you were not there and called their audible. They contacted us by radio and demanded that we turn you over to them in exchange for the rest of their hostages. They also had us give them a phone that could take and make long-distance calls."

Avinash was silent for a long time, figuring out what the entire situation was. "…They want to use me to get to Jonathan Daniels…to get him to shut down all of his facilities here. If they did that…" He glanced over at Lia and then back at Zach. "…then it would be a huge moral victory for them. It would show everybody in the nation that nobody from outside could truly aid them. And…it would make their leader go even more mad with power."

Zach solemnly nodded.

Lia's looked at Avinash, but his gaze stayed fixed on the captain. His mind was still trying to process it all, but his heart could see everything clearly. It knew that Avinash could not let his friends get slaughtered like animals. It knew that there was but one option here. "There's no choice here, Zach. You need to do a trade. Use me to get them out."

"That's not an option. We can't give into their demands. They might just kill them all anyways—"

"You're not looking at things clearly. One life for five is what this is all about."

"I can assure you, I *am* assessing the situation clearly. It's not just one life for five. If they kill the hostages, it'll be a disaster. But if they kill you, it will be an international tragedy. Your death may cause international pressure to close down this entire operation."

"This isn't about politics…this is about human lives. Our *friends'* lives. I'm not going to let other people die for me. I *won't* stand by and let others fight *my* battles!"

The captain's voice remained calm. "This is not a debate. It's my call, and I've made it."

Avinash looked defiantly into Zach's eyes for several long moments, but said nothing. The air around the two of them was tense. All the guards and Lia felt like the situation would explode.

But nothing happened.

268

Without another word, Avinash's gaze tore away from the captain. He took Lia by her hand and walked away from the perimeter without looking back at it.

Avinash and Lia stopped moving when he was far enough away from all the guards to be well out of earshot. He looked up at the black flag of the rebels and watched as it hung in the windless air. The image of his comrades being captive to that flag made Avinash's heart burn with a fiery rage. And the thought of being powerless while they were slaughtered only added fuel to the fire.

Hearing Lia's voice, he looked down at her.

"Avi…"

He could feel her hand trembling.

"I can't believe this is happening."

Looking right into her eyes, he took a deep breath as he played out some scenarios in his mind. There was a long silence as he was lost in his thoughts. He closed his eyes, still holding her soft hand. Neither of the two had ever feared their own deaths since stepping foot in this camp, but the thought of losing those close to them was unbearable.

Lia was silent. She could sense his mind at work. It was the same sense she always got when working alongside him in the operating room. After what felt like minutes, he opened his eyes.

"I need to get in touch with Jonathan Daniels."

"…What?"

"Do you trust me?"

Through the gleam in his eyes, Lia knew what he was thinking. And the thought of that made her heart go mad with fear. "Y—you can't, Avinash. Zach and his men will handle this."

"By the time they have a strategy, the rebels will have killed at least two of the prisoners. Enough have died already at the hands of these savages…and I'll lay down my life before I let any of our friends get killed."

"But you're no soldier—you're not trained—"

"Lia, heart is everything." He slightly smiled as his hand came onto her soft cheek. "You know that better than most."

"But...how?"

He took a deep breath. "The same way General Khau beat the Mongols."

***

"You think this will work?"

Hearing Jonathan Daniels' voice come out of the phone's speaker, Avinash confidently nodded. "I can promise you that my part will get all the hostages out...after that it will be up to Zach and his men."

Jonathan was silent for a long time. Avinash looked up at Lia as they waited for Jonathan's authoritative voice to respond. The two of them were still standing out of earshot from the perimeter of guards. Avinash held the phone between Lia and himself. Although his voice did not show it, the doctor's eyes were full of anxiety.

Jonathan's voice was finally heard. *"Lia, are you there?"*

"I'm here."

"Do you endorse Avinash's plan?"

There was no hesitation in her voice. "I do."

"I only know as much as Zach is telling me about the situation. And from what I know...this may be our best option to get the hostages out...but the price we would pay if the plan goes wrong will be high."

Avinash's voice was as bold as ever. "If that's what the price of courage is, then it's the price I'm willing to pay."

"I'm not doubting your courage, Avinash. What I'm saying is that it's risky. There are countless things that could go wrong."

"But they won't."

"How do you know?"

270

"...I have faith."

After a long moment, Jonathan's smile was heard in his voice. *"A man I once knew spoke like that—it was my brother...you remind me of him. And if you're willing to risk your life in the name of courage, then who am I to stop you?"*

"Then do I have your support?"

"...You do. Get Zach on the line. I'll tell him what we discussed."

***

The compound's security room was in the middle of the hospital. It was well lit with only two doors leading in or out, and they were both thick, metallic doors that could only be opened with a key and security code. Without those, it would take very sophisticated firepower to blast them without bringing down the entire building. Inside, there were countless screens and computers. Another door, as strong as the other two, led to the weapons armory. Some large screens were lined up along the wall and showed live feed from all the security cameras. However, all the screens that were connected to the cameras in the west wing were blacked out.

There were numerous desks and most of them were occupied as many men were working on rerouting the servers to get the cameras back online. The rebels were better equipped than they had thought. Other security personnel were on the phones and radios trying to coordinate efforts to get multiple extraction plans in place.

Avinash was all prepped to go in. He was wearing the same clothing he had worn all day, except for one difference. A hidden camera had been placed on his collar's button. It was small enough to be impossible for the naked eye to detect. As one guard made sure that it was in place, another checked the screen on a nearby laptop to make sure that they were receiving its live feed clearly. He had Avinash walk in a circle to ensure that the feed was coming in without

271

a delay. As he sat at his desk, the guard quickly hit a few buttons to guarantee the connection would not be lost.

The guard next to Avinash spoke in a normal voice. "Testing."

After a half-second, the guard's voice came out of the laptop. *"Testing."*

The guard at the computer nodded as he looked back at Zach. "Video feed is live, and voice feed has a half-second delay. We're good to go, sir."

"Alright." Zach looked at Avinash as he stood beside him. "Want me to go over the plan again?"

"I got it," Avinash calmly replied.

"Whatever you do, stick to the plan. We'll be getting a live feed. Once the rebels have you, they'll try to negotiate with Jonathan. He'll stall them as much as he can. Do whatever they ask of you. All we need you to do is let the camera do a sweep of the room so we know all of the rebels' positions. Once we know the room's layout, we'll get in position utilizing the best extraction plan that fits the situation. Within a few minutes, we'll move in."

"I said I got it."

"Just making sure." Zach glanced at the large screens that were still blacked out. "Last chance to turn around. Nobody will think any less of you."

Avinash did not answer as he kept the image of the black flag in his mind's eye.

"You'll be leaving soon." Zach turned around and went over to the guard on the laptop. "Get in contact with the rebels. Tell them we're handing over Dr. Singh if they release the hostages."

Sensing somebody come from his left, Avinash looked and saw Lia approaching. His gaze locked with hers as she stopped right in front of him. "…Avi…"

He was silent.

"…You don't have to do this."

272

"Yes, I do."

"Zach...he'll figure out a way to get them out."

"It's not about getting them out, Lia. You know that."

As she looked into his eyes, she could see his thoughts. She knew what he was going in to do. She had known even before he called Jonathan. And it was not what he told Jonathan or Zach. It was anything but their plan. A few tears came into her eyes, but she held them back.

His hand went to her soft cheek. "It's about showing these fiends what one good man can do...it's about standing up against evil."

Avinash heard Zach's voice. "It's time. We got word back from the rebels."

"What did they say?" Avinash asked.

"We'll be leaving you in Hall E. They'll be sending out a rebel to bring you in. When you are halfway to the room, they'll release all five prisoners through exit B."

Avinash simply nodded without showing any fear in his eyes. He looked back at the woman standing before him.

Lia's hand came onto his shoulder. "You'll come back, won't you?"

Leaning in, he kissed her on the forehead. "I will always be with you. One way or another."

***

The room was tense. Nobody spoke. Nobody made a sound. The live video from Avinash's camera was playing in the security room, and everybody's eyes were glued to it, including Zach's. He, along with everyone else in the room, watched the live footage as Avinash was roughly taken down the corridor by the armed rebel.

"We have all five hostages."

Hearing his radio go off, Zach looked away from the screen and grabbed his radio. Pressing a button, he spoke into it. "Confirm the last message."

A guard's voice came through the radio. *"Sir, we have all five hostages."*

Zach's tone showed his excitement. "How are they?"

"Rattled, but unhurt. We're moving them safely away from the west wing as we speak."

"Get them examined just in case."

"Yes, sir."

"Keep me posted." Zach quickly put the radio back on his belt. His eyes looked back at the screen. But his eyes suddenly widened.

Where the live footage had been, there was now static.

For several moments, he could not move. He could not blink. He could not speak. All he could do was stare at the static and feel a heavy burden suddenly crush his heart as it began to beat faster and faster. Horror caused his face to lose all color. His eyes looked up at every other screen that had been feeding the live footage.

They were all the same: static.

The faces of every guard in the room were horror-struck. None of them uttered a word as they exchanged glances and stared at the blank screens in terror. Fear gripped each and every one of their hearts. Looking at the guard who had been responsible for the footage, Zach saw that the man's expression mirrored his own. Zach's hand grabbed the guard's shoulder and tightly squeezed it. "What! Happened!?"

The guard stripped his gaze from the screen and looked at his commander. "We…we…lost our feed."

"How?"

"The connections—they—they're all working. Nothing's interfering with it. But…but it seems that…" The guard looked at the

274

static once more and then back at his commanding officer. "That Dr. Singh somehow got rid of the camera himself."

"What the hell!" Zach's rage-filled face turned red. He whirled his head around and looked at Lia. As his infuriated gaze came upon her, he could see that she was not surprised.

Her face was as calm as it had been when Avinash left.

"You..." He took a step towards her. "*You* knew he would do this?"

Her eyes gave him his answer.

"Do you know what you've done!" His roar echoed through the room and down the corridor. He powerfully smashed his fist onto the table.

Again, she was silent and un-rattled. Her composed eyes stayed on the captain.

"You've sent him to his death!"

With a deep breath, she slightly shook her head. "No...I've sent them to theirs."

***

Avinash was roughly shoved onto an empty operating table. Landing on the bloodied table, some of the blood soaked into his clothing, but he ignored it. The whole way here, the rebel had not said a word. All he did was sadistically smile at his new captive.

Without any hint of fear, Avinash looked around the room. This was the same place where he performed thousands of operations. Here, he had saved many of lives and watched countless die. But for the first time, there was not a single patient here. The room was silent—it was an eerie silence. The kind that was the calm before the storm.

The sun was almost at the horizon, and its evening rays came in through the high windows. There was blood everywhere, and its foul stench filled the room. Avinash did not notice it. But that was not the dominant smell in the room. The most prevalent odor was something else.

It was the smell of corpses.

When the rebels came in here, they immediately took everyone captive and shut everything down, including the medical procedures and surgeries. Several wounded had been in the middle of surgery and countless others were about to die if they were not treated. However, the rebels forced all the workers into one corner, leaving the helpless to die.

And now, twenty corpses lay around the room. Three were men. Seven were women. Ten were children. Their motionless corpses were scattered throughout the room. Many of their eyes were open and showed the pain consuming them during their last breath. Their expressions showed that even in their last moments, they were begging for any mercy and compassion that they could find.

But they received none.

However, the odor of the dead and the sight of their corpses did not bother any of the rebels. Each of them had shot down so many that they hardly noticed. However, Avinash took it all in. He could have blocked it out. He had done it many times in this very room, but he did not want to. He wanted to take it all in. He *needed* to take it all in.

It would fuel the fire of what he came to do.

Two rebels stood only a few feet away from him. Their AK47s were loosely aimed at him as they studied their prisoner. Another one was standing atop two tables that were stacked upon each other and looked out the window. His eyes stayed on the perimeter of guards on the grounds. A fourth rebel was at the door. But the other two were at another table. One of those was the group's leader. Avinash was sure of it.

276

The two of them stood next to the phone equipment they had forced security to bring to them. No doubt, they were waiting to hear back from Jonathan Daniels.

Avinash took a deep breath. The leader was a similar age to Avinash. But the rest of these men were in their early twenties. How could they have sold their lives to the devil? Had they been so brainwashed?

Looking back up, Avinash saw the leader come towards him until he was standing directly before him. He wore a wicked smile on his face as he taunted his prisoner. It was the same devilish look the other guard had worn while leading Avinash down here. The leader spoke in his best English. "Doctar Aveenash Singh...you no look so beeg in pason."

Avinash was silent.

"Tha mightee docta is now at my macy...*my* macy!" His devilish smirk grew. "Even thees man is not safe from our flag's powa."

The prisoner's eyes held no fear. In fact, all they showed was the opposite of terror. "Do you think I came here on your terms?"

The leader was silent.

"I came here for *one* simple reason."

"...Wha?"

"Because...I am tired. I am sick and tired." Without warning, Avinash rose to his feet.

All the guards looked at him, but none of them did a thing. Until now, they failed to realize just how big and powerful their prisoner was. As he stood up straight, he towered above them all. His shadow fell onto the leader. And as they looked into his eyes, they could do nothing but stare in awe at the gleam that was in his gaze.

"I am tired of seeing the innocent die. I have seen too many die by your hands. I have seen too many die because of demented and evil people like you. And I am *tired* of picking up the things you break and trying to put them back together."

As he spoke, Avinash could see all the dead. From the first child he had not been able to save to all the corpses that now surrounded him, every face flashed before his eyes. Again, he saw the image of life leaving their eyes. He saw the faces of all the lives these rebels had destroyed in their sadistic quest. And then he pictured the cruel face of the rebel leader. He saw the devilish smiling faces of the rebels as they shot into crowds of women and children. He felt all the heartbreak of their deaths. He felt all the rage that he had built up since coming here. The dam was now breaking. It would no longer contain the flood. All his rage was about to be released.

"But now...*now* I want to see something else."

Without thinking, the leader took a step back.

"Now, there is only one I want to see die." Suddenly, Avinash's face became filled with a fury none of them had ever seen. "And it's you!"

Before any of them could react, Avinash powerfully kicked the leader in the chest, sending him sprawling. As he fell on his back several feet away, the wind was knocked out of him. The guard next to the prisoner instinctively tried to shoot at Avinash from point-blank-range, but the lion grabbed the gun's barrel before crashing his free elbow into the man's face. He followed through by grabbing the rebel by the collar and slinging him headfirst onto the ground.

Swiftly turning around, Avinash still held the AK47 by its barrel. Using it like a club, he swung it at the other guard who had been standing over him. The butt of the gun smashed against the rebel's skull, sounding off a loud crack. The rebel collapsed, and his rifle went skidding across the floor.

It all happened within a matter of moments. Pulling the gun back to his body, Avinash moved with lightning speed as he flipped it around so his finger was on the trigger. The other three rebels realized what was happening. Never before had a lone man stood against this pack of hyenas. As their shock and utter surprise left them, they all frantically tried to aim their weapons at him.

But they did not move quickly enough.

Avinash took aim and pulled the trigger. There was no hesitation in his movements. There was no mercy in his eyes. Today, he possessed the eyes of Khau and the spirit of Veeresh.

Today, he was a lion!

Before the rebel at the door had a chance to defend himself, his chest was riddled with bullets. His back crashed against the wall as he let out the roar of a dying hyena. He slumped onto the ground, leaving a trail of blood behind him. By the time he was halfway to the ground, he could do nothing but feel life slowly leave him.

The guard by the phone fired his rifle at Avinash. But Avinash saw it coming and sidestepped the bullets before the rebel pulled the trigger. The stream of bullets ran inches away from Avinash's head. A second slower, and he would have been killed. Instead, they buried themselves into the wall behind him.

But he did not slow down.

Pulling his trigger, a cascade of his bullets violently injected themselves into the rebel's torso and stomach. Some bullets stopped inside of him while others burst out of his back. The wounded man violently bellowed in pain as the gun dropped from his hands and he collapsed. Falling onto his side, he cried out for mercy as blood seeped out of his wounds. Within a minute, he would be unable to yell. In another, he would bleed out.

The guard by the window leapt off of the bench and fired at Avinash. The doctor dove behind a table as bullets rapidly flew by him. Rising up on a knee, he fired while taking aim of his target. He let out the roar of an angered lion. His snarl echoed through the room and could he heard down the corridor.

The man fled and dodged the first wave of bullets. But he could not outrun the impending doom. By the time he had taken ten steps, the last of Avinash's bullets buried themselves in his back. The man screamed like any hyena would as his blood filled his lungs and flooded out of his wounds. He staggered a few steps before collapsing onto his knees and then falling onto his chest as life was stripped from him.

Avinash tossed his empty AK47 onto the ground. He swiftly turned around as one of the guards he had knocked away came at him with a machete. The man was only two steps from Avinash. But the lion still showed no fear. His eyes held nothing but courage. His eyes showed that he had come here to emerge victorious or meet his death with open arms.

Sidestepping the machete as it came down, Avinash violently buried his knee into the man's stomach. The rebel let out a grown of pain as he was knocked back. Avinash stepped up and gave him a powerful blow to the face. He followed through by crashing his elbow across the man's jaw. While the rebel's head was still spinning, Avinash's strong fist again crashed into the man's face with a roar, completely breaking his nose and cracking his skull. With each blow, the rebel spit out blood. And with each blow, Avinash struck harder and harder.

A few feet away, the leader was back on his feet and pulled out his pistol. He aimed it at Avinash, and his finger came upon the trigger before rapidly pulling it several times.

Seeing what was happening, Avinash grabbed the rebel by the collar and threw him into the line of fire. As the bullets buried themselves into the rebel's back, his back curved inward as his eyes rolled up towards the ceiling. With the cry of a dying hyena, he stumbled a couple of steps before taking his final breath.

Avinash saw the other remaining rebel rise to his feet as well. The lion dove to the right in an effort to dodge the stream of bullets.

As he moved, two bounced off the ground next to him. Two more barely missed his head.

But his luck did not last.

The last bullet painfully cut into his left side. The bullet struck one of his ribs and lodged itself inside his body. The sharp, burning pain was nothing like he had ever felt before. His body recoiled in pain. However, he did not cry out, and his courageous eyes did not change.

Rising to his feet, he saw the leader cast aside his empty pistol as the other rebel charged towards Avinash. He threw several blows, but Avinash knocked them all away. As the rebel sent another fist, Avinash caught it and twisted the man's arm. The rebel let out a scream of pain. But before Avinash could do anything else, the leader came at him from his right.

He powerfully kicked Avinash's knee, knocking his right leg out from under him. Before Avinash knew it, he was on his knees with his foes on either side of him. They mercilessly beat down on him as he did the best he could to defend himself. Their blows beat against his head. Their fists pounded his neck and chest. Their boots hit his torso. He could feel blood continue to seep out of his bullet wound, and it felt like it was on fire. Streams of blood ran down his face and body.

But he would not give in.

Seeing his opening, Avinash shoved the leader away. He grabbed the other rebel's incoming fist before coming onto his feet and stepping up. Still holding his foe, he shoved him several feet until the rebel's back crashed against a bed next to a cart full of medical equipment. Avinash powerfully cross-faced the rebel with his fist, momentarily stunning his foe. He took advantage of his chance and grabbed a long scalpel off of the cart. Without hesitating, he drove the blade right into the rebel's neck. Blood spewed out of the wound, some of it spraying Avinash as well. But he ignored it as he roughly shoved the dying man to the ground.

The leader stood only ten feet away from Avinash. The lion and the hyena looked at one another. Now, without his men and without his guns, the hyena's true colors showed in his eyes. Avinash had showed the leader that he was nothing but a hyena acting out the charade of a wolf.

As the leader looked at the bloodied and beaten standing tall lion before him, all he felt was fear. However, all Avinash felt was courage. He knew that he would pass out from his injuries at any moment. He could see his tunneling vision starting to blur. Soon, color would leave his face. But if he was to die, he would take this last hyena with him.

With a roar, Avinash charged.

CHAPTER 22
PEACE

The first thing Avinash heard was Lia's voice. He could not make out her words but thought it was a prayer. Or maybe it was a poem. The one thing he knew for certain was that it was her angelic voice.

Everything was black. Even with all his strength, he could not open his eyes or move a muscle, and his head was spinning. However, just hearing her voice brought peace to him and made all of his fears disappear. He was not sure how long he stayed like this. He did not know for how much time he laid there. There was no sense of the passing of time. But when feeling returned to Avinash, he felt numbness surrounding his bullet wound. The places where his skin had been cut open were flooded with soreness while his bruised knuckles and hands were difficult to move.

When he finally did wake up, she was the first face he saw. His vision was focused towards Lia, leaving everything else shrouded in darkness. For a minute, he thought that this was the afterlife. His mind was still coming back into the world of the living and did not recognize her at first sight. Instead, he thought he was staring at the face of an angel.

"…Avi?"

Slowly coming to his senses, he weakly smiled. He could feel her hand on his and could see the tears that filled her eyes as she saw him finally beginning to wake up.

Avinash spoke as best he could. But his words were broken and barely audible. "…If this is heaven…then this…is not such a bad place…"

"You're not there yet, buddy."

Hearing the familiar voice and feeling a hand rest on his opposite shoulder, Avinash slowly turned his head, and his gaze reluctantly left Lia. All the blackness was now slowly starting to disappear, and he realized that he was in one of the patient rooms. The darkness was gone by the time he fully turned his head and saw Mirza.

"You had us worried, pal," Mirza said with a caring smile.

"You know me...always the drama king." He looked back over at Lia with his hand still in hers. "Hope it wasn't too bad a scare."

Lia continued to smile as she wiped a couple of tears away. "I knew from before I met you that you were a hero, Avi. But what you did—the way you walked into the fire knowing that death was all but certain, it's...it showed me again who you are."

Avinash smiled without saying anything. He did not know what he could say. The way that Lia was looking at him right now was too perfect.

But after a long moment, the silence was broken.

"How does it feel, Avi?" Mirza asked.

"Truth be told, I wasn't sure that I'd make it," Avinash said. He took a deep breath almost afraid to ask the next question. "...What happened? Last thing I knew, I was charging the rebel's leader...he..." Avinash looked at the ceiling. "...and then everything went black."

"You were saved," Mirza said.

Avinash's eyes came onto his friend. "By who?"

"Turns out the room was not empty. There was a boy and a girl hiding in the corner. When the rebels attacked, they hid there, and were there when you came. They're the ones who saw the whole thing. And when you passed out, they came to your rescue. They applied pressure to your wound to stop the bleeding until Zach and his men barged in. They…they saved your life Avi."

Avinash was silent.

"You want to know the poetic side of all this?"

He nodded.

"The day before, you saved their mother's life. She had come in with a gunshot wound, and you treated her. The two children saw how you stopped their mother's bleeding with your hands, and they did the same thing. It was crude, but they were able to do enough to keep you alive until help arrived."

For a moment, Avinash thought that his friend was lying. It sounded too good to be true. But as he heard the mention of the mother, the face of a woman who had been brought by her son and daughter came to his mind. He remembered seeing her wheeled in with a bullet wound similar to his. He remembered seeing life return to her eyes as he did what he could to prevent her children from become orphans.

"Amazing, isn't it?" Mirza asked.

"…Yeah."

Lia spoke again. "They've been waiting to see you."

He looked over at her with excitement flooding his voice. "They're still here?"

"Yes. They're right outside."

***

Avinash stared at the faces of his saviors. The girl was no older than eight. The boy was twelve. They were both blue-eyed with brown hair. Their normally dirty skin was clean today. Here at the camp, they both received decent clothes and showers. In their eyes, Avinash could see so much life. He witnessed unlimited potential.

Behind them was their mother. She stood on her own two feet now having recovered from her injuries. Also having received a fresh set of clothes, her hands rested on either child's shoulder as she looked down at her savior.

Lia and Mirza stood on either side of the family. There was a long silence as Avinash looked at the brother and sister. He could not imagine innocent faces like these had been able to get their hand drenched with blood in an effort to save his life, and he could hardly imagine that they had witnessed the entire battle without becoming too traumatized.

Avinash smiled at his rescuers as he spoke to their mother. "You have beautiful children."

"They are a blessing."

"I can only imagine." He looked at the boy. Reaching out, he took the boy's hand into his and spoke in the native language. "…Thank you. All of you. What you did for me—it's something that I can never repay you for…it's something that many would not have done."

The mother was the one to respond in her sweet voice. "No, doctor, thank you. Thank you for reuniting me with my children. Thank you for bringing us hope. You have shown my children and my people what it means to be human."

"Everything I've done, I've done only through the grace of God. Today, I've been reminded again of why I use my God-given gifts for the betterment of all." He looked at the face of the son and then the daughter. "I remember why I keep fighting to make the world a better place. It's so that children always have a bright ray of hope to hold on to. It's so that I can hopefully remind people what our role is as men and women: to make the world a better place."

There was silence as the girl and boy shyly smiled at him. Holding onto the boy's hand, Avinash could feel joy radiating off of

286

the boy. It was the joy that any soul received after seeing the fruits of their honest labors.

The mother spoke. "Do you know what my son said to me? He said that you are his hero."

***

The next time Avinash woke up, he saw a new face in the room. This was a face he had only seen a few times before. The brown-haired, white-skinned man was sitting next to his bed. His face was clean-shaven and handsome. Confidently leaning back in his seat, his eyes were locked on a novel in his hands. Avinash could see the back cover of the novel and on it was a city shrouded in mist. But just like here at the camp, the city seemed to be coming out of the mist.

"…The great Jonathan Daniels graces us with his presence."

Hearing Avinash's voice, Jonathan looked away from the book and at Avinash. He slightly smiled as he put the novel down on the table. "I don't think I'm the one who should be called 'great'."

"I wouldn't use any other word, Jonathan." Looking in the other direction, Avinash saw Lia lying asleep on a long sofa. She had spent almost every waking moment here with him. Avinash's eyes came back to Jonathan. "Don't tell me you came down just to see little 'ole Dr. Singh."

"I didn't come to see Dr. Avinash Singh. I came to see the man whose legend has spread like wildfire all through Amaristan."

Avinash was silent for a moment. "…What?"

"Your heroism has gripped the nation. You don't know how many people were praying for your recovery. Hundreds of thousand if not millions were praying for you. And as for your heroic deed…well…"

He was speechless as Jonathan's hand came onto his shoulder.

"It's done more than you could ever imagine. All around the nation, there are now concentrated efforts to fight back against the rebels. Citizens are banning together and pushing them back. Even the international media found out about the famous Dr. Singh's actions, and now many other international powers are starting to send aid and armed forces to help keep the peace. The rebels have been turned on their heels, and after last night, it's now only a matter of time before they dissolve and peace will be restored."

"...What happened?"

"The rebel leader was found dead."

Avinash's eyes widened in disbelief.

"Nobody knows who it was. But he's dead, and their ranks are in chaos."

There was a long silence as Avinash digested everything he was hearing. Was this a dream? How could one act spur so much change?

"A lot to take in, isn't it?"

He looked back up at Jonathan. "...I can't believe it. All I wanted to do was be the best man I could be...I never could have imagined all this."

"It seems like your best is better than you thought."

Avinash smiled but said nothing.

"What can I ever do to thank you?"

Avinash looked up at the wall for a few long moments before his gaze returned to Jonathan. "There are two children here—a brother and sister. They saved my life."

Jonathan nodded. "I've met them."

"I want you to take care of them and their mother. Send them to the best schools you can. Let them be the best they can."

The visitor was quiet for a few moments. "...Even now, after everything you've done, you still look out for other people. You know, Avi, I've met countless people. I've met men and women who have

288

been called guardians and heroes—people who the world admires." He leaned in a bit. "Where did you come from?"

Avinash smiled. "I'm just a boy from a village who wants to make the world a better place."

"You remind me of my brother, Avi. Like you, he dedicated his life to make this world a better place. He's the man who inspired me to do what I've done." Jonathan was silent for a moment. "There are not many men I look up to outside of him. But you are one."

He nodded in thanks.

"So what's next for you?" Jonathan asked.

"...I...I don't know." He again looked over at the sleeping Lia. "There is someone I want to help finish off a list."

Jonathan nodded in understanding. "I see...and I would be honored to make sure that you can do everything first class."

Avinash's gaze met back with Jonathan's. "I appreciate that."

"It's the least I can do." He scooted his chair a little closer. "And then there's your invention."

"What about it?"

"I had some people take a look at your idea. You were having some difficulty with some kinks from what I understand."

He nodded.

Jonathan slightly smiled. "Are you ready?"

"I'm all ears."

"My people figured them out...and as of yesterday, a prototype is in production."

Avinash's eyes widened in surprise.

"We want you to be there when it is tested in a couple of weeks. Once it has a successful test—which I'm sure it will—I'll use all my assets to get in into mass production. Of course, it'll be patented in your name."

The doctor could hardly believe what he was hearing.

"I'm opening up a new division in my charities. We're working on contracts to build up hospitals in a lot of developing countries. If you want, I would like you to be the head of this division. I want you to be the one training the people."

"...*Me?*"

Jonathan nodded. "Can you think of a better man for the job?"

Avinash was silent for a few long moments. "How soon will you need me?"

"It'll be a year at the least, maybe closer to two before it gets going. How much time do you think you'll need?"

Avinash looked back at Lia. "...I'm not sure."

"You can take as long as you want. If you're not ready when the time to start comes, I'll have somebody else do the job. If Mirza wants, I can have him do it until you're ready. And when the time comes, the position will be open for you. You've earned that much."

Avinash's mind tried to digest everything that he was being told. He was almost certain that this was the afterlife where all his dreams were coming true. How could this be reality? "...I...I don't know what to say."

"You'll have plenty of time to take it all in. Either way, we'll be your invention's number one customer." Jonathan was silent for a long moment. "But when you do get out of this bed, where's the first place you'll be going?"

His eyes came back to Lia. He took a deep breath as he looked at her pretty face. "Home."

***

Bihar, India.

The last time Avinash stood here, he was eleven-years-old. But on that day, a pyre had been where he was standing now. It burned with a fiery rage, and its black smoke drifted off into the heavens. In it had been the body of his brother, Akleshwar, as the boy's corpse turned into ashes.

On that day, there had been nothing but tears. His tears. His mother's tears. His father's tears. Every single one of them had been touched by Akleshwar's loving smile when he was alive. That day, Avinash's world seemed to have ended.

But today, there were no tears. There was only one thing: peace.

Today, there was no sign of the pyre. Instead, there was just an open field. Where the pyre had been now grew two yellow flowers. Side-by-side, the two stood with one much larger than the other. However, the smaller one seemed to be supporting the other one, keeping it from falling over.

Avinash took a deep breath. Then another. From here, he had a perfect view of his family's ancestral lands. He saw the seemingly endless fields of sugarcane, rice, and wheat. He observed the numerous temples that his family had built on these lands over the centuries. Some were larger than others, but each had been built with love. In the distance was his parent's large home. They were ecstatic upon seeing him return home.

Most of all, Avinash focused on two things: the spot where Veeresh's home once stood and the original boundaries Khau chose for the family land.

He looked up at the warm skies. The weather was absolutely perfect. There were enough clouds to decorate the sky without hindering the sun's warmth as the sun caringly looking down at the ground. Today, everything was at peace.

Even Avinash.

Avinash slightly smiled as he looked at the heavens. "…Thank you, Akleshwar. Thank you for everything."

His eyes came down to the two flowers. As he saw one supporting the other, he knew that it was a sign. It was his brother who had started all this. It was his brother who was truly responsible for all the good that had happened to him. Had it not been for him, Avinash may have just been another lost soul. But it was his death that sent Avinash down this path.

"I'll see you soon…and I know that you can see all this. And…and I know your smile is bigger than ever. I'll do everything I can to bring your smile onto as many faces as I can."

Slowly, Avinash looked away from the flowers. His heart was as full as ever. He held back any tears of joy that were forming in his eyes. For the first time since his childhood, Avinash was truly happy. The peace that he had longed for was finally around him. The place that tormented his dreams for so long was the place where he finally found tranquility. It filled his soul. It was pouring out of his spirit. And it consumed his heart.

He saw somebody coming his way. Lia was walking across the plains. She was too far away to speak to, but he could see her perfectly. As Lia came towards him, he could see that she was dressed in a yellow *shalwar kurta*. Her beautiful eyes and smile were directed at him. Her long hair was blowing in the soft wind. Their eyes locked. In the same way that Veeresh and Pari had spoken to each other without words, so did Avinash and Lia. She could see everything that he was feeling. It was all around him. In his gaze, he shared his peace with her. He gave her a part of the tranquility that he found here. He let her feel all of it.

And slowly, Avinash walked towards her and into the new day.

Glossary of Foreign Terms & Names

Allah – Arabic name for God

Allahu Akbar – "God is the Greatest"

Assalam-O-Alaikum – "May God's peace be upon you"

Ayurveda – a system of preventive medicine and health care that
    developed in India more than 5,000 years ago

Babaji – paternal grandfather

Beita – son

Bhabi – sister-in-law

Bhagwan – Hindu name for God

Bhojpuri – native language in India's region of Bihar

Bihar – northeastern Indian province on the border of present-day
    Nepal.

Brahmin – highest caste in Hinduism

Delhi Sultanate – first Islamic dynasty over India

Dholka & Tabla – musical instruments resembling drums

Dhoti – a garment worn by male Hindus, consisting of a piece of
    material tied around the waist and extending to cover most of
    the legs

Henna – dye prepared from the Henna plant used to decorate the
    body

Hijab – head scarf worn by Muslim women

Janeu – holy thread that is worn by the Hindu Brahmins of India

Jai Bajrang Bali – Hindu battle cry

Kameez – loose body shirt

Kufi Hat – a brimless, short, and rounded cap worn by men in many
    populations in North Africa, East Africa, Western Africa and
    Asia

Kurta – an upper garment for men and women, originating in South
    Asia

La Ilaa Illallah – "There is nobody worthy of worship other than
    God"

Layla & Majnun – famous classical Arabian love story

Ma ji – mother

Mangal Panday – an Indian soldier who played a key part in events immediately preceding the outbreak of the Indian rebellion of 1857

Masjid – Islamic place of worship

Namaste – respectful Hindu greeting

Pita ji – father

Qur'an – holy book in Islam

Rus' – modern day greater Russia

Sepoys – an Indian soldier serving under British or other European orders

Shalwar - a pair of light, loose, pleated trousers tapering to a tight fit around the ankles, typically worn with a *kameez*

Sherwanis – long coat-like garment worn in the Indian subcontinent, very similar to a British Frock coat

Sitar – Indian musical instrument resembling a guitar

Sultan – Arabic term for ruler

Thobe – an ankle-length Arab garment, usually with long sleeves, similar to a robe

Vagbhata – one of the most classical writers of Ayurveda

Walaikum – "And unto you"

ABOUT THE AUTHORS

Ammar Habib

Ammar Habib is a bestselling author who was born in Lake Jackson, Texas in 1993. Ammar enjoys crafting stories that are not only entertaining, but will also stay with the reader for a long time. Ammar presently resides in his hometown with his family, all of whom are his biggest fans. He draws his inspiration from his family, imagination, and the world around him.

Other works by Ammar include:
Dark Guardian
Dark Guardian: The War for Peace
Crossroads: A Story of Hope and Love

To learn more about Ammar, please visit:
www.ammarahsenhabib.com

Anil Sinha

Anil Sinha is a general surgeon who has had an active practice in Lake Jackson, Texas for nearly two decades. Born in Bihar, India, he moved to New York City in the 1970s before receiving his medical degree from Texas A&M University and completing his residency in New York City. Much of the historical aspects of the novel were inspired by his family's history. He currently lives with his loving wife, Laura. During his free time, he enjoys playing golf, fishing, hunting, and working on his ranch.

To contact Anil, please write to:
gulfcoastsurgicalclinic@gmail.com

IN LOVING MEMORY OF TAXI

CPSIA information can be obtained
at www.ICGtesting.com
Printed in the USA
LVOW04s0906041016

507279LV00009BA/145/P